Welcome To The Space Navy!

CW01560469

The Space Navy Series

Books One & Two

(Including the Kindle novellas)

"Josiah Trenchard and the Might of Fortitude"
"Josiah Trenchard and the Morgenstern"

By

JONATHON FLETCHER

Jon 7/3/18

For Wib; my nesting partner…

CONTENTS

ACKNOWLEDGEMENTS

I would like to thank all those who supported me over the years, especially Mum and Dad, Jane and Alex, my friends Pete Pugh, Mark Collins, Paul Bird, Zyggy (who doesn't play guitar) and Dave Thomas (the nicest man in the world). Special thanks to my wife who is my biggest critic and helps me to see my books with a new perspective. I simply could not do this without her, she is my best friend and the love of my life. Finally, I would like to thank those special people on Twitter and Facebook who have helped me to promote my #SpaceNavy books world-wide and also the lovely fans of my work for your excellent reviews and support.

Honour, strength and unity!

PROLOGUE

"MARS"

Bullets whined through the air like angry mosquitoes and the ground heaved as a massive explosion tore the road into shreds. The sound of the explosion was deafening to the two soldiers who were running for cover. Even their rasping lungs shook and rattled with the deep resonant boom. The air that they desperately tried to suck in smelled of sulphur and builder's dust. The foreboding purple sky gave everything a sickly, pinkish hue. The ruined landscape of Mars' largest city, Belatu-Cadros, was as close as they had ever come to the depths of hell itself.

The two troopers ducked behind the crumbling corner of a demolished building and instinctively covered their heads with their arms until the hail of dust and debris had subsided. When the explosion had spent itself, the younger of the two looked to his comrade and grinned, pushing up the protective visor of his black helmet to reveal clean eyes on a dirt streaked face.

'What's pissed these guys off so much anyway?' he called above the constant sound of gunfire, clearing his throat loudly and spitting thick, black mucus to the ground.

The older of the two soldiers squared his broad shoulders, grinned back at his comrade and snapped his visor up too. 'For god's sake Trench, don't you *ever* watch the news?'

A stray bullet pinged off the masonry above their heads and the two soldiers ducked. In the distance, someone was screaming. The sound ceased abruptly after a short burst of gunfire.

'Politics bores the hell out of me Bird,' a grinning Josiah Trenchard replied. 'I don't care why these fuckers are pissed at the government this time; I'm just here for a little payback and to make sure that they stop shooting at poor munters like me!'

A United Worlds attack gun-ship roared overhead. Its deafening jet engines rattled the buildings as it passed slowly overhead, causing a thick orange dust to rain down. The gun-ship hovered for a moment in the purple sky. The gunners, who were hanging out of the side hatch, strafed a nearby building with their mini-guns, decimating the structure and silencing the sporadic gunfire that was coming from the insurgents hidden within. As relative silence fell, the gun-ship sped off over the massive chimneys of the distant atmosphere processing plant and then dwindled slowly into a tiny dot against the vast extinct volcano of Olympus Mons.

'Whatever the reason they originally started all this,' began Bird, 'we must still find out where they're getting their weapons from, and that means interrogating the insurgent leaders.'

There was another erratic burst of rifle fire from a nearby building.

'Come on Trench,' shouted Bird above the din, waving his arm in the direction that he intended them to go. 'Let's move it. This low gravity is making me sick to my stomach. The sooner we finish, the sooner we can get back to base for a shower and some scran!'

'Sounds good to me,' replied Trenchard eagerly.

The two soldiers snapped down their visors once more and dashed across a dangerous stretch of open ground, their black uniforms covered with dirt and thick orange dust. They reached the door to a large, officious looking building and booted it open before carefully entering; rifles raised and torch beams dancing through the hazy air.

Bird lowered his rifle and let it hang from the strap while Trenchard covered the room. It was a large entrance lobby, deserted and covered with the same orange dust. Bird studied the display on his portable G.P.S. unit and once satisfied, he raised his wrist towards his mouth and pressed the communicator switch on his bracelet cuff-link radio.

'Lieutenant Bird to mobile command H.Q. Come in, over,' he called.

There was a burst of static before the reply came through.

'Mobile command H.Q. here. What is your status, over?'

Lieutenant Bird spoke calmly and clearly into the radio. 'We have suffered heavy losses to our squad. Only Sub-Lieutenant Trenchard and I have reached the target building. Requesting backup. What are your instructions, over?'

There was a pause while H.Q. passed the information up the chain of command. After what seemed like an eternity, the very short reply came through, *'Backup currently unavailable at this time. Proceed as planned, over.'*

Another gun-ship roared overhead, the vibrations from its engines dislodging a heavy rain of dust. Lieutenant Bird gave Trenchard a worried look. 'Instructions confirmed. WilCo. Lieutenant Bird out!'

Trenchard pulled a sour face. 'They still want us to go in without any backup?' he said incredulously. 'After all those we've lost?'

Lieutenant Bird nodded grimly. 'Looks like, yeah,' he replied.

'But what about our fucking squad?' raged Trenchard. 'Do they think we're bloody expendable? We lost some damn good troopers today!'

Bird scowled. 'Command must think that finding the insurgent leaders is top priority, whatever the losses. No other squad has made it this far behind enemy lines.' Then Bird paused and fixed Trenchard with a sombre stare. 'Don't you want to find out who's behind all of this?'

Trenchard nodded grimly. 'I swear,' he said angrily as he activated the laser target pointer on the top of his rifle, 'that if I get out of this alive, I'm going to stick my boot so far up the Captain's arse that he will be able to taste the dog shit that I just trod in!'

Lieutenant Bird grinned and switched his own laser pointer on, the pencil thin beam of red light showing up clearly in the dusty atmosphere. 'Lead on mate,' he ordered.

Bird and Trenchard worked their way slowly and ever deeper into the concrete structure. The room that they were looking for would be right at the heart, in the most protected underground bunker. They rounded a corner and found an inert body lying on the cold concrete floor. The body was covered with blood. The young woman, barely a teenager, was dressed in the desert camouflage uniform of the local Rubente Dextera militia. Her hand still grasped her pistol and her eyes stared blankly at the ceiling.

'Another one!' exclaimed Trenchard.

Lieutenant Bird knelt by the body to check for a pulse. The woman was still warm, but quite dead.

'Just like the others,' said Bird softly. 'Throat slit and left to bleed to death. It's a very clean cut too.'

'Special forces?' asked Trenchard with a furrowed brow.

Bird thought for a moment. The wound was very long and precise. 'No,' he replied thoughtfully. 'This is more like an execution.' Then he prised the pistol from the dead girl's grip and examined it thoughtfully. 'This pistol is navy issue,' he said with a scowl. 'It's an older model than ours, but it's definitely military, made by Pap-Corp. Someone's definitely supplying the insurgents with illegal arms.'

'If the insurgents are using those weapons on us, then who the hell is getting all Ninja on them?' Trenchard hissed.

'I don't know,' Bird said quietly, dropping the pistol and staring thoughtfully into the distant gloom ahead. 'But we need them alive to question.'

Trenchard gestured to the bloody boot prints that led off down the corridor in front of them. 'Whoever it was has fucking small feet!' he observed.

'…and they're not far ahead of us,' said Bird, a dark, foreboding expression falling across his face.

The two soldiers dropped into a walking crouch and carefully made their way along the corridor, aiming their rifles into the gloaming darkness ahead of them.

They found three more bodies along the route before finally arriving at the entrance to a control bunker. They carefully edged around the door, which was hanging off its hinges, blasted into pieces by an explosive charge. The room was full of computers, communications equipment and tactical display banks. The scene inside was utter carnage. Bodies lay everywhere, the command staff of the Martian insurgents. Every single one of them was slashed and drained of blood, which pooled onto the floor, resembling used engine oil in the dim, red emergency light of the bunker. In the very centre of the room a slim figure, dressed head-to-toe in black, was finishing off the last of the unfortunate command staff with what looked like a short sword. The figure expertly slashed the terrified man from shoulder to gut, spilling his blood and internal organs onto the cold concrete floor. The man crumpled and lay twitching on the floor next to the disfigured bodies of his fallen comrades.

Trenchard and Bird inched gently into the room, the tiny red dots from their rifles aimed steadily at the lithe black figure's head and chest. The figure looked down and studied the red dots on its chest for a moment, then it cocked its head to one side inquisitively before looking straight up into Bird's eyes as if daring him to fire.

'Don't move!' shouted Lieutenant Bird. 'You are under arrest by order of the United Worlds peacekeeping force under section…'

The figure suddenly leapt, more quickly than it would seem a human was capable of. Bird and Trenchard reacted a moment too slowly and strafed the room, attempting to keep up with the figure that leapt and dodged their every volley. With a sudden rush, the figure swung off a roof girder and lunged at Trenchard, catching him with its sword across his neck and chest. He dropped his rifle and clutched desperately at his throat with his gloved hands, in a vain attempt to stop the warm flow of blood that was pouring from the gash. Then he fell to the floor gasping for air.

Lieutenant Bird angrily attempted to zero in on the black-clad figure and managed to skim a bullet across its thigh. The figure howled with pain and anger. It brought the sword down hard in a wide arc that sliced cleanly through the metal barrel of Bird's rifle. At the same time, the figure leapt feet first at Bird's stomach. Bird's broad frame crumpled like a squashed beer can and he whacked his head violently on the sharp edge of a console. Despite his helmet, he fell to the floor unconscious.

Trenchard couldn't speak. The blood was filling his convulsing windpipe, bubbling and popping as he choked.

He was losing his grasp on his throat as well as on consciousness. The black-clad figure dropped onto its haunches beside Trenchard's face and calmly wiped the blood off its sword on Trenchard's uniform before sliding it expertly into a sheath tied to its back.

As Trenchard slid into the numbness of unconsciousness, the figure brought its masked face close to Trenchard's ear and whispered. The voice was soft, feminine, and had the slight hint of a chocolaty Japanese accent.

'*You're lucky…*' she said as she pulled Trenchard's dog tags out from beneath his uniform and studied them. '*…Sub-Lieutenant Josiah Trenchard. My orders weren't to kill United Worlds troopers. But this was fun. We must do it again. Catch you next time?*'

The figure reached over and activated the inbuilt distress beacon that was part of Trenchard's bracelet cuff-link radio. Then she stood up and raced away down the darkened corridor. The last thought that went through Trenchard's oxygen starved mind before everything went black was… *she's got a really nice arse.*

CHAPTER 1

"A MAN OF WAR"

Four years later...

The heavy metal hatch screeched slowly open and Commander Josiah Trenchard stomped angrily down the creaking ramp. He stopped at the base of the ramp and threw his heavy harness to the scuffed tread plate floor with a resounding clunk. He'd had a hard day. He had a pounding headache and was keen to get out of his sweaty, blood-stained uniform as quickly as was humanly possible. He looked down at his black sleeves which were spattered with blood and bone fragments from troopers in his platoon; people he knew well, good friends. They would be coming back from the crappy little ice-moon below in a plastic body-bag. That was, if they could find all the bits.

He scratched irritably at the long scar on his neck that was just visible as it disappeared underneath his crumpled uniform. It always itched when he was sweaty and stressed. The underwater tunnels that he'd been fighting in had been hot as hell and humid to match. He was desperate for a shower but he had a job to do first. He needed to get this over with.

'Okay, bring them down,' he shouted impatiently to the waiting troopers inside the sturdy little craft, an edge of sadness and weariness creeping into his voice.

One by one, twelve dishevelled prisoners, brow beaten and manacled together, were ushered down the ramp by the battle weary United Worlds troopers. Trenchard studied the prisoners closely as he pulled a crumpled packet of cigarettes out from his inside jacket pocket. He lit one and took a long, satisfying drag. Hardly anyone smoked these days but Trenchard had an addictive personality. Whether it was booze, coffee or nicotine, Trenchard usually required each in large quantities. He was getting some dirty scowls from the nearby Techs, but they could all go and screw themselves. They hadn't just been into battle. He needed this cigarette more than he needed air right now. He let the smoke linger inside his lungs for a long moment as he savoured the head rush, before blowing the smoke out of his mouth to one side. Then he ran his grubby, yellow stained fingers across his greasy shaved scalp and thought back on the day's events as he took another long, satisfying drag.

A stocky man strode over and stood beside Trenchard. His insignia identified him as Trenchard's Lieutenant Commander. He too was glaring angrily at the prisoners and then he spoke quietly to Trenchard through gritted teeth.

'This should have been a straight forward mission, damn it boss! I've just about had enough of the bloody insurgents stirring things up. What the fuck do they want with one of Jupiter's moons anyway? I mean, Europa for fucks sake! It's a pissy little moon in the arse end of nowhere. There's absolutely nothing whatsoever of value here!'

Trenchard grunted in agreement. 'I think these fuckers just like to cause mischief wherever they can,' he replied.

Not much had changed since the Martian uprising four years ago, Trenchard thought to himself as he scratched reflectively at his scar again. It was a solid reminder of the uprising in Belatu-Cadros. That was where the insurgents had first learned to fight, learned to make bombs and learned to kill. He had beaten the "Red Right Hand" on Mars, but they had managed to regroup and grow stronger on other planets. The war against the Rubente Dextera still raged relentlessly across the United Worlds despite the best efforts of the Space Navy.

'The insurgent leaders must have persuaded the colonists on Europa to declare independence somehow. If there's one thing that the United Worlds government hates, then it's pokey little back water colonies trying to avoid paying their taxes by suddenly getting all holier than thou!' Trenchard groused.

The massive star-ship that Trenchard was currently based upon, the "Hand of Valour", had been sent to Europa to deal with the recent uprising. It had arrived in orbit of Europa and Trenchard's platoon had been blasted towards the small moon, expecting an easy victory. He played back the journey from the Hand of Valour to the surface of Europa in his head, remembering the sudden thrust of acceleration as they blasted off. He recalled the shaking and jostling as the tiny Space-Air-Water drop-ship fell through the thin atmosphere of Europa. He could almost feel the sudden jolt of deceleration as the tiny ship plunged into the icy ocean and dived towards the atmosphere processing station, deep beneath the ice on the ocean floor. That was where the trouble had really started.

'I don't understand it boss,' said the Lieutenant Commander bitterly. 'It should have been a piece of piss to gain entry to the atmosphere processor. These guys are supposed to be civilian engineers and technicians. It was a straight-forward op!'

Trenchard nodded. 'It should have been,' he agreed, 'but that was before the fucking R.D. armed the colonists and taught them how to make I.E.D.'s. They're spreading their political hatred to as many people as will listen to them. It was only a matter of time before something like this happened. It's fucking Belatu-Cadros all over again.'

The Lieutenant Commander gave Trenchard a respectful smile and a nod. Every trooper knew about Belatu-Cadros. It was where the war against the terrorists had begun in earnest. In the early days, the enemy were only fervent amateurs and they had done enough damage as it was. Someone had obviously taught the Europan colonists the same guerrilla tactics that had been used on Mars. They had started blowing up barrels of oil, packed with nails and bolts, as the troopers gained entry to the airlocks. Trenchard shuddered as he felt the heat of the explosion in his mind. He could see the troopers falling all around him, feel their fear and taste the air that was thick with smoke and the tinny smell of blood and burning flesh.

'How many did we lose?' asked Trenchard grimly.

'At least half of the squad,' replied the Lieutenant Commander, 'mostly to deep tissue shrapnel wounds.' He turned and spat onto the ground. '*Bastards!*'

Trenchard looked down at the deep, fresh wound on his own arm as he pulled back his ripped sleeve and scratched at the skin around it. He winced in pain, idly plucking shards of metal from the wound. He would have another scar; another permanent reminder of battle and death. It had been a hard battle. Too hard. He was remarkably pissed off.

'I don't know about you,' said Trenchard, 'but I feel like I want to rip someone's head off and piss down their neck!'

The Lieutenant Commander grinned. All it would take was one more little push and Trenchard might just forget that he was supposed to set a good example to the other troopers. The chained prisoners who were standing in a line in front of him were the ring leaders. Most of them were from other colonies, far away. They were R.D. insurgent agitators, trying to persuade the people of Europa to revolt against the rule of the United Worlds. Well these guys would pay, Trenchard thought grimly.

'Is that all of them?' he asked his Lieutenant Commander.

The stocky man nodded and replied, 'All present and accounted for Sir.'

For a moment, something caught Trenchard's eye. On the other side of the vast hangar bay, other S.A.W. craft were returning from the frozen surface of Europa. Trenchard watched a couple of the missile shaped craft land with a thump and whistle of engines. Through the rectangular hole at the end of the runway the white moon of Europa hung in the blackness like a well-worn billiard ball, criss-crossed with dark scarlet cracks. He would be glad to see the back of that crappy little moon he thought as he dropped the spent cigarette to the floor and stubbed it out with his blood splashed boot. He walked over to the prisoners and eyeballed them angrily before beginning his well-rehearsed tirade.

'You fuckers picked the wrong people to mess with today,' he shouted. 'In case you hadn't been watching the I.N.N. news reports recently, President Smith has just brought back the death sentence for terrorists.'

In the background, another S.A.W.'s hatch opened and a weary trooper stomped out. He was wearing a scruffy red ribbon tied around his greasy dishevelled hair, which he pulled off and wrung the sweat out of before replacing it onto his head. He saw Trenchard tearing shreds out of the prisoners and began to walk over, grinning broadly. The grinning trooper stopped just behind Trenchard with his arms folded, seeming to take great pleasure in the entertainment.

'Section forty-two allows me to execute terrorists on sight! I'd quite happily carry out the sentence right here,'

Trenchard threatened, dramatically drawing his pistol from its holster and clicking a round into the chamber.

'Smith's wrong!' said one of the prisoners in a trembling but determined voice. '*You* are wrong! We want freedom to self-rule, not martial law forced upon us by thugs like you!'

Trenchard narrowed his eyes and walked closer to the prisoner. The man was defiantly staring at him with unbridled hatred in his eyes. Trenchard finally snapped. He'd had enough. He pressed the pistol hard to the man's forehead. The man did a good job of putting on a brave face, but Trenchard could see the terror welling in his eyes.

'Do you think that blowing up booby traps packed with sharp metal is the answer?' he growled. 'Do you think that it's *honourable* or even *fair*? You might not like the United Worlds but at least we keep the peace. You lot would be kicking ten tons of shit out of each other if it wasn't for us! Would you prefer that? Don't you realise that we're protecting you useless bunch of fuckwits?'

The prisoner's face reddened but he remained tight lipped.

'Unfortunately, unlike you *criminals*, "thugs like me" have to follow the rules.' Trenchard pulled back the pistol, disarmed the mechanism and slid it safely back into its holster. It had left a perfect red imprint of the barrel on the man's forehead. 'But mark my words,' he continued, 'if any of you terrorist arseholes put so much as one bollock out of line, I will put you down like a fucking rabid dog! Understood?'

The prisoners remained solemnly silent. Trenchard placed his hands behind his back and tried to relax his aching shoulders. 'Take them away,' he ordered, completely exhausted.

As the prisoners shuffled dejectedly away towards the holding cells to await transport back to Earth for trial, Trenchard became aware of childish sniggering behind him. He turned around to find the trooper with the bright red head-band, leaning lazily on the butt of his rifle and chuckling with obvious glee.

'Very impressive Trench,' said the man in a broad Geordie accent. 'You made them fuckers shit their pants all right!'

Trenchard scowled at the grinning trooper. 'Haven't you got something better to do Dasilva?' he growled.

Lieutenant Commander Dasilva smiled and winked. 'Whey aye, but I couldn't miss the show man. It was champion!'

Trenchard looked around to make sure that the prisoners were out of ear shot and then broke into a broad grin himself. 'Piss off Eddie!' he said. 'Do you know how hard it is to keep a straight face with you pratting around behind me?'

'Aye well, you seemed to manage all right enough,' said Dasilva with a chuckle, then his face dropped and became suddenly serious. 'Did you lose many?'

Trenchard grimaced. 'Twelve... you?'

'Most of the squad,' replied Dasilva, 'just four of our lot made it back, and Commander Fisher took some shrapnel to his hand.'

'Shit!' said Trenchard as helpfully as he could. 'How's he taking it?'

'Fisher?' said Dasilva, 'Ahh, he'll be all right. The man's as tough as old boots. He's got footballs for knackers! He's more upset about losing good troopers. That prick reporter on the news is going to have a field day with this!'

Trenchard took another cigarette from its packet and offered one to Dasilva, who refused.

'I just have this creeping feeling that maybe...' Trenchard began in a soft voice that was almost a whisper. He tailed off, deep in thought. 'This sort of thing used to be sorted out peacefully by the politicians. The United Worlds is supposed to be a democracy Eddie. We're meant to uphold the law and protect the people. Recently, things have been... *different*. High Command didn't even give them a chance to negotiate this time; we just waded straight in, feet first. This mission wasn't honourable.' Trenchard narrowed his eyes and stared at Dasilva. 'Know what I mean?'

Dasilva looked around nervously. 'Yeah, I know mate,' he hissed out of the corner of his mouth. 'But keep it to yourself man, or Ciaputa will have you up on a subordination charge.'

Trenchard's shoulders slumped and he sighed deeply. 'Oh… I don't know Ed. I'm probably just tired, but this doesn't feel *right* anymore. It's not what I signed up for.'

Dasilva gave a quick nod of affirmation. 'You can't do anything about it mate, other than vote that is. Smith and Chang are running things right now and they're talking tough! Pretty soon there'll be another election and the government will change again. Someone else will be in charge and they'll try diplomacy again instead of the hard line. Trust me, you'll see.'

Trenchard nodded knowingly. 'I hope you're right Eddie,' he said. Then he paused and stretched, cracking his aching back. 'I could do with a fuckin' big drink,' he sighed, stretching some more and clicking the bones of his neck.

'With a bit of luck,' said Dasilva, 'we'll all be back at base on Cairn soon and we should all be due some leave after that mess down there,' he said, jerking his thumb towards Europa. 'Fancy a pint in Mike's and then a curry?'

Mike's Bar was the local haunt for the troopers at their home base on Cairn. The thought of its sticky floor and sticky beer was very tempting. Trenchard was about to reply when the dull, toneless voice of the ship's Guardian computer echoed over the tannoy system.

'COMMANDER JOSIAH TRENCHARD, REPORT TO COMMODORE CIAPUTA ON THE BRIDGE IMMEDIATELY.'

Dasilva looked up and listened to the message with a puzzled expression. 'What does that frigid old bitch want?' he asked with more than a hint of bile.

Trenchard shrugged. 'God only knows, but it can't be good. I'll see you later Ed.'

With that, Trenchard picked up his heavy harness from the floor and trudged off towards the bridge, past the tail fin of the S.A.W. where the Space Navy's proud slogan of "Honour, strength and unity!" was painted in bold white letters. It was a motto by which Trenchard had tried to live his life. Recently, it was becoming harder to adhere to.

As he left, Dasilva shouted cockily after him, 'Keep your hands in your pockets mate, or she'll freeze your bollocks off!'

The bridge was a shielded dome that was built onto the outside of one of the massive rugby ball shaped habitation pods that rotated continually around the hull of the Hand of Valour on giant metal spokes to provide gravity within. The domed floor of the bridge faced space-side, with the main hull and engine core of the ship above the crew's heads. An iris shaped hatch in the ceiling slid apart gracefully with the sound of grating metal and Trenchard was lowered down on a circular platform towards the deck below. He waited respectfully at attention for a moment as he studied the bridge watch-standers busying themselves at various control stations set around the curved walls of the compartment. At the front of the bridge was a large reinforced rectangular window that gave a view of space ahead. Clustered around a large tactical hologram in the centre of the room were several high-ranking officers. Trenchard coughed politely and a female officer in her late forties, who was wearing an immaculate bright scarlet uniform, seemed to notice him for the first time. By the look on her face, his very presence appeared to annoy her somewhat.

'Ahh, there you are Trenchard,' said Commodore Constantine Ciaputa in a clipped, tight voice that sounded like the lid of a heavy, wooden box snapping shut.

Ciaputa handed a tablet screen that she was holding to an aide who rushed over from one side. She shooed the aide away irritably and the young officer dropped his head and respectfully backed away again.

'You sent for me Sir?' enquired Trenchard as politely as he could muster. He was tired, dirty and aching. He was in no mood for another telling off from his boss. Ciaputa was the worst kind of officer. She had worked her way up the ranks by doing as little as possible and brown-nosing her superiors. She was now the commanding officer of the Hand of Valour. Trenchard severely doubted whether she had ever seen any combat action at all.

'Yes Commander, I did,' replied Ciaputa with a curled lip. 'At ease.'

Trenchard relaxed his shoulders and placed his hands behind his back, widening his stance. Ciaputa studied Trenchard as if he were something that she had found crawling around under a rotten tree stump. Then she seemed to come to an internal decision.

'I've had word from Admiral Fife at High Command. A new posting has become available and you have been selected.'

'Sir?' said Trenchard with a raised eyebrow.

He didn't like the sound of this. He was comfortable aboard the Hand of Valour. The quarters were quite big compared to some of the smaller ships in the fleet. The food was good and the water wasn't rationed. He had respect here. He had worked hard to get where he was and didn't want to leave so soon. Had he done something wrong? Ciaputa seemed to be taking pleasure from Trenchard's disquiet. She smiled a greasy smile as she continued.

'The first prototype Wolverine class vessel has just come into operation. Four of the hunter-killers are being sent into the asteroid belt on a seek-and-destroy mission. One of the Wolverines, the Might of Fortitude, is short of an X.O. It seems that the Captain of the vessel has specifically requested you to be his executive officer... although god only knows why?'

'Thank you, Sir,' said Trenchard as politely as he could manage.

It was astounding how Ciaputa could congratulate and belittle in the same breath.

'The Breath of Vengeance is going to meet us when we dock at Cairn. You will transfer over to her immediately upon arrival. I'm afraid your leave is cancelled as the mission has been brought forward and you are required aboard the Might of Fortitude straight away. That is all.'

With that, Ciaputa turned back towards the glowing green tactical hologram. She snapped her fingers at the aide who rushed back over and handed her the tablet screen once more. Obviously, the audience was over. For a moment, Trenchard didn't move. He was still shocked by the sudden re-deployment. Ciaputa glanced irritably back at Trenchard over her shoulder, seemingly annoyed that he was still here.

'*Dismissed,*' she said sharply and then turned back to her work.

Trenchard stepped back onto the elevator platform and left the bridge in an even worse temper than before. No leave, he thought angrily. Why the hell did the Captain of the Might of Fortitude need him so damned urgently anyway? The Wolverines were a little bigger than the old Hunter class, but they were still cramped fucking sewage pipes compared to the Hand of Valour. This day had started shitty and had just gotten worse and worse.

Deep below the rocky surface of the desolate planetoid Cairn, was a blast shielded, circular bunker. Its twelve-foot-thick concrete walls were resin bonded and electronically shielded. The "War Room" could withstand any attack from orbit and all attempts at espionage. The room resembled a cave or basement. It had a clammy, dank feel and the atmosphere within was oppressive and the lighting subdued.

The man in the centre of the room was clearly agitated; he paced back and forth with his hands clasped tightly behind his back and a tight-lipped expression on his stony face. He wore the bright red uniform with four diagonal black stripes of an Admiral and he looked as if he had the worries of the whole navy bearing down upon his shoulders.

Suddenly, the reinforced titanium blast door screeched open and another figure walked casually into the room. This second man was tall and broad shouldered. His face too was stern and had the polished ebony skin of an Afro-Caribbean lineage. His uniform was also bright scarlet but had a single downward pointing black V that ran from his shoulders towards his stomach. There was only one man in the whole fleet who had the privilege to wear that uniform; Admiral of the Fleet Adisa. He came to a halt in front of the first man, who had stopped pacing and was staring into Adisa's eyes as if his life depended upon it.

"Well?" asked Adisa in a deep resonating voice, emphasised by the acoustics of the War Room.

The other man spoke in what could only be described as a dour Scottish accent.

'The Breath of Vengeance is preparing to leave Sir. The Wolverines will be launched on schedule,' he said. 'I will personally be overseeing the mission.'

'…and is your man aboard?'

The Scottish man nodded curtly. 'He will transfer over in a couple of days once the Hand of Valour returns to Cairn. He'll be meeting the Captain of the Might of Fortitude as planned.'

Adisa paused and screwed up his mouth, deep in thought.

'This had better work Fife,' he said. 'We're placing a great deal of trust in this man of yours. I checked his record. He's not exactly an exemplary officer.'

Fife took a deep intake of breath before answering.

'His mission reports are exemplary. He was fundamental in our victory at Belatu-Cadros on Mars, and on Horizon, Cubecca, Thalos...'

'Admitted,' replied Adisa. 'He also has seven reports for insubordination, four aboard the Hand of Valour which were lodged by Commodore Ciaputa and several other disciplinary matters on his record still pending. He smokes, he drinks...'

'*He fights hard!*' Fife snapped, cutting Adisa off in mid-sentence.

Fife was probably the only Admiral in High Command who would have dared to interrupt Adisa like that. Taking a deep breath, Adisa narrowed his eyes and fumed quietly for a moment with tightly drawn lips.

'He might not be the most... conventional officer in the navy, but he's a born fighter. Don't worry Sir. If anyone can pull this off, he can...' said Fife firmly.

'You had better be right!' Adisa growled.

CHAPTER 2

"MEMORIES"

Commander Skelat was a real bastard. He knew to be true this because he'd had a lot of people point it out to him over the years. He had very few redeeming qualities. He liked being in charge and he liked pushing people around. He was one of the old-school troopers in the navy. He had been part of the British Army back on Earth, before the United Worlds Space Navy had even been thought up. There, he had been a drill sergeant and his reputation preceded him like a bad smell. He was a hard-nosed, vicious little bugger and those were in fact, his best qualities. Currently he was bawling at his platoon, as was his habit on a bright morning after he'd had his morning bowel movement. It was said that Commander Skelat suffered from haemorrhoids and that was why he was always in such a bad mood first thing in the morning. It wasn't true. Whether he had piles or not would make little or no difference. Skelat was a bully, simple as that.

'Move it, move it, MOVE IT!'

The parade ground was covered by thick red dust from yet another storm that had blown down last night from the slopes of Olympus Mons. The fine particles of pumice bit at the back of the trooper's throats as they stood to attention in the purple light of dawn on Mars. Lieutenant Bird and Sub-Lieutenant Trenchard were handing out the new rifles that had just arrived by transport, fresh from the Papaver Corporation's munitions factory. Each was carefully removed from a large wooden crate as the wind whipped up the polystyrene packaging and sent it dancing away across the parade ground. The rifles were covered with a thin film of oil and Trenchard fumbled with the one that he had just picked up. The rifle slid from his grip and clattered to the dusty ground.

'Be careful with those Trenchard, you festering little bum boil!' Skelat yelled angrily.

'Yes Sir, being careful Sir!' Trenchard shouted back through gritted teeth as he picked up the rifle.

'Those are brand new, straight from that Froggy little twat's shiny factory!' Skelat barked. 'I don't want to have to be the first officer to send one back broken, do you hear?'

'Yes Sir.'

Bird caught Trenchard's eye and winked. Trenchard rolled his eyes and pulled the last rifle out of the crate. Then Bird and Trenchard joined the end of the first row of Troopers and faced Commander Skelat and Lieutenant Commander Hedges square on. Skelat took a deep breath, swelling his considerable chest out to bow in front of him like the prow of a ship. Then he snarled his top lip, making his neatly trimmed moustache curl up under his flattened, once broken nose.

'Right, you 'orrible little lot. This,' said Skelat, holding one of the rifles out in front of his puffed-up chest, 'is the new model 15-C, void capable case-less assault rifle. That's a bit of a mouthful, I here you say, as the actress said to the bishop…'

There was a marked silence at the appalling joke. Skelat snorted and carried on after a pause.

'So the Johnnies at High Command 'ave decided to nickname it the "Vicar".'

Skelat deftly swung the rifle around and slapped a full ammo cartridge into the bottom of the rifle. There were a series of uncomprehending stares from the troopers.

'I know what you're thinking. You're thinking that V.C.C.A.R. doesn't spell Vicar. But it sounds a lot better and people like a nickname, don't they? You lucky lot are going to be the first to field test this marvellous new piece of kit.'

There were several groans from the troopers.

Skelat raised an eyebrow. 'Did I here a flippin' complaint?'

'No Sir!' shouted the platoon in unison.

'I didn't fucking hear you lot of testicle inhibited bastards!'

'*NO SIR!*' shouted the platoon at sufficiently raised volume to satisfy Skelat's ego.

Skelat eyeballed the troopers. 'Now, this particular Vicar ain't the nice kind that you invite round for tea and fucking cucumber sarnies, oh no he's not. He's the sort of Vicar who sticks a crucifix up the enemy's arse and then drowns them in the bloody font!'

There were a few reserved chuckles from the troopers. Skelat wasn't renowned for his humour, but he did have his moments.

'This weapon fires the standard ten-millimetre case-less rounds and is powered by a gas cartridge in the stock. It has a targeting laser guide attached above the barrel and soft foamy grips so your little tingies don't suffer from vibration damage, which I'm sure you'll agree is an 'ealth and safety nightmare! It also has a warming mechanism in the chamber to avoid misfires, in the event that you have to discharge your weapon in a vacuum.'

Trenchard raised a hand. Bird gave him a hard stare out of the corner of his eye and gritted his teeth.

'*What are you doing?*' Bird whispered urgently through his clenched teeth.

'*Having some fun…*' Trenchard replied with a glint in his eye.

Skelat's eyes narrowed. 'What's the problem Trenchard?' he growled from snarling lips.

Trenchard cleared his throat. 'I just wondered why you would ever need to fire it in a vacuum, Sir?'

'Were you indeed…' snarled Skelat, his eyes narrowing even further.

'Yes. I mean, wouldn't your domestic cleaner be pissed that you've broken her Hoover?'

Several of the troopers smirked or sniggered. Even Lieutenant Commander Hedges, who was standing right beside Skelat, stared down at her boots, her shoulders shaking uncontrollably with silent laughter.

Skelat's left eye twitched so violently that it almost closed shut. He passed the rifle firmly to the quaking Hedges next to him, clicked his neck bones and walked forwards to stand right in front of Trenchard. Skelat leaned in so closely to Trenchard that their noses almost touched. Trenchard could see the Commander's veins throbbing in his face.

'Do you think you are a funny little fucker, Sub-Lieutenant Trenchard?'

'No Sir,' said Trenchard, deliberately quietly in order to annoy the Commander further.

Out of the corner of his eye, Trenchard could see the main gate to the compound. It had a barrier and a simple wooden guard hut. A crowd of civilians had suddenly converged upon the gate. The sound of distant shouting reached Trenchard's ears on the dusty air. Several other troopers had noticed too and a few of them chanced quick glances towards the commotion.

'What was that Trenchard? I must be going deaf!' screamed Skelat, reaching a near apoplexy of anger.

'NO SIR!' shouted Trenchard, his eyes now fixed on the gate.

Skelat finally noticed that he didn't have Trenchard's full attention. 'What are you looking at Trenchard? What's so fucking interesting that you…'

BOOM!

The troopers all instinctively hit the ground and scrabbled to cover their heads with their arms. Only Skelat remained standing resolute, with his fists on his hips. A black cloud of smoke was mushrooming up from the gate area. When the smoke had cleared sufficiently, the troopers could make out a large blast radius, black at the centre but with smears of red flesh around the outer edges. The barrier and the guard hut had gone, smashed to smithereens. The surviving troopers at the gate were picking themselves up off the ground and staggering around helplessly in bemused shock. Then, just as they were recovering, the angry mob burst into the compound and began to club the stricken troopers back to the ground. The throng were followed in by at least twenty figures, all dressed in local R.D. militia uniforms. They were armed. Even at this distance, Trenchard could see that they were carrying navy issue assault rifles, although much older models.

At the first shot, Skelat broke his silence and bellowed a single order; one word, but it was enough to motivate every single trooper in the platoon.

'*MOVE!*'

Trenchard was jolted awake by turbulence and the dream instantly began to fade. He was slumped into one of the more comfortable chairs in the rear compartment of a shuttle that was transferring him from the Hand of Valour over to the Breath of Vengeance. The journey back from

Europa to Cairn had taken a couple of days which had been taken up with paperwork, packing his things and saying his farewells to what was left of his platoon. He'd stayed awake most of last night drinking coffee with Dasilva and they had recounted endless stories to each other. When he had settled into the comfortable seat in the shuttle earlier this morning, he had been so tired that he must have dozed off.

As the vivid dream faded, Trenchard rose groggily from his seat and staggered forwards towards the cockpit, using the seat backs to support him. Out of the cockpit window he could see the troop deployment carrier Breath of Vengeance looming ahead. It was slightly smaller than his last ship, the Hand of Valour, but it was no less fearsome a sight. There were many more hangar bays on the habitation pods to accommodate the hundreds of drop-ships and shuttles needed for ferrying troops down to a planet's surface. There were also four distinct shapes strapped to the rear of her hull, missile shaped hunter-killers; the brand-new Wolverines. Trenchard switched his gaze from the Wolverines to the back of the pilots' heads.

'How long till we dock?' he asked with a deep, rumbling, early morning voice.

The co-pilot turned around to face him. 'Just a few minutes Sir,' she said. 'You should return to your seat and strap yourself in.'

Trenchard raised a brow. 'Why? Are you that bad at landing?'

The co-pilot chuckled. 'No Sir, it's just regulations.'

Trenchard grunted and was about to return to his seat when the co-pilot spoke up again.

'Sir?'

Trenchard looked back into her face. She was very young, as were many sailors these days. Her eyes still sparkled with hope that had yet to be knocked out of her by the relentless war against the insurgents.

'What is it, Able Spaceman… Gerrard?' he said, reading the name off her lapel badge.

The young woman blushed. An odd reaction, Trenchard thought to himself.

'I just wanted to say that it's been an honour meeting you Sir!' she said with an excited note in her voice.

The pilot, an older male, let out a deep sigh of exasperation. Trenchard glanced towards the pilot to see that he was gently shaking his head from side to side. Then Trenchard looked back towards Gerrard in confusion.

'Erm, thank you?'

Gerrard gave Trenchard a quizzical look. 'You don't know who I am, do you Sir?'

Trenchard shook his head. 'Should I?'

Gerrard took a deep breath. 'My father served with you on Mars Sir. Your actions in the battle for Belatu-Cadros saved his life. I was fourteen when the uprising happened. Dad was brought back to us with no legs, but he was still brought back to us. I'll always be grateful for that.'

Trenchard felt the kernel of a memory forming at the back of his mind. 'Gerrard… Hector Gerrard?'

At the mention of her father's name, Able Spaceman Gerrard beamed. 'Yes Sir!'

'He was a brave man. I'm sorry that I wasn't able to save his legs. He took the full force of a shrapnel-packed I.E.D.'

Trenchard paused for a long time as the stark memory flashed through his mind. That first day of the battle for Belatu-Cadros had been disastrous for the United Worlds. It was etched into every trooper's memory, for those who had survived the bombings. Trenchard had recounted most of it to Dasilva over several espressos and it must have been sitting at the back of his mind even in sleep, haunting his dreams. Dasilva hadn't been there when the battle had started, but more United Worlds troopers had been shipped in as quickly as was possible and Dasilva had been in the second wave. They both bore battle scars from Mars.

'How is he these days?'

'He's okay. He managed to get a pair of Pap-Corp's new artificial legs. He's back in the navy now Sir, it's only a desk job, but it's at Star-spires. We're very proud of him Sir.'

Trenchard nodded then asked, 'How old are you now Gerrard?'

'Eighteen Sir.'

'You've done well to get to A.S. by now. I take it you joined the academy junior cadets when you were sixteen?'

'Yes Sir. My father inspired me to join the fight against the terrorists. He and I owe you a great deal Commander Trenchard.'

Trenchard felt a little uncomfortable. He wasn't used to this sort of adulation, particularly from pretty, young, eighteen-year-old girls. Especially when he knew their fathers.

'I was just doing my job,' he managed with a tight smile.

'Well keep on doing it Sir!' said Gerrard. 'Strap in.'

'What?' said a suddenly confused Trenchard.

'We're on final approach. I need you back in your seat Sir.'

Trenchard nodded and carefully made his way back to his seat. Hector Gerrard's daughter, he thought as he stumbled along the passageway; an eighteen-year-old co-pilot. Jesus, that made him feel old. He'd managed to cram a lot into four years. After Mars, he'd been promoted to Commander and had toured the galaxy aboard the Hand of Valour. That was all behind him now. His future lay ahead aboard the Breath of Vengeance which drew nearer with every passing second.

CHAPTER 3

"A BIRD IN THE HAND"

A short while later, Trenchard stepped out of the shuttle into the hangar bay of the Breath of Vengeance and grumpily threw his heavy kit bag to the floor. Able Spaceman Gerrard was happily waving at him out of the cockpit window. Trenchard threw her a forced smile and stepped off the ramp, making sure to put his right foot first. It was admittedly an ancient naval superstition, but walking onto a new ship with the wrong foot could get you shunned for weeks. "left footers" were deemed to be unlucky.

The place was bustling with urgent activity. Shuttles loaded with armaments and supplies were arriving constantly from the nearby dusty ball of rock that was misleadingly named "planet" Cairn. Far out on the edge of the Solar System, beyond the Kuiper belt and just inside the icy Oort cloud, Cairn was either a very large asteroid or a dwarf planetoid, depending upon your viewpoint. It was a remnant of the planet forming process and was slightly smaller than Neptune or Pluto. The one thing that Cairn had going for it was an immensely dense core, which gave the small rock almost exactly the same gravity as Earth. For that reason, the Space Navy had chosen it as the location for their supply base and naval training academy.

The surface of Cairn was packed with pressure domes that held offices, classrooms, storage warehouses and training areas, to say nothing of the bars, restaurants and cinemas where the battle-weary troops could spend their shore leave. Trenchard hadn't even had so much as one pint of "Old Speckled Gobshite" with Dasilva in Mike's Bar. Everyone else was down on Cairn having a good time. Trenchard was completely sober and in a fouler mood than usual.

He still couldn't work out why he had been chosen for this mission, or who had specifically requested him. It was annoying and a little mysterious. It wasn't the way that the navy usually worked, and that made him feel nervous. Someone was playing games with him, but who?

As Trenchard surveyed the organised chaos, a small female officer came rushing over through the bustling crowd of technicians, mechanics and pilots. Trenchard calmly took a cigarette out from its packet. A disparaging look from the Techs who were re-fuelling a shuttle right next to his put him off lighting it, so he just let it hang limply from his lower lip.

The woman came to a halt in front of him, panting heavily. Trenchard could tell that she was a Warrant Officer from her insignia, but just like Gerrard, she looked terribly *young*. The navy were pushing recruits through the academy faster recently. That inevitably had a knock-on higher up the ranks. It was also dangerous. Officers needed experience. The woman standing in front of him didn't look old enough to legally buy a beer, let alone operate weapons systems. Or was that just the jaded perspective of his ageing mentality? She had bright red hair, not ginger but dyed a distinctive red colour. She had about her the air of a bouncy Labrador puppy. Trenchard looked her up and down with disdain as the woman saluted and caught her breath.

'…and you are?' Trenchard asked with a sneer.

'Warrant Officer Hilary Cochran Sir, but everybody calls me Scarlet,' the woman said through panting breaths as she smiled hopefully.

'I'm sure they do Warrant Officer Cochran,' Trenchard said, deliberately keeping things formal. '…and which fucking genius put you in charge?'

Cochran stared at him blankly, her cheeks beginning to redden. 'Sorry Sir?'

'I was sent for,' Trenchard said testily. 'I still don't know quite why or by whom.'

'Yes Sir. The Captain is waiting to see you Sir, he will explain everything,' Cochran clarified, tripping over her words nervously.

She was probably still used to the extremely structured protocol of the academy and these larger ships. She obviously wasn't expecting Trenchard's informal and rather blunt squaddie approach.

'…and that would be Captain who?' Trenchard asked, his patience wearing thin.

'The Captain ordered me not to say Sir,' Cochran replied. 'He says that he "wants to see the look on your face", Sir.'

Puzzled and increasingly annoyed, Trenchard thoughtfully chewed on his cigarette for a moment and then picked up his kit bag. 'Better lead on then Cochran,' he said exasperatedly.

'Yes Sir,' said Cochran, turning and bustling away across the hangar bay towards the elevator.

Trenchard watched her closely as she walked away. Cochran was definitely a little too eager to please, but his masculine ego couldn't help but notice that she had a nice backside. Trenchard had always had a thing for bottoms. He liked a woman with, what he described as "a bit of meat on them". He'd once got a black eye for voicing that opinion out loud in Mike's Bar to a young female officer when he was more than a little drunk. He smiled to himself at the memory and followed the nice bottom towards the distant elevator, wondering just who the Captain was that had specifically "requested" him in person.

'*Eighteen!*' the crowd shouted in unison as Cochran led Trenchard into the packed-out mess hall. The smells of fresh coffee and stale cooking fat from the evening meal, drifted across the room and the clanking of cutlery being washed echoed out of a metal hatch at the far end. Towards one side of the mess hall it seemed like every member of the crew had gathered around just one table, eagerly peering over one another's shoulders at a seated figure that Trenchard couldn't quite make out. Pieces of paper were changing hands, as were notes and coins. There was obviously some kind of gambling going on.

'What's the bet?' Trenchard shouted to Cochran over the hubbub of the crowd.

Gambling was a common event aboard star-ships. It was a good diversion from the day-to-day drudgery of daily duties and there was always someone ready to bet on something.

'Captain Collins bet Captain… *our* Captain, that he couldn't eat twenty of the canteen chilli-dogs,' Cochran replied over her shoulder.

'Fat fucker is he?' Trenchard snarled, a little unkindly.

Cochran gave him a disapproving look, but ignored the comment.

'I was hoping that I wouldn't miss the end of the bet. I've got fifty quid riding on the Captain in Kittinger's book.'

Trenchard looked over towards the table. He could make out a tall figure with dark hair in a Captain's uniform who towered above the rest. He had his arms folded and a despairing look on his face. That must be Captain Collins, thought Trenchard. The seated figure at the table was still partially obscured by the crowd but Trenchard was beginning to suspect that he might know the competitive eater in question. Only one person that he knew could possibly stomach that much chilli-dog. The same person who at the academy, Trenchard had bet couldn't force a whole heaped plate of Spaghetti Bolognese into his face in one go. The bastard had done it too. It had cost Trenchard a week's beer money.

'*Nineteen!*' the crowd roared.

The tall man looked sharply at his watch with a scowl. 'You have thirty seconds!'

Trenchard elbowed his way to the front of the crowd, where his suspicions were confirmed. Sitting at the table, with chilli sauce running down a napkin that was stuffed into his shirt collar, was a mighty man. He wasn't what you would call fat, but the man had a frame like an oak barrel. He was easily as tall as Captain Collins and broad with it. He had a jolly face with piercing dark eyes and his hair was shaved either side and then plaited into a long pony tail at the back.

'Twenty-five seconds!'

The man clocked that Trenchard was watching him, winked and then stuffed the last chilli-dog into his mouth in one go to a wild cheer from the crowd. He stood up, ripped the napkin off, threw it into the air and spread his arms wide in celebration.

Captain Collins shook his head forlornly, ripped up his betting slip and threw the pieces into the air in despair. 'You've fucking done it again, eh?' said the Canadian Collins, shaking the big man's hand.

'Pleasure doing business with you!' said the large man, wiping chilli sauce away from the corners of his mouth with the back of his hand.

'Here's your winnings. See you later at the mat-stat briefing,' said Collins, handing a bottle of rum over to the big man before turning and walking away, shaking his head and muttering.

The big man turned towards Trenchard with a beaming smile. He held his fist to his chest and let out an extremely loud belch and then grinned. 'Trench!' he shouted as he extended a hand like a baseball glove.

'Bird!' exclaimed Trenchard. 'I should have fucking known,' he said, warmly shaking the man's outstretched hand.

The big man smiled, 'Hey, that's *Captain* Bird to you,' he said, pointing to the downward red V on his black sleeve.

'What are you doing here?' asked Trenchard in surprise. 'When did you get promoted?'

Captain Bird smiled. 'About a month ago,' he said. 'They're short of Captains for the new Wolverines and with the pirates cutting the supply lines in half, High Command have made this mission a priority.' Captain Bird put his big meaty hand onto Trenchard's shoulder and laughed a deep booming laugh. 'It's good to see you again Trench. Let's go to my cabin and I'll tell you all about it. I bet you could use a drink?'

Bird waved the prized bottle of rum in front of Trenchard's face.

Trenchard grinned. 'You just said the magic fucking word, mate!'

Captain Bird led Trenchard through a maze of corridors to his temporary quarters aboard the Breath of Vengeance. The room was small and spartan but it had a table and two chairs which Bird pointed Trenchard towards as he opened a metal locker and took out two shot glasses. The glasses had the design from Mike's Bar etched onto them and had clearly been "rescued" from the bar on some drunken escapade long ago.

Trenchard smiled when he saw the glasses. 'You still have those?' he asked.

Bird nodded and grinned, idly turning on the holographic viewer on the wall. 'Of course. After what we went through to get these, they're my most prized possessions.'

Trenchard nodded towards the viewer 'Is there something on that you desperately want to catch mate?'

Bird looked at the viewer as if he didn't even recognise it. 'What? No, that's just automatic. I like the company,' he said turning down the volume as the evening news programme began. 'How've you been?' Bird asked as he poured two shots of "Black Void" rum from the bottle, then took the other seat himself.

'Good,' said Trenchard as he took a deep swig of the strong, spicy, caramel flavoured spirit. 'I'm in command, correction, *WAS* in command of a pretty good platoon. That was, until some twat "requested" my transfer. Which leads me to my first pertinent question; why the hell did you request me specifically? I haven't even seen you since we were posted on Mars and that was… what, four years ago?'

Bird ignored the direct insult; he was used to Trenchard's unique view of the world. He sipped his glass thoughtfully before answering. 'I need someone as my X.O. who I can trust on board the Might of Fortitude,' he began. 'There's a lot of bad feeling in the ranks these days. They're throwing recruits through training quicker than I can eat a Cornish pasty, to say nothing of this Technologist cult that all the rookies seem to be in to. It's completely fubar!'

Trenchard grinned. Fubar was old naval slang. It stood for "fucked up beyond all recognition".

'Fortunately, I've been able to hand pick my crew,' continued Bird. 'So I've been able to avoid any potential trouble makers. Admiral Fife owes me a favour or two,' he said winking. 'I need someone as my second in command who I know has got my back covered. Ever since that vicious bastard Chang was elected as Vice President, he seems to have been steering things his own way. He's trying to spread what he did on Mars to the rest of the United Worlds. President Smith's policies are becoming more and more... *sinister*.'

Bird threw Trenchard a glance that meant "do you understand?" Trenchard understood completely. The Space Navy used to be a proud force, policing the colonies, upholding the law and keeping the peace. In recent months, Chang's influence on President Smith had seen a complete lack of mercy. He had cracked down hard on the pirates and the insurgent terrorists and had pressured Smith to re-introduce public executions for the worst offenders to make examples out of them. Everyone knew that section forty-two was just the thin end of the wedge.

Trenchard settled for simply replying, 'I know what you mean…'

'Long story short,' continued Bird more brightly, 'Tempers get frayed when you're stuck in a tin can for months on end. I want someone as my second in command with a good deal of common sense in case the shit hits the fan while we're in deep space; someone who knows how to keep order in the ranks and doesn't take any crap from the rookies. Someone I trust completely. In short, you Trench.'

Trenchard swigged down his glass and Bird poured them both another.

'I'm flattered,' he said. 'I'll endeavour to repay your faith in me.'

'One more thing,' said Bird as he reached into his pocket. He pulled something silver out and dropped it into Trenchard's full glass of rum.

Trenchard looked at him as if he had gone insane. 'What the hell?'

Bird smiled. 'It's an old tradition aboard the hunter-killers,' he explained. 'These Wolverine's and Hunters are unlike any other ships in the navy. They're a different breed of crew. Usually you would have to go through weeks of training to even be allowed to step aboard one. Unfortunately, we don't have the time for that. I was rushed through the Perisher command course by Admiral Fife. Every officer who tries out for Wolverine command or exec must undertake the Perisher, but we don't have time in your case! You'll have to make do with these honorary dolphins.'

Trenchard looked into his glass and saw the silver badge lying at the bottom. He had heard about the tradition. It dated back to when submariners qualified in their basic training. They had to know every inch of the submarine like the back of their hand. If they passed the course, there would be a ceremony up on deck where the Captain would give them a large glass of rum with their dolphin badge at the bottom. The crewmember was supposed to swig down the rum and catch the badge in their teeth.

Trenchard gulped down the large measure of rum in one and bit into the metal badge. It had an oily, metallic taste. He spat it out into his palm and studied it. Two arched dolphins faced each other with the United Worlds emblem at the centre; a star surrounded by eight planets. He carefully pinned the badge over his left breast pocket.

'How's that?' he asked.

'Well at least you look the part,' said Bird. 'You'll have to learn the rest as you go, but be careful. The crew can be vicious if they suspect you're a skimmer. Just don't let them know that you haven't passed the Perisher, or they'll eat you alive.' Bird seemed to relax and poured another shot. 'Tomorrow I'll give you the grand tour of the vessel before we launch. Until then… a toast,' he said, raising his glass. 'To the Might of Fortitude; long may she sail!'

'The Might!' replied Trenchard as he clinked his glass to Bird's and swigged down the shot in one.

Trenchard's smile abruptly faded. The viewer screen had suddenly caught his attention. The news broadcast picture was showing a courtyard area with four stout wooden posts mounted into the concrete. Four people were being tied to the posts by U.W.S.N. troopers.

'Turn that up,' snapped Trenchard with a grim expression on his face.

Bird moved his hand near to the holographic projection and manipulated a virtual control in mid-air. The volume increased and the news presenter's voice could be heard narrating over the pictures.

'...*transmission is coming to you live from the naval headquarters of Star-spires on Earth. These four insurgent agitators were convicted today for their part in the Europa uprising. Each has been sentenced to death by firing squad, under section forty-two of the criminal code, an amendment recently introduced by President Smith's administration...*'

Captain Bird studied Trenchard's anguished face. 'You know them?' he asked.

'I arrested them,' he replied coldly. 'They were responsible for the deaths of twelve troopers in my platoon.'

On the screen, black canvas bags were forcibly placed over the chained prisoner's heads. One young man was clearly distraught; tears were streaming down his face as the bag covered his head. He was shaking and a dark patch gradually spread on the front of his trousers. It was the same man whom Trenchard had held a pistol to his forehead on board the Hand of Valour. The others had blank, almost disbelieving expressions on their faces as the black bags dropped down.

'*We will be switching to audio only in a moment when the actual punishment is carried out...*' said the presenter quietly.

Four troopers stepped forwards. Their visors were down and blacked out and they were wearing black breathing masks over their nose and mouth in order to protect their identities. At a command from their officer, they raised their rifles and took aim.

The screen went black.

Four shots rang out with a loud retort…

After a moment of silence, Trenchard snarled, 'Turn it off!'

Bird waved his hand through the screen's sensitive airspace and the picture disappeared. He looked thoughtfully at his friend, who had a tight-lipped expression and thunderous eyes.

'Did they deserve that?' Bird asked.

Trenchard looked straight into Bird's eyes. 'I don't know,' he replied.

CHAPTER 4

"LESSONS"

Extract from the Central Computer Network:
ccn.unitedworlds.co.ert/history/space_navy

In the early days of the United Worlds, there was no single police force to keep the peace across the many different colonised planets. Each world had its own militia, army, navy, air and space force. Territorial disputes were common. The central government on Earth realised that a single military organisation was needed and so the United Worlds Space Navy was created. Its mission was to keep the peace and crack down on any criminal activity or border disputes.

Huge military star-ships were constructed and troopers were recruited from every single colonised planet. The plan was to have a multi-cultural peace-keeping force with representatives from all corners of humanity. Unlike previous military organisations, there was no distinction drawn between the different fighting forces and so it was decided to use one single rank structure for the whole of the Space Navy. Thus, infantry troopers who fought on planet surfaces would have a similar rank structure as their comrades aboard the star-ships. In theory, this would build a better team spirit. To be a part of the

Space Navy was considered a great honour. Many stayed on after their initial tour of duty and became career troopers. They took the motto of the Space Navy, "Honour, strength and unity", entirely to heart…

Trenchard awoke with a start and tried to open his eyes. They were crusted with sleep as if he had been unconscious for days rather than hours. The bright light above the bed dazzled his vision and he blinked furiously. As he looked around he saw a white room with lines of beds along the walls. In confusion, he tried to raise himself off the pillow, which was damp with sweat. With an effort, he struggled into a sitting position and his vision gradually became clear. A blur beside the bed resolved itself slowly into the familiar shape of Bird, who was sitting and reading from a palm held computer device.

Bird looked up and smiled as Trenchard stirred. 'Morning Trench,' he chirped brightly. 'We thought that we lost you for a while there.'

Trenchard tried to speak but found that his throat was dry and hurt like hell.

'Whoa!' cried Bird. 'Don't try to speak; your throat was nearly cut through by that black suited bastard. The surgeons have managed to repair everything, but you'll need plenty of rest before you can talk properly. You lost a lot of blood. It's going to leave you with one hell of a scar.' Bird leaned closer and clasped Trenchard's hand warmly. '*You were lucky there mate…*'

Trenchard nodded in understanding and pointed to the palm computer in Bird's hands. Bird duly passed the machine over to Trenchard. Trenchard tapped at the screen and a small holographic projector shone the words that Trenchard was typing into the air above the screen in glowing green letters.

HOW LONG HAVE I BEEN OUT?

'Just over a week mate,' replied Bird. 'The Martian uprising is mostly under control now. There are just a few sporadic outbreaks of fighting and the occasional roadside bombing, but we've got the R.D. on the run. Dasilva sends his regards.'

WHAT HAPPENED ON THE MISSION?

Bird shuffled uncomfortably and looked down for a moment. 'I'm not sure. The insurgent leaders were all dead, killed by that guy with the sword who cut you up, so we were unable to question any of them and find out who supplied their weapons. They were all navy issue weapons though, older models, but they had definitely been made by the Papaver Corporation. The thing is, High Command have ordered the matter to be closed. They've ordered both of us never to mention that fellow in black with the sword. I had a personal visit from Rear Admiral Turner. She was very clear on the point. It was really weird. They just don't want to know anything about it.'

IT WAS A WOMAN. SHE WAS JAPANESE.

'What?' Bird exclaimed in shock. 'A woman did all of that? She must be one hard bitch! It felt like a freight train slamming into me when she drop-kicked me. I've never met any lass in training who could floor me like that.'

ASSASSIN!!!!

There was a long silence as Bird contemplated the number of exclamation marks that Trenchard had typed after the single word.
'The question is,' Bird said eventually in a hushed tone, 'why did she leave both of us alive when she could easily have finished us off?'

There was an uncomfortable silence for a long moment. Bird clearly had something else on his mind. He stared at Trenchard and took a deep breath.

'There's something else that I need to tell you mate. It's about Lorna...'

Suddenly, a dark shape loomed over Trenchard's bed. In a flash, a thin silver object sliced through the air. Bird sat still for a moment with a face full of shock, before the top of his head slid slowly to one side and fell to the floor, cut through cleanly just above the nose. As Bird's body toppled to the floor spraying blood over the pristine white sheets, the dark shape loomed over Trenchard, crawling up his bed like a huge black spider. Trenchard couldn't scream, he couldn't even move. He stared in terror at the black clad figure that was crawling up the bed towards him. The spider-like figure stopped and inch from his face and cocked its head to one side quizzically. Then it spoke, the voice feminine but steely, with a slight Japanese lilt.

'*You wanted to know why I didn't kill you?*' it hissed. '*...because I wanted to save you for later of course. Catch you next time!*'

The figure raised the small sword high into the air and then brought it scything down towards Trenchard's wildly staring eyeballs.

Trenchard awoke with a start for the second time. He was sweating and breathing heavily. He looked about him at the small bunk room that he had been allotted aboard the Breath of Vengeance. There were no shadowy figures poised with a sword to decapitate him. It was just another dream. As his heart began to slow down, he struggled into a sitting position on the edge of the bed and ran his hand over his sweaty shaven head and down his neck. He tried to rub away the cramps in his shoulder that he always got when sleeping in a new bed.

Why the hell was he dreaming about the assassin again? He hadn't had nightmares like these since he was in the hospital on Mars. Perhaps it was seeing Bird again, stirring up old memories and emotions? Perhaps it was seeing the execution of the prisoners that he had delivered into the hands of the authorities? He stood up and walked over to the utilitarian steel wash-basin and filled the bowl with cold water. He bent down, splashed his face and felt the icy water wash away the terrors of the night. Then he straightened up, grabbed a towel and began to pat down his face. As he looked down at the white towel he noticed a spot of blood. Looking up into the mirror he saw that his neck scar had opened slightly in the night. It sometimes ripped where the scar had healed the skin too tightly. But it hadn't done that for months now. He must have been tossing and turning all night long.

Wearily he began to pull on his uniform. There was no time to ponder on the meaning of the dream now, he had work to do. It was probably just one too many shots of dark rum with Bird last night in his cabin. He had a whole ship of new people to meet and a lot of new things to learn today. The woman in his dreams would have to wait. One day he would find out who she was and on that day, he would pay her back for the permanent scar she had given him and give her a few more of her own in return.

The asteroid belt spanned the view in every possible direction. Huge spinning lumps of iron and ice floated between even more massive dark foreboding mountains of cratered rock. Suddenly, the empty space on the edge of the belt was rent apart by the arrival of a massive object which was travelling many times faster than light. A whirling singularity stretched the fabric of space-time into eye-watering shapes. The magnificent hull of the Breath of Vengeance emerged gradually from the gaping maw in an unholy parody of birth. As the prow of the ship protruded into the void, it was surrounded by violent electrical bolts of bright blue and purple which arced and danced around the immense particle gathering tube. Once the whole ship had pushed through, the spinning singularity disappeared with a bright white flash of light and the Breath of Vengeance coasted gently to a full stop.

Inside the ship, Commander Trenchard was standing by an observation window looking out thoughtfully at the Might of Fortitude as he chewed on an unlit cigarette. The spacecraft was clamped to the side of the Breath of Vengeance by huge robotic arms. He absent-mindedly rubbed his shiny new dolphin badge with his right hand, thinking of Bird's words the night before. How different could it be serving on one of these smaller ships, he thought to himself? There would still be the confined living quarters, the zero-gee sickness, the crap food and the short tempers. Life aboard any navy star-ship could be tough. He'd become used to it over the years and now he couldn't imagine doing anything else. Surely this couldn't be too different?

Further thought was derailed as Captain Bird walked over to meet him, whistling a cheery shanty tune. Bird's metal-soled boots made a loud clanking sound on the metal deck as he approached. Trenchard straightened and performed a cursory salute, which was waived away by Captain Bird. He stopped next to Trenchard, beside the many inches' thick window and gazed lovingly across the vacuum towards his pristine new command.

The Might of Fortitude looked a little like a cold-war submarine. The main hull was torpedo shaped with a pointed nose cone at the front and a long, streamlined middle that tapered towards the main engine at the rear. Mounted slightly forward from half way were four "fins"; conning tower-like projections that were arranged in a cross at ninety degrees from each other. The Might was docked to the Breath of Vengeance by a hatch on the top of one of these fins. At the front, spaced evenly on the nose cone, were four rocket torpedo missile tubes and the dark, metallic blue hull was dotted with several fearsome plasma cannons and mass driver turrets.

Trenchard looked on in admiration, always one to appreciate a well-constructed vessel. 'She's a fine ship Captain Bird,' he said without taking his eyes off the spacecraft.

Bird nodded. 'The Might and her three sisters are the best hunter-killers in the fleet,' he said wistfully. She's actually the original prototype and is equipped with the latest stealth shielding tiles and low emission magnetic fusion drive. She has a lot of little extras that none of the other Wolverines have. We're field-testing her for High Command. If the new gadgets work well, then they'll be rolled out to the rest of the Wolverines in the fleet.'

'So, what's the mission?'

Bird gestured broadly out of the window with his hand. 'As you are no doubt aware, the asteroid belt is positioned between Mars and Jupiter. People generally think of it as a disc or hoop, but it's more like a hollowed-out sphere. There are millions, perhaps billions of shards of iron and rock left over from the early days of the solar system.'

'Yeah, I went to the lectures at the academy too,' said Trenchard with a sneer. 'You sound like our old tutor.'

'Not only does the belt present a formidable practical barrier to space travel, it's also the perfect hiding place for pirates. If they power down and sit still, it's very hard to tell the difference between a pirate cruiser and a floating lump of iron. The pirates hide out here between the asteroids and launch surprise attacks on passing cargo ships. Every ship that travels from the inner to the outer solar system has to drop out of Watters' for a short while to pass through the belt. That's when they're vulnerable.'

Trenchard nodded. 'Yes, I've seen some of the confidential reports on the attacks. I've even boarded some pirate hulks myself. Never seen much about it on the news though?'

Bird nodded. 'Do you think the United Worlds government could reveal the true scale of the problem out here? It's too much of an embarrassment to them. As the area straddles the trade routes between the inner and outer solar system, their activities have gradually become a very real threat to the inner planets, especially the Earth. The larger naval vessels like the Breath of Vengeance can't navigate safely between the asteroids in many sectors and so it's the responsibility of the smaller, sub-light speed, Hunter and Wolverine class vessels to track them down using stealth tactics. Here in the Koronis sector, the belt is particularly dense and is also right next to a major clear path through the belt, so it's a natural haven for pirate ships.'

'So, it's a search and destroy mission?'

'Mainly,' Bird replied, 'but if we're able, we are to board the pirate ships that we find and salvage what we can. Sometimes their supplies are better than those we have in our own stores on board. Weapons and ordinance can also be salvaged and re-used. If we capture a ship, we hang around until a slower cargo hauler shows up to pick up the prisoners and cargo. Then we blow up the pirate vessel to prevent it being used again and escort the hauler back out of the belt.'

'Sounds like you know the ropes pretty well?' said Trenchard.

'My last posting was as X.O. on one of the old Hunter class. I've led squads over to pirate hulks more times than you've had hot dinners mate!'

There was a pause as Trenchard digested this. Then he screwed up his face in puzzlement.

'One thing I've never worked out,' he said. 'Why do they make the damned things streamlined? I mean it's not like they ever enter an atmosphere, is it? They could make them brick shaped and it wouldn't make any difference in space. It's even got tail fins for Christ sake!'

Bird smiled. That was just like Trenchard. He couldn't stand unnecessary "faff".

'Well, the tail fins do allow for vectoring of the steering jets,' he said by way of an explanation, 'but there's also another very good reason. It just looks *striking*. It's all very well sending a flying brick into battle against pirates, but they're much more likely to be impressed by something that looks the part. The designers made these things look deadly because it's psychologically more intimidating to the enemy. Humans have thousands of years of programming built into their brains to tell them what looks dangerous and what doesn't. Her designers took advantage of that. It also instigates a feeling of pride and even love in the crew that pilot her. It's hard to love a brick.'

Trenchard grunted and ran his eyes over the vessel's hull again.

'You could if you had a big enough drill bit,' he said dryly.

Trenchard wondered just exactly how many plasma blasts the hull would withstand. He had heard that the pirates were getting better equipped all the time. He was about to entrust his life to the engineers that had built the Might of Fortitude for the lowest possible cost in the shortest time. The navy always had a strict budget to stick to. Pirates stole what they needed and improved their ships all the time.

'Have you got your magnetic boots on?' Bird asked. 'As we leave the wheel and approach the Might, we're going to lose gravity'.

Trenchard nodded and banged the heel of his magnetic soled boot onto the metal floor making a clanking sound. 'Aye Sir and I've got my heavy suit on. It's not the first time I've been aboard one of these smaller ships.'

Trenchard could feel the weight of the heavy suit underneath his uniform. It had weights sewn into the fabric and special elastic bands to keep the muscles under tension. It helped to reduce muscle wastage on long voyages by putting extra load on the wearer's limbs, in the lower gravity compartments of the vessel.

Bird smiled. 'Lesson number one. It's referred to as "boat" not a ship. Call it a ship to a member of the crew and they really will realise that you're a "skimmer".

Trenchard looked blank.

Bird laughed at Trenchard's obvious confusion. 'That's what they call all the sailors in the rest of the fleet; comes from old rivalry between submarines and surface fleet ships.'

Trenchard pulled a sour face. He was starting to realise that he did have a lot to learn.

'Well, let's get down there,' said Bird. 'The sooner we board, the sooner you can stow your kit and make yourself at home. Come on mate.'

With that, the two comrades clanked off towards the lower levels of the Breath of Vengeance where the Might of Fortitude was berthed.

CHAPTER 5

"THE MIGHT OF FORTITUDE"

By the time the pair reached the airlock hatch that led onto the Might of Fortitude, they had left the rotating spokes behind and there was no gravity whatsoever. The only thing holding them down was their mag-boots. Trenchard had already started to feel space sick.

Bird looked at his friend's green face and smiled, reaching into his pocket. 'You still get sick?' he asked with a grin.

Trenchard nodded, gulping in air to try and ward off the wave of nausea.

'Here,' said Bird, handing a small plastic bottle to Trenchard, 'take one of these.'

Trenchard took the bottle and read the label, "Proteus Pharmaceuticals Anti-Gravity Sickness Tablets. One to be taken every four hours."

'Zee gee pills?' said Trenchard with a raised brow. 'It's a long time since I've had to take these.'

Bird grinned again. 'That's 'cos you've gotten soft, working on these big ships all the time. You'll find that you will need these more often aboard the Might. Most of the missions that these boats undertake involve zero gee at some point. While we're in flight, the Might will spin and there will be nearly normal gravity at the ends of the four fins, but for now, every part of the ship is zero gee.'

'Great!' said Trenchard, as he gulped down a tablet and gazed around the airlock.

A long line of crewmembers, each held down by their magnetic boots, were passing cargo and supplies along a human chain from a vast cargo lift through the small airlock and into the Might. They were watched over like a hawk by a Logistics Officer who ticked items off on a touch screen computer as they were loaded aboard.

'That's a lot of supplies,' observed Trenchard.

Bird nodded. 'It could be a long voyage mate. It would be no good to run out of bog paper or coffee half way through.'

'Where do you store all the crates?'

'Anywhere and everywhere. In the head, underneath bunks, even in the wardroom.'

As the junior rates worked they sang an ancient seafarers shanty to make the work pass more easily; a jaunty song about drinking and sailing, adapted for the space-faring age. The most important thing about the song was the beat.

'There are mighty fine girls in every port,'
'Haul away boys, haul away!'
'And I've laid me down with every sort,'
'Haul away boys, haul away!'
'But I've never seen a girl with a finer arse,'
'Haul away boys, haul away!'
'Than the mighty fine girls that I've seen on Mars…'
'Haul away boys, haul away!'

As the song continued along similar lewd lines, Captain Bird and Commander Trenchard passed by and one of the men shouted 'Officer on deck!' All the officers and lower ranks saluted, leaving the cargo momentarily floating in mid-air. Waiting for them by the airlock was Warrant Officer Cochran with her vivid, bright red hair and a young Lieutenant Commander that Trenchard didn't recognise. As they stopped by the hatch, both officers saluted. Cochran still looked like an over eager puppy, but the new face looked, if anything, a little worried. He was a tall man with short black hair and deep, haunted, sunken eyes. He had a full, close cropped beard and dark bushy eyebrows. Trenchard had the feeling that the man reminded him of somebody that he knew.

'Trenchard, you've met Warrant Officer Cochran,' said Captain Bird smiling.

Trenchard nodded to Cochran. 'Unfortunately… yes,' replied Trenchard.

Cochran's face fell. She obviously wasn't used to being disliked.

'…and this,' said Bird, turning to the other officer, 'is Lieutenant Commander Peter Pugh.'

Trenchard clasped Pugh's outstretched hand and shook. Pugh had a strong grip but his palm was a little sweaty.

'Pugh?' he said. 'Do you have a brother posted aboard the Hand of Valour?' Trenchard asked.

The man's face brightened. 'You know little Jimbo!' he exclaimed excitedly.

'I've met Jim once or twice in the pub,' said Trenchard being as non-committal as he could.

'He's doing very well serving under Commander Fisher I'm told,' said Pugh happily. 'I was hoping that I might get the chance to see him while we were docked at Cairn, but the mission has been brought forwards.'

'Yes, I know,' said Trenchard tersely, casting a sour glance towards Bird.

'Pugh is my Warfare Officer in the control room and will assist you in command of the troops during off-vessel operations, Commander Trenchard. I'm sure that the two of you will get along famously,' Captain Bird said with a wink.

Trenchard grunted. He would have preferred to choose his own team but it seemed that Captain Bird had other ideas. Bird had personally handpicked the whole crew. He must have seen something worthwhile in Lieutenant Commander Pugh. His brother served with Trenchard's Geordie friend Dasilva and was, by all accounts, a steady officer who never put a foot wrong. Time would tell if diligence ran in the family.

Pugh turned towards Captain Bird with a furrowed brow. 'Captain, I still think that it's a bad idea to launch this early,' he said with obvious concern. 'We still haven't had the time we need to de-bug all of the systems. Lieutenant Sivia reports that the plasma cannons are still juddering on their tracks and none of the escape pods release mechanisms will…'

Captain Bird placed a comforting hand onto Pugh's shoulder.

'I'm reassured by your concern Pugh, but we'll have to straighten out the kinks while we're out there. We're close to finding Harlequin now, so very close. If we can take him out, then the whole of the pirate organisation will be plunged into disarray. They'll be too busy fighting between themselves over who will be their new leader to pose a significant threat to the space-lanes. The time to strike is now. We don't want to disappoint Admiral Fife now do we?'

Bird squeezed Pugh's shoulder and Pugh gave a worried little nod of acceptance.

'No Sir.'

So, that was the mission target, thought Trenchard. Harlequin was the pirate's mysterious and enigmatic leader. All that was known about them was that they wore a space suit painted in a bright red and black jester pattern. It wasn't even known if they were male or female. Whoever they were, they were a magnificent strategist and had a reputation for being ruthless and cunning. If they were going after Harlequin, then the mission was extremely important and also damn bloody dangerous. Trenchard made a mental note to bawl out Bird in private later for not telling him about Harlequin sooner.

'Shall we?' asked Bird, waving his arm for Trenchard to enter the main hatch.

'I'd fucking love to!' Trenchard replied gruffly as he stepped aboard the Might of Fortitude, right foot first.

Over the next hour, the party of four officers toured the whole spacecraft, Cochran making a snagging list of faults on a touch screen pad as they went. They took in everything from the engine room that housed the fusion drive, through the escape pods, air re-cycling store, mess, cabins, missile room and launch gear, before finally ending up at the entrance hatch to the control room. Unlike the larger vessels, the room that the Might of Fortitude was controlled and operated from was referred to as the "control room" rather than the "bridge", another hangover from its ancient submarine lineage.

The control room was situated at the extreme of one of the four fins where the gravity would be highest in flight. As Trenchard climbed down the metal ladder into the control room, a wave of stifling air and body odour hit him from the multitude of electronic equipment and body heat which was produced in the cramped space. As he settled his mag-boots onto the floor with a clunk, he looked about the room. It was roughly oval shaped, set at the top of the opposite fin to the main hatch, the deck being space-side and accessed by the metal ladder through a hatch in the overhead that led into the rest of the ship. Every available surface was festooned with pipes and cables of multiple colours. The various control stations were crammed in around the curved walls and a small rectangular reinforced window slit gave the actual view of near space towards the front.

In the centre of the deck stood the virtual reality control station or "Conn", where the officer on deck would stand to oversee operations. This one station could, if required, control every single function of the ship automatically with the aid of the on-board Guardian computer system.

The Conn was more like an upright body splint than a chair. It held the legs steady, enabling the torso and arms to move freely through virtual reality. Captain Bird had already been strapped into the leg braces with help from Warrant Officer Cochran. He then placed a black visor over his eyes from which small metal tubes extended and clamped around his forehead and temples. From Captain Bird's point of view, the control room no longer existed. He could see everything around the ship, as if he were part of the ship itself. He could operate any control by merely waving his arms in the air in front of him or, with practice, by merely thinking about what he wanted the ship to do.

Trenchard gazed around the rest of the cramped control room as the watch-standers settled into their positions. He had been on the old Hunter class vessels before but the layout of the new Wolverine class was slightly different. There was more automation for a start and so therefore fewer crewmembers in the control room. At the front, underneath the view slit, sat two junior ranked helmsmen in charge of steering and thrust. To their right sat an officer who was staring deeply into a glowing green tactical hologram showing near space and another next to him at the navigation plotting station. Behind them and overseeing their actions stood Lieutenant Commander Pugh, the Might of Fortitude's Warfare Officer.

To the left of the helm were the communications station, scanner control, and Warrant Officer Cochran who was settling into the weapons fire control station.

Trenchard assumed his place behind Cochran, just behind and to the left of the Captain. Glancing back, at the rear of the control room, he could just see the technical station and damage control, manned by two junior engineering officers. Finally, Trenchard eyes came to rest on a brass plaque that was bolted to the back of the Conn. It had a picture of a dolphin inscribed into the metal and underneath the words "We hide with pride!" This was the traditional motto of the Space Navy's hunter killer spacecraft and reflected their skill at stealth tactics. All the crew were ready, tense and expectant, concentrating on the job at hand. The feeling of concentration was tangible, like mist in the air.

'Guardian,' Captain Bird announced out loud, 'transfer all automatic controls to respective manual stations and pipe the boat to harbour stations!'

'CONTROL TRANSFERRED,' said the monotone voice of the ship's Guardian computer software. 'ALL CREW TO STATIONS READY TO LEAVE HARBOUR.'

The control room hummed with new power. The vessel seemed to come alive like a bear rousing from deep hibernation.

'All stations check in,' ordered Bird.

One by one the officers called out to confirm that they were ready.

'Clear moorings,' ordered Bird.

'Moorings cleared, aye, aye Sir.'

Captain Bird tapped the air in front of him. To an onlooker it appeared odd, but inside the virtual reality he was operating controls that only he could see.

'Captain Bird to Breath of Vengeance. We are squared away and ready to launch.'

The voice of the controller came over the ship-wide communicator system. '*Prepare for launch of Wolverines. Release clamps.*'

The Guardian software answered him, 'DOCKING CLAMPS RELEASED.'

Outside, the huge docking clamps that held the Might of Fortitude in place clicked and slid back with a hiss of compressed air and a loud clunk. She was now free from the Breath of Vengeance and ready to manoeuvre on her own. Navigation lights flickered on and blinking red and green lights shone out to port and starboard.

The controller's voice reverberated again. '*Launch in five, four, three, two, one...*'

'Fire manoeuvring thrusters,' ordered Captain Bird.

Outside on the hull of the Might powerful thruster jets fired, pushing the vessel away from the hull of the Breath of Vengeance. Manoeuvring jets now fired and she began to spin gracefully outwards at an angle from the hull. Gradually she gained distance, spinning like an arrow in flight. Inside the Might of Fortitude, gravity finally took hold and the crew felt the weight of their bodies press them to the deck once more. The mag-boots that Trenchard was wearing automatically released as the gravity came back on and he stretched the aching muscles at the back of his legs. Being in the boots was like standing on a ladder for any length of time, all your muscles were pulled and stretched in odd ways. It always gave Trenchard cramps in his calf muscles. Finally, the nausea that Trenchard had been experiencing began to subside as his inner ear became accustomed to gravity once more.

The three other Wolverines then slowly came into view from underneath the Breath of Vengeance, each spinning elegantly. As the ships formed up into a diamond pattern, a new voice came over the tannoy in a thick Canadian accent that Trenchard recognised from the chilli-dog eating competition in the mess.

'*This is Captain Collins aboard the Gift of Stealth. Permission to engage main thrusters,*' he said.

'*Permission granted to engage main thrusters on my mark,*' said the controller's voice. '*Good luck Captain, may you have clear skies and calm seas. Thrusters in three, two, one...*'

'Fire main thrusters,' ordered Captain Bird.

'Firing main thrusters, aye, aye, Sir.'

Everyone on board felt the judder as the main engines came on line. The tactical hologram showed the four Wolverines peel off into different directions, heading for different sectors of the asteroid belt.

When they had gained enough distance, Captain Bird pushed a small button on the black visor, just above the bridge of his nose and the small metal tubes retracted. He removed the visor and placed it safely back onto its stand next to the Conn. He looked tired and rubbed his forehead with his fingers.

'Christ, these things still give me a headache,' he complained. 'Well done everyone. That was first class. Kittinger, begin sweeping the area for exhaust trails. Schmidt, plot a safe course to the first waypoint. I don't want any stray rocks damaging the paintwork. This boat is brand spanking new and Admiral Fife will have my guts for garters if I bring her back damaged.'

He was met with a chorus of 'Aye, aye Sir.'

Bird carefully un-strapped his legs, stepped out of the stiff harness and stretched. 'You'd think that they'd design something better than Velcro to hold your damned legs in!' he grumbled to himself. 'Cheap sons of…' He caught Trenchard's eye and winked. 'Well, what do you think?'

Trenchard nodded appreciatively. 'Nice shi… er, boat! Let's hope that she doesn't fall apart in the first battle.'

This comment received a disapproving glance from Lieutenant Commander Pugh.

Captain Bird chuckled. 'There's nothing you two can do up here for now. Most of the systems are switched to automation. Pugh, why don't you take Trenchard down to meet his troopers? I'm sure that you'll want to introduce yourself?'

Trenchard smiled a broad smile. 'It's been a while since I've had to break in a new platoon. Come on Pugh, let's go squeeze some balls!'

Trenchard headed up the ladder followed by Pugh, who cast a despairing glance towards Captain Bird as he left.

Aboard the Breath of Vengeance, a lone figure dressed in red stared out of a huge plexi-glass observation window. The expanse of the asteroid belt stretched out almost to infinity in front of him and the four Wolverines could still just about be made out as small dots disappearing into the darkness; tiny points of light alone in the void. The sun was a distant orb, still bright but diminutive and lonely looking. The rocks that orbited here were cold and dark; gravestones marking the deaths of the many sailors who had dared to traverse this forbidding and lonely place, hunting ground of the pirates.

A second figure walked over and stopped beside the first, waiting respectfully. This man was wearing the uniform of a Captain, black with a downward pointing red "V". After a few minutes of silence, the Captain brought his clenched fist up towards his lips and coughed politely.

The red clad figure seemed to notice the Captain for the first time and sighed deeply before speaking. 'Are they away safely Overvoorde?'

Captain Overvoorde nodded. 'Yes, Admiral Fife. The launch went ahead as scheduled without a hitch.'

Fife nodded, but he seemed distant and pensive.

'Is everything alright Admiral?' Overvoorde asked carefully.

The Admiral was renowned for being moody, but this was a dark meditation even for him. Fife finally broke his gaze from the distant, diminishing pin-prick that was the Might of Fortitude and turned to face Overvoorde.

'Yes. Fine. I'm just concerned about this mission. There's a great deal resting on the backs of those Captains out there.'

Overvoorde raised a curious eyebrow. 'But it's just a run-of-the-mill sweep Sir. Those are the four best vessels in the fleet and four of the best Captains. What could possibly go wrong?

Fife pouted. 'Nothing Overvoorde, I hope to God! Nothing at all...'

CHAPTER 6

"WILD TIMES"

Four years and a great number of beers earlier…

The two comrades burst into the pub like wild bulls on stampede in Pamplona. They pushed their way through the throngs of drinking, cavorting sailors and headed straight for the bar. Then they sat down heavily on two swivelling bar stools and settled their elbows onto the sticky bar top. Mike, the bar owner, sighed wearily and put down the glass that he was polishing with a filthy bar towel. He walked over and stood in front of the two troopers and rested his hands upon his hips.

'It's been a while since I've seen you two reprobates in here, eh?' he observed. 'Where've you been hiding?'

Lieutenant Bird smiled broadly at Mike and proudly replied, 'Saving the United Worlds from the burgeoning threat of the evil insurgent terrorists of course! Don't you watch the news?'

Mike raised an eyebrow. 'You two were on Mars?' he asked, picking up the glass again, spitting on the towel and resuming polishing.

Trenchard nodded. 'That we were Mike,' he said in a croaky voice. His throat was still bandaged and he was only just starting to regain the use of his voice. '…and this is the first time that we've been for a run ashore since we returned from that shitty hell-hole, so you can leave the bottle!'

Mike duly reached down a full bottle of Black Void rum and set it onto the bar top in front of them. He then pulled two shot glasses from under the bar and set them on the counter, picking up the bottle and pulling the cork with his teeth before pouring two brimming shots. The two troopers raised their glasses and then Bird proposed a toast.

'To fallen comrades!'

Trenchard glazed over for a moment, lost in thought.

'To fallen comrades…' he said eventually in a subdued voice.

Trenchard clinked his glass into Bird's and the two young men guzzled their drinks down in one. Trenchard grimaced as the alcohol stung the sore inside lining of his throat. The assassin's blade had cut deeply, not only into his neck, but into his soul. He was still suffering from nightmares and sleeplessness. He held the shot glass up to the light and studied the finely etched design on the side.

'You know,' he croaked, 'I must get myself a couple of these glasses one day.'

Mike raised an eyebrow again. 'You're joking! Do you know how much it costs me to get those glasses printed? Three-dee glass printers don't come cheap you know.'

'Couldn't we buy 'em?' Bird asked, as he poured them both another shot.

'Of course you could,' grinned Mike with a twinkle in his eye. 'The next time you two have any money left after you've spent the night in here, I'll gladly sell you a couple.'

Bird grinned. 'Fair point,' he said.

Mike suddenly became serious once more.

'So, you two were at Belatu-Cadros? I hear things were pretty rough out there?'

Trenchard stared at his rum as he remembered the battle. 'They were,' he growled.

Flashes of orange dust, howling storms and the cacophony of rifle fire filled his mind. Visions of his pals, blown apart by the insurgent's explosives, still haunted his dreams. A picture of his friend's face flashed through his mind, their lower jaw blown clean off. Then Lorna's face inevitably filled his thoughts. He shook his head to clear the image, took the bottle, filled his glass to the brim and swigged it down. It stung a little less this time.

'We lost all of our squad...' Bird said with a deep breath. 'Only Trench and I made it out.'

'Yeah, I heard about the bombs... what is it you guys call 'em?'

'I.E.D.'s. Improvised Explosive Devices. They're just chemicals packed with metal, not too technical, but they do a lot of damage,' said Bird as he studied Trenchard. His friend had gone into a deep, dark place inside his head. 'The insurgents used fuel cans and packed them with nails. Not a good way to die!'

'Is that where you got that?' Mike asked, pointing at the dressing on Trenchard's throat.

Trenchard looked up. 'Something like that,' he growled, remembering the cold sting of the assassin's blade. Abruptly, shouting and bawling came from the far corner of the bustling bar. The three men looked over towards the noise and Mike's face fell.

'Not them again,' he complained as two large men began pushing and shoving at each other.

'What's the score?' asked Bird, studying the men carefully. They were not dressed in navy uniforms, but dull brown, full-body flight suits.

'They're cargo hauler pilots,' Mike explained disconsolately. 'They're on a lay-over while their cargo's being unloaded. They've been in here every night and every night there's been trouble.' Mike leaned in closer to the two troopers and spoke more softly. 'I'll tell you what. You calm them down and save me from calling the navy police again and you can have those shot glasses and the bottle on the house.'

Bird smiled and pushed himself up off his bar stool. 'Deal,' he said. 'Come on mate!' he ordered Trenchard and began to make his way over towards the two arguing pilots.

Trenchard shook his head and stood. 'Thanks for that,' he hissed at sarcastically Mike, before following his comrade across the bar.

By the time Trenchard and Bird reached the two men, they were engaged in a full-blown row. One of the men had the other by the scruff of his collar and was drawing his fist back for a punch.

'*Gentlemen!*' Bird announced as he clamped a restraining hand down onto the man's quavering fist. 'Why don't we all calm down eh lads? There's no need for fisticuffs.'

The two men looked around and stared at Bird. Lieutenant Bird was himself a large man, but the two pilots must have had Viking somewhere in their lineage. They were both blonde, bearded and around seven foot tall. Trenchard stood behind his best buddy and looked up at the two. One had a large scar on his forehead, the other was missing one of his front teeth. Clearly, they both enjoyed a fight.

'What's it to you, squaddie?' said the man with the scar.

The word "squaddie" was obviously meant as an insult. The pilots knew that troopers were proud of being navy sailors; matelots to the core. The noise of several chairs being pushed back echoed across the suddenly silent bar. A wide circle of empty space abruptly appeared around the four men. If someone had been playing a musical instrument, it would have chosen this moment to stutter to a stop.

Bird's smile disappeared and was replaced by a stern grimace. 'What it is to me buddy, is that the owner of this bar is a personal friend of mine and he'd rather not have it smashed up by a pair of visiting truck drivers. So why don't you just sit down, relax and have a quiet drink before someone gets hurt?'

The scarred man swung at Bird. Bird ducked instinctively. Trenchard tried to move but took the full force of the punch to his eye and went skidding across the floor. Instantly, Bird brought his heavy boot up into the scarred man's groin and he fell like a rotten oak in a storm. The man with the missing tooth grabbed Bird by the throat and began to throttle him with his arm locked around Bird's neck. Trenchard shook off the punch as he felt his eye begin to close up. He scrabbled to his feet and punched the toothless man in his ribs.

The punch had little effect. The man with the scar was already recovering from being kicked in the happy sacks and was already half way to his feet. Bird was starting to turn blue in the face. Trenchard looked around. Everyone else was keeping well out of it. Brawling in a bar was frowned upon. Anyone caught by the M.P.'s would find themselves on "nines" for two weeks. He had to end this quickly before someone called the police.

Trenchard stooped and picked up a chair. He swung the chair in a high arc and brought it down heavily onto the back of the man who was choking Bird. The big man crumpled into a heap on the floor, knocked out cold, leaving Bird clutching at his bruised throat and gasping for air. Then Trenchard turned, seething, towards the man with the scar and brandished the broken chair leg which he was holding high in the air.

'Just try it, you filthy piece of shit!' he spat angrily, baring his teeth and glaring through his one good eye.

The scarred man paused, about to leap from his position on the floor. He looked at the broken and splintered wooden chair leg. Nearby troopers were finally beginning to close ranks behind Trenchard and Bird to back them up. He seemed to think better of taking any more action and relaxed his shoulders, loosening his fists and holding his palms outwards in a pacifying gesture. Trenchard relaxed ever so slightly and looked across at Bird, who was still red in the face.

'You okay?'

Bird nodded and assumed his position, shoulder to shoulder with Trenchard. The scarred man staggered to his feet and began to help his dazed colleague off the floor. Trenchard raised himself to full height, puffed out his chest and mustered what he could of his failing voice.

'Now piss off back to where you came from and don't come back!' he shouted to rapturous cheers from the sailors around him.

Like Moses parting the sea, the crowd of onlookers made a corridor for the exiting cargo pilots who left to much jeering and shouting. Bird and Trenchard staggered back to their stools at the bar to be met with a huge grin by Mike who was already pouring them another shot of rum.

'You boys are pretty handy in a fight.' Mike said cheerily. 'Consider the drinks tonight "on the house".' Then Mike leaned in closer and winked. '...and you can keep the glasses too. You've earned it. You're both stalwarts,' he said with a nod of his head before making his way out into the room to retrieve the broken pieces of chair and mop up the blood and spittle.

Bird looked at his friend. 'You took quite a knock to that eye,' he said. Then he stared at Trenchard's neck with concern. 'Hey, did you know that your neck's bleeding?'

Trenchard shrugged. 'It does that sometimes. Don't worry about it. I'll recover.'

Bird clasped a meaty hand onto Trenchard's shoulder. 'You're a good mate Joe. You're always there when I need you and you're a damned good trooper! I just want you to know that I'll always have your back.'

'Thanks mate,' replied Trenchard, wincing at the throbbing pain in his eye and holding the cold shot glass to his eyelid. 'Same goes for me. Just try and keep us out of bar fights, would you? I get enough fighting when I'm on the job.'

Bird laughed. 'I'll drink to that,' he said, raising his glass. 'Here's to fighting hard… and drinking harder!'

Trenchard raised his glass. 'Here's to good mates,' he croaked, before downing the first of what would be many more glasses of rum that night.

CHAPTER 7

"THE ONIBABA"

As the Might of Fortitude coasted gently between the asteroids, inside one of the vast metal fins, Pugh had mustered the fifty troopers of the Might's platoon into an inspection parade. They were standing on the metal deck beside one of the two ship-to-surface drop-ships that sat there patiently, like a brooding sperm whale waiting to dive out of the airlock hatch below. The troopers were lined up in two perfectly neat rows. Each trooper was immaculately turned out, not in fancy parade dress but combat armour, ready for battle. Black helmet and armour were worn over black combat fatigues and a cross-chest harness carrying ammo and grenades. Each trooper had their protective visor pushed up so that their faces could clearly be seen and each was carrying a shining Vicar rifle.

On away missions, Trenchard and Pugh would each command one squad of twenty-five troopers, but Trenchard had absolute command of the whole platoon. He was master of all he surveyed and he rather liked that fact. He'd spent years being bawled at by irate

Commanders like Skelat. Now it was his turn to break in another new platoon.

As Trenchard approached with his hands clasped firmly behind his back, Pugh shouted at the top of his voice, 'Platoon, *ATTENTION!*'

The fifty troopers snapped into a stiff attention, their pristine assault rifles clasped tightly to their sides.

Trenchard came to a halt beside Pugh and eyeballed the troops. His first impression was vital. 'At ease!' he growled, '…and take the helmets off. I want to see your faces.'

The trooper's stance widened with their rifles relaxed to the floor and out to the side. Helmets were quickly removed and held under one arm. Well, at least they were well drilled, Trenchard thought, mildly impressed by their moves. Now let's see what they're made of. Without speaking, he walked over to the front row and began his inspection. Trenchard ran his eyes critically over each sweating trooper as he passed. He couldn't help but notice that every single one of them was very young, much like the rest of the crew.

'Pull that webbing tight!' he ordered gruffly as he passed a young woman.

She immediately clasped a strap on her front and pulled the fastener that held her spare ammo and grenades.

Trenchard moved along the line, stopped by a lanky young man and stared straight into his eyes. 'What the fuck is *that?*'

The trooper did well to retain his composure and kept his eyes fixed steadfastly forwards. 'What the fuck is what, Sir?' he shouted back.

Oh, a comedian, Trenchard thought. Time to have some fun. He leaned closer in. 'The badge sonny,' he snarled.

The lanky trooper had a small pin badge of a cute kitten attached to his webbing. He risked a glance down and then pulled his eyes back to the front again, a bead of sweat running down his forehead.

'That's fluffy, Sir! She's my lucky mascot Sir! My girlfriend gave it to me just before I left for the academy.'

There was a wave of chuckling from the rest of the platoon. It stopped quickly with a glare from Trenchard. Trenchard growled deep in his throat as his eyes narrowed. 'Are you fresh out of the academy son?'

'Yes Sir, three weeks, Sir!'

'No personal adornments are allowed on uniforms sonny, you know that. Pocket it now!'

Then the young trooper made his big mistake. He looked Trenchard straight in the eyes and spoke back. 'But… Captain Bird says…'

Trenchard steamed. His eyes narrowed even further.

'I don't give a rat's knackers what the Captain said son, this is MY fucking platoon! Pocket it now or I'll have your balls for breakfast!'

Some of Trenchard's spittle hit the trooper's face and he cringed. The badge was removed quickly by the blushing young man. Trenchard took a step back and addressed the whole platoon.

'You can forget whatever you were used to. I'm in charge now and in this platoon, my word is fucking *law!*' he bawled. '*What is my word?*'

'Sir. Fucking law, Sir!' shouted the platoon in unison.

'I'm sorry, but I seem to be suffering from a build-up of ear wax!' Trenchard shouted, cupping his hand to his ear. 'What is my word?'

'*SIR. FUCKING LAW SIR!*' bellowed every man and woman in the platoon at the top of their voices.

Trenchard smiled a self-satisfied smile and took a step back. 'From now on, this trooper is to be referred to as "*Mrs Fluffy Kitten*".' Trenchard relished each syllable, like a wine connoisseur savouring an oak aged Chardonnay. 'Anyone who does not, will be on nines for two weeks. Got it?'

'*AYE, AYE SIR!*' shouted the platoon.

The trooper's face dropped and his cheeks flushed bright red. "Nines" was navy punishment; extra duties and leave cancelled. It could also include a fine. Nobody would be foolish enough to argue with that. Trenchard stepped close to the lanky trooper once again and pressed his nose close to his red face.

'Any problem with that son?'

'No Sir!'

'Good. Because if you want sympathy, you'll find it between shit and syphilis in the bloody dictionary!'

Trenchard stepped back and folded his arms behind his back. 'Has anyone in this platoon been out of the academy for more than three weeks?' he shouted.

There was a moment's pause and then one solitary trooper stepped forwards, a suspiciously young woman with a closely shaven scalp. Her face immediately reddened like a beetroot. Trenchard walked over to her, subconsciously scratching at the scar on his neck. He was becoming irritated. There didn't seem to be a single experienced hand in the entire platoon.

'What's your name trooper?' he asked.

'Lieutenant Ellen Stofan, Sir!' the woman shouted back in a strong Scottish accent.

'I didn't ask for your first name love. This is not a fucking date!'

'Sorry Sir.'

'How long have you been on active duty?'

'Almost two years Sir.'

Finally, thought Trenchard, someone with a little experience.

'Where were you stationed?'

'United Worlds H.Q. on Earth, Sir. Star-spires perimeter guard.'

'For two years?'

'Aye Sir.'

'Have you ever been in action Stofan? Ever been in combat?'

'No Sir, just guard duty.'

'Guard duty? At the safest and most heavily guarded place in the whole of the United Worlds?'

'Aye Sir.'

Stofan's voice began to quaver.

'Ever fired your weapon in anger Stofan?'

'No Sir.'

Trenchard sighed. 'Step back in line,' he growled disappointedly.

The woman hadn't done anything wrong but Trenchard had a sour taste in his mouth. There was nobody with any real experience in the whole platoon. He felt like he had been stitched up. Either things were so bad that there were not enough experienced troopers to go around anymore, or somebody deliberately wanted an ineffective fighting unit aboard this boat. Either way, the realisation made him nervous. His gaze wandered along the line. At the back, trying unsuccessfully to remain unnoticed, was a huge man that Trenchard was certain he had seen somewhere before. He looked older than any of the other troopers and his grizzled face had a multitude of battle scars. He must be a veteran. Surely he had some experience?

'You there, tall fellow at the back,' called Trenchard. 'Step forwards.'

The tall man hesitated and then reluctantly stepped past his comrades and stood before Trenchard. He was nearly seven foot tall and broad with it. He had forearms the size of beer kegs and massive hands like dinner plates. As Trenchard studied the trooper's hands, he could just make out tattoos on the knuckles of each hand that read "Drink" and "Feck". Suddenly it all fell into place and Trenchard knew where he had seen the man before. His heart sank.

'Patrick McGagh!' Trenchard exclaimed. 'I never thought that I'd lay eyes on your ugly face again. It's been a long time since Mars. What are *you* doing in my platoon?'

The word, "you" was spat out by Trenchard with extreme bile. McGagh turned slightly and looked Trenchard directly in the face. He'd been bawled at by the best and Trenchard's act didn't impress him. He had a weathered face that looked like it had seen battle many times before. McGagh was clearly not afraid of a fight. He snarled as he spoke in a thick Northern-Irish accent that rattled like a bullet in a tin can.

'Transferred here Sir, two days ago.' McGagh's voice also had an unmistakable undertone of hatred. Clearly there was no love lost between the two men.

Trenchard studied the big man and his gaze fell upon his rank insignia. 'You're still only ranked Leading Spaceman? Mars was four years ago for Christ's sake McGagh. How have you managed to avoid promotion in all that time?'

McGagh's face remained impassive. 'Don't know Sir. Must just have the knack for it, Sir.'

Trenchard leaned in closer and his eyes became suspicious slits. 'Where were you transferred *from* McGagh?' he asked.

McGagh paused and frowned. 'Naval prison on Unity Island, Sir…'

Shit, Trenchard thought. Someone's dumped this loose cannon onto me. The naval prison was where the worst repeat offenders were discarded. It was where the navy abandoned its problems.

'What were you in there for, or shouldn't I know?' he asked carefully.

'Drinkin' and fightin' Sir,' said McGagh. 'Put two officers into hospital Sir, on account of what they said about my mother.'

'I'm guessing it wasn't a first offence?'

'No Sir. Not by a long chalk.'

'So how did you end up here in my platoon?'

'I was offered this posting or twenty lashes in Union Square.' McGagh looked Trenchard squarely in the eye. 'I had no choice... Sir!'

Trenchard screwed up his face in thought. 'Who offered you this posting?'

'Admiral Fife Sir,' McGagh snapped.

Trenchard stepped back. Clearly this was a last chance posting for McGagh. If a trooper got lashes then the next step was being dishonourably discharged from the navy. But why had Fife offered McGagh the chance to serve aboard the Might of Fortitude? He must have had his reasons. Trenchard decided to shelve that thought for later.

'You always were a vicious bastard McGagh,' Trenchard observed.

'Yes Sir,' McGagh replied politely, although his eyes were burning with internal hatred.

Trenchard leaned closer. 'You enjoy fighting a little too much.' he whispered. 'I won't put up with any of your shit aboard this boat, trooper,' Trenchard threatened. 'You try anything like you did on Mars and I'll have your nuts for cuff-links. Understood?'

McGagh eyeballed Trenchard for a long moment before replying through gritted teeth, 'Understood, Sir.'

'You're going to wish that you took those lashes McGagh. Step back in line trooper.'

As McGagh stepped back into line Trenchard resumed his place next to Pugh and whispered out of the corner of his mouth, *'This is the worst bunch of fucking munters that I've ever seen. Why are there no experienced officers in the platoon?'*

'This is the best we could get Sir,' Pugh whispered back, an edge of panic in his voice. *'They can't train recruits quickly enough. We were lucky not to get raw cadets.'* Then Pugh paused while he formed a pertinent question in his mind. *'McGagh was a last-minute addition though. What did McGagh do on Mars, Sir?'*

Trenchard sucked air through his teeth. *'Nothing good. I'll tell you later. Better get this lot moving…'* Trenchard rolled his eyes. 'Right then,' he exclaimed as he turned to address the troops again.

'Okay you lot. The first thing we're going to do with you useless sons of bitches is get some E.V.A. suit training in. You're going to need it if we're in combat against pirates. I want every one of you suited up in thirty minutes and ready for inspection. Then we…'

…and then the whole ship was rocked by a massive explosion. Everyone was thrown off their feet as the deck shook violently. The explosion was so hard that the ship stopped spinning momentarily and for a brief second the artificial gravity failed. Anything that was not bolted down began to rise into the air and then as the gravity was restored, came crashing back down again. Red emergency lights flashed on and an alarm klaxon sounded.

Trenchard picked himself up off the floor and helped the stunned Pugh to his feet. 'What the hell was that?' he shouted above the alarm.

He got his answer from the shipboard Guardian computer a moment later.

'RED ALERT. ALL PERSONNEL TO GENERAL QUARTERS. COMMANDER TRENCHARD TO THE CONTROL ROOM IMMEDIATELY!'

Pugh and Trenchard exchanged worried glances.

'Get them into action stations,' Trenchard shouted at Pugh, 'and then meet me in the control room.'

'Aye Sir!' Pugh shouted as Trenchard ran at full pelt towards the control room.

Pugh turned and bawled at the squad, 'Okay you lot, grab your rifles and load up. I want you standing ready with your rifles loaded in one minute. MOVE!'

The troopers began bustling about. Most of them looked unsure of themselves. Only McGagh readied his rifle in double quick time and then started to help others who were struggling with theirs. When he was sure that he was not being observed, Pugh moved over towards a metal locker on the far wall. Carefully, he opened the locker and reached inside. On a shelf inside the locker was a small metal canister with a valve on the top. Pugh quickly turned the valve on top of the canister until it was fully open and a sharp hissing sound began to emanate from the valve. With a quick glance around him, Pugh surreptitiously shut the metal locker again and followed Trenchard out of the hangar bay, carefully closing and locking the hatch behind him.

Trenchard raced down the ladder into the control room to find Captain Bird already plugged in to the Conn, directing a heated battle.

'What just happened?' Trenchard shouted rather unhelpfully, running his eyes over the tactical hologram and scanner control, trying to make sense of the information.

Captain Bird was grimacing with concentration, his temple thumping with the V.R. data streaming through his brain.

'A large black ship jumped us as soon as we were out of communication range of the other Wolverines,' Captain Bird shouted in reply. 'She must have been waiting for us, powered down. We strolled right past her without noticing. They took us from the aft. One of the tail steering jets is damaged and we're listing off centre.'

'Bandit is coming around for another pass!' Warrant Officer Van Allen shouted from the tactical station.

'*BRACE!*' Bird bellowed.

Through the view slit at the front, an ugly black space-craft thundered into view. It had no visible viewing ports and a multitude of weapons scattered across its pitted surface. It looked like a junkyard, randomly welded together from chunks of other space-craft that had been captured and salvaged along the way. As the crew gazed in horror at the approaching monstrosity, Trenchard could make out a crudely sprayed, helmeted white skull design, picked out in a deep crimson, blood streaming from its eye sockets and a malevolent grin on its face. Either side of the grimacing skull was a rough drawing of an assault rifle, the mark of the Martian space pirates. Plasma bolts seared from the turrets of the approaching ship and the Might shuddered and rolled.

'They have plasma!' Trenchard yelled. 'Where the hell did pirates get hold of military grade plasma cannons?'

Bird turned his head towards where he thought Trenchard was standing. 'Where's Pugh?' he shouted.

At that moment, Pugh descended the ladder into the control room, sliding down with his feet clamped to the outside of the ladder rail. As he hit the deck he called out, 'Here Sir!' above the din.

Captain Bird nodded. Then calmly and deliberately, with the black ship bearing down on them at full speed, he powered down the whole ship, turned off the V.R. Conn and disconnected himself from the leg brace.

Inside the hangar bay, McGagh looked up and sniffed the air. He turned to Stofan who was standing next to him. 'Do you smell that?' he asked.

'Smell what?' replied Stofan, concentrating on her rifle.

'That musty smell,' said McGagh. 'It smells like…'

Next to Stofan, one of the troopers keeled over and collapsed onto the floor.

'Gas!' exclaimed McGagh.

Around him, the troopers began to drop like flies. McGagh made a move for the door. He scrabbled at the control mechanism, only to find it locked from the outside. Gradually the big man dropped to his knees. His last view before unconsciousness took him was that of the deck of the hangar bay filled with the slumped bodies of the whole platoon.

Trenchard stared at Captain Bird in disbelief. 'What the fuck are you doing? Get the defences back on line now!' he yelled.

Bird ignored him, walked over to the communications station, pushed Petty Officer Hall out of the way and calmly leant forwards towards the console in front of him. Pushing a button, he spoke carefully into the microphone.

'This is Captain Bird to S.S. Onibaba. We surrender and are standing by to be boarded. Over.'

Trenchard looked at Bird as if he was insane. 'The fuck we do!' he spat and made a move towards the Conn.

At a nod from Bird, Pugh quickly drew his side-arm and pointed it straight at Trenchard. 'Remove your weapon please Commander,' Pugh said levelly, 'and move to the front of the control room.'

Trenchard stared at Pugh. 'What?'

'All of you,' said Pugh. 'Leave your stations and move to the front of the control room.'

By now Captain Bird and Chief Petty Officer Schmidt had both drawn their own side-arms and were pointing them steadfastly at the other crewmembers. Captain Bird looked up and spoke out loud.

'Guardian. Lock down all internal doors and hatches. Bypass emergency override, then unlock the main airlock and send out a docking lock on signal to the approaching ship. Priority override code delta five five nine.'

'CONFIRMED,' the Guardian answered dutifully.

By now, Trenchard and the other crew had been relieved of their weapons and herded towards the front of the control room by Pugh and Schmidt. A beeping from the communicator panel got Captain Bird's attention and he pressed a button. Immediately the air in the centre of the control room was filled by a large floating hologram. The figure in the hologram was wearing an E.V.A. suit, with their helmet already in place, presumably to conceal their identity. The helmet was sprayed bright yellow and a crude smiling face had been drawn across the visor.

Standing behind the man were several other space-suited pirates. Each had similar masks, skulls, demons, snarling animals; intended to conceal and intimidate. The punishment for piracy was death by firing squad. The pirates knew that and were taking no chances.

'*Good morning Captain Bird,*' said a man's voice from inside the smiler faced helmet. '*I am the Captain of the free trade ship Onibaba. I trust everything has gone to plan?*'

Bird looked slightly unsure of himself. 'Where's Harlequin?' he demanded.

'*I'm afraid our leader is detained on another matter and has sent me in his stead,*' said Smiler.

'But the deal…' Bird started.

He was cut short by Smiler who interrupted. '*The deal hasn't changed. You're just dealing with me now. Have the bridge emptied and clear the route to the bridge from the airlock. I'll meet you there in a few minutes. Onibaba out.*'

And with that, the hologram abruptly flickered off. There was an ominous silence in the control room, disturbed only by the beeping and clicking of machines.

Captain Bird turned to Pugh. 'Did you knock out the troopers?'

Pugh nodded. 'They'll all be sleeping soundly by now Sir.'

Bird motioned to the crew at the front of the control room. 'Take them down to the crew quarters and lock them in with the others,' he said. 'Lock any trouble makers in the hold and make sure all the inner hatches are fast.'

Pugh nodded and without a word he and Schmidt escorted the crew out of the control room at gunpoint. Trenchard made a move to leave with the others.

Bird turned to Trenchard and placed a restraining hand onto his shoulder. 'Not you Trench. I need to talk to you… alone.'

His face thunderous, Trenchard stood and waited patiently until all the other crewmembers had exited up the ladder and he and Bird were alone. Then he exploded with rage.

'What the buggery-fuck are you doing?' he screamed.

Bird leaned back on a console and relaxed a little, but kept his pistol trained on Trenchard. 'I'm sorry it had to happen like this Trench,' he said. 'I wanted to talk to you before we left Cairn, but there was no time.'

'No time?' screamed Trenchard. 'What about last night in your cabin?'

Bird looked uncomfortable. 'I had to get you on board first. I couldn't take the chance that you'd act… like this,' he finished, waving at Trenchard with the pistol.

'Why are you giving the prototype Wolverine to the pirates?' Trenchard demanded. 'Don't you know what an advantage this will give them?'

'That's exactly why I'm doing it,' said Bird sadly. 'Look… you know the way the United Worlds are going.' Bird paused looking uncomfortable and distracted. 'We're supposed to be a free democracy, but dictators are slowly and surely taking over. That vicious little bastard Chang is bad enough as Vice President. You know what he did on Mars, how he handled things? Imagine what would happen if he were to gain absolute power?'

Trenchard's mind raced. In a way, he could see Bird's point of view, but he had no time to debate politics. The pirates would be boarding right now. Somehow, he had to escape and mount a defence.

'These pirates and the insurgents may not be perfect, but they're the only thing standing between Chang and complete dominance of every civilised planet. These new Wolverines could potentially wipe the pirates out completely. They're a game changer. So, I decided to give them a fighting chance.'

'You fucking *traitor!*' Trenchard snarled. 'You were on Mars! You saw what the insurgents are capable of! Christ, I lost twelve good troopers on Europa to I.E.D.'s. I had to pick up pieces of their fucking bodies and put them in a plastic bag. There are other ways to make a difference Paul. What about the crew?'

'Harlequin promised me that they wouldn't be harmed. They're going to be dropped off in life pods near a well-used trade route where they can be picked up.'

'…and you trust Harlequin?' said Trenchard, aghast.

'I trust him… enough. What other choice do I have?'

'You could have talked to me.'

'I wanted to. I was hoping that you'd see things my way. I still do…'

There was a long pause before anyone spoke again.

'What happened to you Paul?' Trenchard asked with a sigh. 'What happened to the man that I trained with; the man who fought next to me against people like them?' Trenchard flicked his eyes upwards towards where he knew the pirate ship would be docking.

'Some things happened to me recently Trench,' Bird explained soberly. 'I've had my eyes opened to what's really going on. I couldn't, in all conscience, carry on fighting for what is slowly becoming a military dictatorship. I know you've been thinking along the same lines. I saw your face when those insurgents were put in front of the firing squad.' Captain Bird stared deeply into Trenchard's eyes, looking for some sign that he had convinced him. There was a loud clang from somewhere on the hull. 'That'll be the Onibaba docking. They'll be here in a moment. You don't have long to consider this mate. Join us, I promise you'll come to no harm.'

'I'd rather eat a bucket of fermenting rat shit!' Trenchard growled.

Bird chuckled mirthlessly. 'That's your choice Trench.' The sound of metal-soled feet clanging down the corridor outside echoed darkly through the control room. 'But it might be the last choice that you ever make,' Captain Bird admitted sadly.

CHAPTER 8

"SMILER"

Ten pirates filed slowly into the control room, clanking down the access ladder like an army of ants in their Extra-Vehicular-Activity space suits. Trenchard was pushed roughly to the back of the control room under cover from the pirate's mish-mash of captured and stolen weaponry.

'Watch it sonny! Trenchard' growled angrily at the pirate that had pushed him.

The pirate's helmet was painted with the face of a snarling bull. The pirate didn't react for a moment and then brought the butt of his rifle up and hit Trenchard square across the chest. Trenchard fell backwards against the damage control station, rubbing his chest and glaring angrily at the space-suited figure.

'*Shut up or I'll break your teeth!*' the pirate threatened, his voice sounding strangely distant through the communication unit of the suit.

At that moment, Captain Smiler clanged down the ladder into the control room. His E.V.A. suit was slightly less beaten up than the others and sprayed the same bright yellow as his helmet. He came to a halt in front of Captain Bird at the front of the control room and stood for a moment, examining him. Then he seemed to come to a decision. He reached up and undid the clasps that held his visor in place. With a hiss of compressed air, the visor rose and Smiler's face was revealed to Captain Bird. From where Trenchard was stood he couldn't quite see the man's face. It was definitely a man though. His voice, although altered by the echoing helmet, was deep and resonant. He had broad shoulders and slim hips.

'Captain Bird,' said Smiler. It was more of a statement that a question.

'Yes,' replied Bird nervously, 'and you are?'

'None of your business,' snapped Smiler. 'The ship?'

'She's powered down and waiting for you to assume command.'

'Control systems?'

Captain Bird looked up. 'Guardian. This is Captain Bird, authorisation alpha omega nine five three two seven. Transfer command of the vessel to Captain… to this man standing in front of me.'

'VOICE SAMPLE REQUIRED FOR AUTHORISATION,' the Guardian prompted.

Captain Bird looked pointedly at Smiler. 'You have to say something to the computer,' he said.

Smiler shrugged and began to speak. 'I once knew a girl from Carolina, who had the most hairy…'

'VOICE SAMPLE ACCEPTED. CONTROL TRANSFERRED.'

All the pirate's attention was focussed on the two Captains. Trenchard saw his chance and cautiously began to shuffle very slowly towards the access ladder in front of him. His ploy of taunting the pirate who'd hit him had worked and now the ladder was directly between him and the nearest pirate. It would make it harder for them to grab him as he ascended. Somehow, he had to stop these bastards getting away with the boat. That meant getting out of the control room. He hadn't worked out yet what would come next.

Smiler looked very pleased with himself. 'Well done Captain Bird. I now have control of the entire ship?'

Bird nodded and shuffled uncomfortably. 'You do. I've held up my side of the bargain, what about the crew?'

Smiler grinned. 'Which crewmembers are with us?' he asked.

'So far… Pugh and Schmidt. They've taken the command crew to their quarters and locked them in. All the other crewmembers are confined to general quarters as you requested and the troopers are knocked out cold in the hangar bay. The Guardian has disabled all the automatic locking mechanisms. The ship is yours.'

'Good. That will make it easier to kill them if they won't join us.'

Bird's face fell. 'But you promised…' he tailed off.

'What good is a ship without a crew?' Smiler asked smugly.

Trenchard inched further towards the exit ladder. Everyone's attention was on Smiler and Bird. Bird's hand started to move cautiously towards his side-arm.

'We need crew with experience of operating this prototype,' snarled Captain Smiler. 'Anyone who joins us will be treated well, as a comrade. Those who don't will be pushed into the airlock and… disposed of with the rest of the jetsam. I believe you call it "ditching gash"?'

Smiler drew his weapon and pointed it straight at Bird's face.

'I'm afraid we can't trust you and your friends Pugh and Schmidt. You could be spies trying to locate Harlequin. I promise their deaths will be quick. Thank you for delivering your ship to us Captain Bird.'

'It's called a boat, dumb-ass!' Bird snarled as he tried to bring his own pistol to bear.

With a grin, Smiler pulled the trigger. There was a flash and a loud bang echoed off the walls of the cramped control room. Captain Bird's face was frozen for a moment in complete shock as a line of blood trickled down his forehead from the entry wound in his skull. Then Bird slowly slid to the floor, leaving a trail of blood splashed all over the scanner control station.

Trenchard took advantage of the distraction and planted a heavy kick firmly into the groin of the pirate nearest to the ladder. Despite the armoured suit, the pirate crumpled to the floor with a satisfying groan and Trenchard leapt for the ladder as all the pirates swung around to see what the noise was.

Smiler snapped his visor down and turned abruptly to see what was going on. 'Stop him you useless idiots!' he screamed.

The pirates made a grab for Trenchard's legs as he disappeared up the ladder but their restrictive E.V.A. suits made them slow and clumsy. Trenchard exited the top of the ladder and slammed the hatch down, spinning the locking wheel tightly. It wouldn't delay them long, but he could move a lot faster than them. He pelted towards the next ladder. He had to get out of the command fin as quickly as possible and make his way aft towards the engine room. The only problem was that there were several locked hatches between here and there and the Guardian computer had control. He would have to release them manually if he could, which would take time; time that he couldn't afford.

In the hanger, the sleeping giant McGagh stirred. He sat up groggily and held his aching head in his hands. He tried to work out what had happened and then remembered the gas. He was probably the first to wake because of his enormous frame. He could take more whiskey than any other man he knew, so it stood to reason that it would take more gas to knock him out cold. Rising awkwardly to his feet, McGagh staggered over to the hatch and pressed the control to open it. Nothing happened.

'Guardian?' he shouted hoarsely.

There was no reply, so he shuffled over to the comatose form of Stofan who was lying in a crumpled heap where she had fallen. He kicked her shoulder with his boot, which gained no response, so he knelt beside her and took her head in his massive hands. A couple of rather harsh slaps to her face brought Stofan out from her slumber.

'Ow! Wha….' she slurred through the drug-induced haze.

'Wake up petal,' McGagh growled with a grin. 'Something's up. We've been drugged and locked in the hold. We need to get the hatch open and find out what's going on, pronto.'

Stofan finally focussed and sat up. She nodded and pushed McGagh's helping hands away.

'Go and help the others. I'm okay,' she said, rubbing the base of her skull with her hand and swaying to her feet.

As Trenchard raced up through the command fin, the gravity started to become noticeably less and less. By the time he got to the centre of the ship, it would be zero. He hated being in the central core; he had an inner ear problem that made him feel sick and dizzy in zero gee. Better dizzy than dead he thought as he raced along another ladder. The ship's corridors were strangely quiet and deserted. All the crew had been at general quarters when the Guardian had locked down the ship. They were all stuck in various sealed compartments. There were no crewmembers bustling from one part of the boat to another on urgent errands. They were all trapped. He would have to worry about them later; there was nothing that he could do for them now.

The murder of his friend played on Trenchard's mind as he climbed. The pirate Captain had killed Bird in cold blood. Bird should have known never to trust the pirates. They killed all crew and passengers of ships that they boarded to prevent anyone identifying them. What the hell had Bird been thinking? This was not like him. Bird was no longer the man that he once was. Trenchard tried not to think of all those late nights in Mike's Bar on Cairn, of all the close scrapes they'd gotten into on Mars. Bird was a legend in his own lifetime. He'd saved Trenchard's life more times than he could remember and when the crunch came, Trenchard hadn't been able to reciprocate. Damn! That smiling bastard would get what was coming to him. Trenchard would see to that personally. For now, he had to concentrate. Somehow, he had to save the ship. If the pirates caught up with him, he was dead.

With some effort, Trenchard pulled himself into the central core. It was a wide metal tube that ran the entire length of the ship. As there was zero gravity in here, there was no point having a distinction between walls, floor and ceiling. There were just four long ladders running along the core which led from the entrances to the four fins towards the fore and aft of the ship. Trenchard pulled his magnetic boots off the metal ladder and started to pull his free-floating body along towards the engine room at the aft. No-one seemed to be following him yet, he couldn't hear any boots clanging up the ladder behind him, but he couldn't take a chance. He raced along the core as fast as he could, his arms burning with the effort, until he finally reached the mid hatch.

The hatch was similar to those he had seen on other star-ships. It had an electronic opening system but also had a backup manual pneumatic system in case the vessel lost power. He quickly grabbed a lever set onto the circular hatch and pulled it from "auto" to "manual". A light on the hatch that indicated it was locked turned from red to orange. Trenchard pulled a steel bar from two clips set in a recess on the hatch. He then pushed the bar into a square hole located in the centre of the hatch and started to pump the bar up and down. He was rewarded with the sound of compressed air being pumped into the locking mechanism of the hatch. Shhh, shhhh, shhhh, shhhh…

'Psst!'

Trenchard stopped pumping. He was almost certain that the hatch mechanism hadn't made that last sound.

'Pssssst!'

There it was again. Trenchard spun around in the zero gee to see the cover to an engineering crawlspace, halfway up the curved wall of the core, standing wide open. Sticking out of the crawlspace with a beaming smile on his tanned face was the Chief Engineer, Lieutenant Devinder Sivia. Trenchard had met Sivia on a tour of the engine room. He was a Sikh, one of the few practising religious officers in the navy. The sight of the tanned, smiling, fully bearded face below a regulation black turban was both a surprising and a welcome sight.

'Lieutenant Sivia,' exclaimed Trenchard with surprise. 'How the hell did you get there?'

Sivia grinned broadly, showing off a beautiful collection of perfectly white teeth. 'All the doors locked automatically. We couldn't get out of the engine room. The Guardian's overridden the door lock and we couldn't get the pneumatic override to work. It must be faulty. I wanted to find out if it was just a local malfunction or the entire ship, so I crawled through the snipe tube. Everywhere is locked down. What the hell's going on?'

Every sailor in the navy knew the grubby engineers as "snipes". They were hard-working men and women who barely ever saw daylight or atmosphere and it was rumoured they drank engine oil instead of coffee. Older sailors would taunt the new recruits that had to venture down to engineering with, "The snipes will get you!" Sivia took great pleasure in perpetuating this myth by keeping a coffee mug full of engine oil next to his workstation and occasionally appearing unexpectedly from a snipe tube, scaring the rookies half to death.

'Pirates have taken control of the ship,' Trenchard blurted out. 'I haven't time to explain. The Captain is dead. We have to stop them getting the ship underway and somehow send an S.O.S.' Trenchard pointed to the snipe tube, ignoring Sivia's shocked expression. 'Does that go all the way to main engineering?' he asked hopefully.

Sivia nodded, his grin gone and his face suddenly serious. 'Sure,' he said, climbing out of the confined tunnel. Then he pulled a short length of string out from the pocket of his dirty overalls and tied one end onto the crawlspace cover. 'Follow me in. It's dirty and cramped in here mind. Grab the string as you go and pull the cover shut or they'll know what we're up to.'

With that, Sivia climbed back into the snipe tube and scuttled away on all fours like an insect crawling up a drainpipe. Trenchard took a deep breath and followed him in, pulling the cover shut as he went. Just as the cover closed with a gentle click, four space-suited pirates appeared out of the ladder at the far end of the core and started to make their way slowly towards the mid hatch.

Ten agonising minutes of bruised elbows and scraped knees later, Trenchard fell out of the inspection tunnel onto the metal deck of the engine room. The floor of the engine room was on the outer hull of the vessel and so there was partial gravity here but it felt like standing in a swimming pool. As Trenchard caught his breath Lieutenant Sivia and a junior engineer helped him to his feet.

'Are you okay Sir?' asked Sivia.

'Fine,' replied Trenchard, looking around him, 'for the moment at least.'

The room they were now in was essentially the engine control room, full of circuit boards and panels that controlled the various operations of the Might of Fortitude. The actual reactor core was further aft from here, just before shaft alley and was protected by thick shielding. At least there was partial gravity in here, Trenchard thought as his nausea subsided slightly.

'How do we stop them taking the shi… boat?' Trenchard asked Sivia, a deeply serious expression replacing the usual grumpy look on his face.

'If they have control of the Guardian,' replied Sivia, grinning at Trenchard's schoolboy error, 'then there's only one way to bypass that. We could take out the main circuit breaker; it protects the electronics in case of a power surge. Essentially, it's the main fuse. The only problem is that the reactor will scram, it'll shut down automatically. The whole boat will be dead, cold iron, and we'll be running off batteries only.'

'How long can we survive on batteries?' asked Trenchard, a sinking feeling in his stomach.

'Lighting and heating will last for around twelve hours, but the air will run out long before that as the scrubbers and burners stop working, perhaps four to six hours?'

Four hours! It wasn't long, but it was better than nothing.

'What about sending an S.O.S. from here?'

'No can do I'm afraid. All the communication equipment is forward from here next to the control room. Even if we could get up there, they could block the signal internally. But…' Sivia tailed off thoughtfully. 'If I could get to one of the forward sensor domes, I could disrupt the sensor beam and concentrate it into a pulse, send a sort of Morse-code signal. The range would be extremely limited but any passing ships would pick it up and we're still pretty close to the main trade routes. We might even be able to hail another Wolverine or Hunter if they pass close enough.'

'Sounds like a plan,' said Trenchard. Then he looked towards the hatch that led from the passageway outside into the engine room. 'Is there any way you can block that hatch? Slow them down a little.'

'We can weld it shut. That'll buy a little time.'

Trenchard nodded and Sivia looked towards one of the junior engineers who went to a storage cupboard and selected a plasma torch. He moved over to the sturdy metal hatch and began to weld a seam around the edge, the metal dancing and dripping under the searing heat of plasma.

'Can I get out of the ship from here?' asked Trenchard. 'I need to get the circuit breaker as far away from those bastards as possible.'

Sivia jerked his thumb towards the back of the room. 'There's an outer hatch at the back of this compartment to allow us to inspect the engine housing and vents from the outside. We've got four E.V.A. suits prepped and standing ready. We'll have to cycle the airlock by hand once the main power is off, which will be slow, but it's possible.'

'Right then,' said Trenchard firmly. 'Let's get to it! Where's your weapons locker?'

CHAPTER 9

"SPACE WALK"

Trenchard was suited up in the cumbersome E.V.A. suit and waiting inside the airlock for the engineering crew to cycle the air and open the hatch in front of him, when the nerves finally kicked in. Until now the adrenaline had been keeping him going, he hadn't had time to think about what he was about to do. Now that had passed, he had started to feel a pit open in the bottom of his stomach. He had the circuit breaker and the spares in his inside pocket. He also had a selection of weapons from the engineering weapons locker strapped to the outside of the spacesuit. It was regulation that all critical areas of military star-ships kept a store of weapons loaded and ready for action for just this sort of emergency.

The attitude of the navy was always D.G.U.T.S. - don't give up the ship. No deals, no surrender. A Captain would rather deliberately scuttle a ship than hand it over to an enemy. In the old days, that had meant breeching the hull and letting water flood in so the ship would sink. Out here in space it meant setting the reactor to self-destruct; a very final act from which there was no return. Trenchard had left orders with Sivia and the other snipes that if the pirates got the circuit breakers back, they were to try and blow up the ship rather than let it fall into enemy hands.

Trenchard pondered this gloomily as he waited in the cold darkness. The inside of the E.V.A. suit smelled of sweat and for some obscure reason, there was a faint odour of menthol. Probably one of the engineers liked to chew menthol gum, Trenchard thought. They were doubtless a recovering smoker. Smoking wasn't permitted on these smaller vessels. On Cairn and the bigger vessels there were designated smoking areas. These hermetically sealed rooms had extra fine filters to extract the smoke particles and additional fire dampers. Smokers were few and far between in this enlightened age. The equipment was bulky and expensive, so smaller vessels simply couldn't afford the cost, or the space. Trenchard hadn't smoked since leaving Cairn. Mike had the equipment fitted inside his bar as a great number of his clientele were smokers. Trenchard's last drag had been over a cold beer in Mike's Bar. He was suffering the effects of withdrawal. God, he could murder a cigarette.

Whoever the last occupant of the suit had been, they had left the inside feeling damp and cold from their sweat. His visor was beginning to mist up already from his own breath and hot body. He reached over to the control on his left arm and turned the internal demister onto full and the visor started to clear. His neck scar was already itching but there was nothing he could do about that now that he was inside the suit. He just had to try and ignore it.

The whole of the Might of Fortitude was now dead inside. An eerie silence had replaced the ever-present background hum of the engines and there was no light, bar dim emergency lighting that was slowly but surely draining the batteries. The ship was truly "cold iron". The pirates would have realised by now what Sivia had done. They would be desperately attempting to force their way into engineering. Trenchard had left the snipes welding every spare piece of metal to the hatch in an attempt to prevent the pirates gaining access.

Abruptly, the hatch in front of him opened with a hiss and a clunk and he stepped gingerly out onto the blue-black surface of the hull. It was almost a relief to be outside the ship and to see the dim light of the distant stars. Although zero gravity made him feel sick, he had no problem with heights and so the dizzying effect of being in open space had never bothered him. He was always a little taken aback by the sheer vastness of space though. On a planet's surface, there was always a horizon. Out here there was nothing except black airless void in every direction. He felt his stomach tighten and his breathing became shallow and quickened.

The stealth tiles that were glued to the hull felt spongy under his feet, which was unexpected. It was like walking on springy foam cushions. They were reasonably fragile but they prevented radar and most other types of scanning beams from bouncing off the hull. Beneath the tiles was the solid steel outer hull of the Might itself and that felt comforting and sturdy. What was his next move? He hadn't thought much further ahead than getting outside of the ship. While he was suiting up, the pirates had begun to hammer on the outside of the hatch that led into engineering. It wouldn't be long until they figured out what he was up to and came after him. The pirates were smart, too smart. They obviously had inside information about the Might of Fortitude that Captain Bird must have given to them before the launch. What other secrets had he told them before they killed him?

Trenchard shook the memory of Bird's death from his mind and looked back towards the hull of the Might of Fortitude. He had come out next to one of the rear tail fins. The main engine was to his right and the long, streamlined hull, stretched onwards to his left. The ugly, black, pirate ship Onibaba was docked on the opposite mid fin behind him, rotating gently along with the Might.

Looking around, he took in the local area. This part of the asteroid belt was sparsely populated with the slowly turning, megalithic chunks of rock and ice. The nearest asteroid was an unclassified pile of rubble that was held together loosely by gravity. It resembled a freely floating sack of potatoes. It would be a good place to hide; there were plenty of nooks and crannies that he could wedge himself into.

The light from the distant sun was dimmer here. Everything had the blue cast of twilight. It gave the already freezing void an extra hint of frostiness, foreboding and sinister. He had about two hours of air with him in the suit and a spare gas bottle tied to his belt. That gave him four hours if he was lucky and didn't need to exert himself too much. At least he would suffocate at the same time as his shipmates he thought darkly. The thought gave him a strange comfort. He just had to hope that Lieutenant Sivia could make it to the scanner array by then and send the S.O.S. Then they had to hope that someone was in range and would hear it and come to the rescue. It was a slim chance, but if he could just…

WHAP!

A sizzling burst of energy flew past him and exploded against the hull to his right, singeing one of the stealth tiles. He hadn't heard the impact so much as seen the flash and felt debris hit his suit. He turned quickly and looked to his left towards where the burst had come from. Five, no, he counted six space-suited pirates who had just exited from an inspection hatch towards the front of the ship near the forward sensor domes. They had fired a flare at him, a mix of chemicals designed to give off a bright glow in the oxygen-less vacuum of space. It was a warning shot. They wanted him to surrender and give them back the circuit breakers. They were armed with traditional rifles but obviously didn't want to damage the circuit breakers by firing directly at him. That gave him an edge.

He studied the pirate's rifles. Even from this distance he could see that they were old models, not intended to be fired in the vacuum of space. The rounds would probably ignite well enough, unless the chambers became too cold. It was very cold out here in the void. Trenchard looked down at his own rifle. The Void-Capable Case-less Assault Rifle, or "Vicar" for short, was standard navy issue. It was deliberately designed to be fired in space. He pressed a small control next to the handle and a tiny element began to gently warm the firing mechanism. His rifle wouldn't miss-fire. That was a certainty. That gave him another edge.

Trenchard pushed off from the hull of the Might of Fortitude with a huge leap and simultaneously fired the steering jets on his backpack. He kept the burst short to save the precious fuel. The thrust was just enough to propel him towards the nearest asteroid. He held up his left hand and looked into the mirror that was fitted onto the back of the glove. The pirates had pushed off towards the asteroid after him. They were burning far more fuel in order to catch up. Their tanks wouldn't last as long on full throttle. They would run out of fuel. Did they know that? Did they even care? Another warning shot from the flare gun zoomed past him and disappeared into the dark interior of the asteroid, illuminating a large cavity between two enormous lumps of solid iron. It was almost like an invitation to come inside, lighting the way for him.

It seemed to take an age to reach the asteroid. There was no feeling of speed out here as there was nothing to judge his speed against. He was probably travelling at hundreds of meters per second by now but he felt as if he were standing still. Minute by minute the opening in the asteroid loomed gradually larger and larger. Another object suddenly shot past his head, small and fast. It was a bullet. The bullet smashed into the iron surface of the asteroid in front of him and shattered into a thousand tiny fragments, spinning away into the void. Their rifles did work after all.

Trenchard reached the opening and risked a quick glance backwards before the darkness of the interior swallowed him up. The pirates had gained some ground but were still more than thirty meters away. Let's see if I can't lose them in here, Trenchard thought to himself as the asteroid enveloped him like the jaws of a mighty yawning whale.

Inside the Might of Fortitude, an inspection hatch cover slid quietly open and Lieutenant Sivia peered cautiously out. He had crawled as far as he could in the hidden compartments and engineering crawlspaces behind the walls. He was now just outside the hatch to the scanner room, located in the main hull, just forward of the fin that housed the control room. The pirates had obviously thought that the crew might try and get a message out this way and had cleared the scanner room of the watch-standers and posted a guard outside. Blood was pooled on the floor where some unfortunate crewmember had made a stand and been swiftly dealt with.

One pirate stood on guard, holding a rifle listlessly and looking bored. His helmet was lying on the floor next to him. Most of the others must either be inside the control room or chasing after Trenchard, thought Sivia. Although the pirate was for the moment looking the other way, if Sivia dropped out of the shaft to the ground, despite the low gravity in this part of the ship, the guard would undoubtedly hear him and bring his rifle to bear. Sivia wouldn't stand a chance. How to get into the scanner room, Sivia thought? How do I get past a space pirate who is looking out for Space Navy crewmembers?

Three minutes later Sivia crawled out of another snipe tube, one compartment down from the scanner control room. This was an area by an exterior inspection hatch that led out of the ship towards the front, allowing the technical crew to affect repairs on the forward scanner arrays and torpedo tubes. Just as in main engineering, there were four E.V.A. suits lined up ready to use. They looked similar to the pirate's suits but they were too new, too clean. Sivia desperately searched around the room, through the cupboards full of tools, sealing tape and reels of wire. Then he chanced upon something that might work; a pot of sickly yellow grease that the engineers referred to as "baby shit" due to its yellow colour and terrible smell. Sivia grinned from ear-to-ear and set to work on the nearest suit.

'He's done what?' Captain Smiler shouted angrily.

Inside the control room Smiler's X.O. stood in front of him with her helmet under her arm, looking rather sheepish.

'We think he's taken the circuit breakers with him outside the ship. He just entered one the asteroids. Our men have followed him in but it's going to be hard to find him in there.'

Smiler scowled for a long moment before replying. 'Tell them that if they don't recover those circuit breakers, they won't get back aboard this ship! That should motivate them a little.'

There was a moment of uncomfortable silence before the Executive Officer replied.

'What about Commander Trenchard?'

Smiler snarled. 'I don't care about him, just the circuit breakers.'

Then Smiler grabbed his own helmet from a nearby console and moved towards the exit ladder.

'I'm going back to the Onibaba,' he said with a frustrated tone in his voice. 'I can't make head nor tail of the command systems here so I'm going back to use ours and contact Harlequin.'

Then he stopped and turned back towards his X.O.

'Try not to fuck up any more while I'm away, would you?'

Trenchard was playing a deadly game of hide and seek with the pirates. He had worked his way deeper inside the loose pile of gently floating lumps of rock and iron and had turned off his suit's lights and propulsion jets. He was waiting, crouched in a natural alcove that had been splintered from one of the larger rocks. All he could hear inside his suit was his own tense, heavy breathing, coming in short, nervous gasps. The scar on his neck was itching terribly now and he was desperate for the toilet. Suddenly, he spotted movement and all was forgotten.

The pirates must have split up to search for him more quickly. He could see one of them, a fearsome skull painted across his helmet. The pirate was feeling his way along the solid iron walls of this part of the asteroid. The pirate's spotlight played along the rough walls of the inner space, illuminating minerals and ores that danced and glittered in the bright beam. Trenchard couldn't see any of the other pirates; they must have explored down different openings. He waited for the pirate to pass in front of him, about ten feet ahead. Then he braced his feet onto the rock behind him and launched himself towards the back of the pirate.

He hasn't seen me, thought Trenchard as he floated forwards. Don't look round, *don't look round.* As Trenchard neared the man's back, he pulled a combat knife out from its sheath on his belt. As he reached within arms distance, he grabbed the air hose that connected the pirate's backpack to his helmet and sliced through it with one deft swipe. The terrified man grasped desperately behind him at his unseen attacker but Trenchard had already moved, spinning past him and brought the knife up in a diagonal thrust into the man's ribcage. The pirate spun away erratically, his struggling becoming gradually less and less frantic. He left a trail of perfectly spherical blood droplets in his wake, frozen solid like ruby marbles. Trenchard could see the man's lips moving. Even though he couldn't hear the words, he knew that the man was warning his comrades. One down, five to go, thought Trenchard grimly.

PING!

A bullet zipped past Trenchard's visor and impacted into the wall sending splinters flying. Shrapnel hit his visor making a sharp pinging sound, rattling like hail on a tin roof. As he turned, he could see another pirate gaining on him at full speed and there was nowhere to hide.

The guard stationed by the scanner room was bored. He'd had no company, no food or drink since being posted here three hours ago. Man, he could murder a bacon sandwich, he thought to himself. Dreaming of white bread, crispy streaky bacon and brown sauce, the pirate almost didn't notice his comrade approaching down the passageway. Along the corridor came another pirate dressed head to toe in his E.V.A. suit with his helmet still in place. They must have just come over from the Onibaba, thought the guard idly. I wonder if they've brought lunch? The guard smiled broadly at the new arrival as he got nearer.

'Hey shipmate, you can take off the hard top now you know,' he called out.

The new arrival came to a stop in front of him. It was only now that the figure was this close that the guard noticed something unusual about their E.V.A. suit. The skull painted across the new arrival's visor looked a little… greasy?

'Mate, what the heck is that bloody awful smell?' the guard asked, wrinkling his nose up. 'Have you just dropped one?'

The new arrival reached up with their left hand and popped his visor up. The face beneath beamed a broad smile.

'No, but you have mate!' Sivia said as he brought the large spanner that he was hiding behind his back, up sharply, smashing it across the side of the guard's face.

The surprised guard dropped like a stone with a satisfying crunch as his jaw crumbled. Sivia bent and dragged his unconscious body inside the scanner room, closed and locked the hatch behind him and thrust the spanner into the mechanism to prevent anyone else from opening the hatch. He pulled a handful of plastic cable-ties out from his inside pocket and bound the unconscious pirate's arms and legs. Then Sivia stood up and turned towards the scanner machinery.

'Right then,' he said out loud. 'Let's see if anyone's listening out there, shall we?'

McGagh gave a grunt as he heaved on the end of his rifle. The barrel of the rifle was wedged in to a minute crack that the troopers had managed to open up between the hatch and the frame. A group of the strongest troopers were hauling as hard as they could on the hatch, using any hand hold that they could find purchase upon with their fingertips. The pneumatics that held the hatch closed were whining and complaining but they still held fast. With a bellow of anger from McGagh, the rifle slipped out of the crack in the hatch again and the hatch slammed shut with a resounding clang. McGagh finally lost his temper and began clubbing the stubborn hatch with the butt of his rifle, taking his frustration out on the solid metal.

'Stupid, fecking…'

'Hey, McGagh!' Stofan shouted. 'That's not going to do us any good, you daft sod.'

McGagh stopped swinging and turned towards Stofan, panting and glaring. 'No. But it makes me feel a hell of a lot better,' he growled.

'Is this what you lot do for fun?' called a new voice from somewhere above their heads.

The whole platoon snapped their eyes up to where the voice had come from. Several rifles were aimed at the figure who was sticking half way out of a snipe tube, high up on the bulkhead. It was a young engineer and she was beaming down at their surprised faces with obvious glee.

'How did you get up there?' called out an amazed Stofan.

'Snipe tube,' shouted the young woman, jerking her thumb back towards the tunnel behind her. 'Come on. Pirates have boarded the boat. The Captain's dead. I can lead you nearly all the way to the control room through here.'

After a short silence while the troopers mulled over the news of Captain Bird's death, McGagh piped up, 'Where's Commander Trenchard?'

'In an E.V.A. suit, outside in the asteroid belt with the boat's main circuit breakers,' the young snipe called. He's trying to stop them from getting underway. He left orders to attempt to re-take the control room.'

Stofan's gaze moved from the figure in the tunnel down to the deck. It was a drop of some twenty feet.

'We need to build some stairs. Move it!' she shouted.

Instantly the troopers began lugging heavy crates and ammunition boxes over towards the wall, stacking them on top of one another to form a surmountable pile.

'Better load up,' said Stofan to McGagh.

McGagh nodded and ripped the cover off a nearby ammo crate. He clicked a cartridge home into his own rifle and then began handing the other live rounds out to the busying troopers.

CHAPTER 10

"ALPHA MIKE FOXTROT"

Trenchard brought his rifle up and around in an arc, strafing the area where the pirate was floating towards him. The volley just about cut the pirate in half, his lunch spilling out from his ripped open guts and floating away into the cold vacuum, becoming instant frozen dinner. With the sudden decrease in pressure the man's lungs expanded and ruptured. Salmon pink foam began to spew from lips that were beginning to turn an icy blue. Two down, four left. Trenchard had no more time to appreciate the pirate's gradual death from exposure to the freezing vacuum as two more of his shipmates rounded a corner and raised their weapons.

Trenchard pushed off from the nearest floating boulder and sailed out of their range. The next few minutes were a limb-wrenching race for life through the asteroid's interior. Each time the pirates came close, Trenchard hit a wall of floating rock and pushed off in a different direction, spinning and rolling to avoid random bursts of rifle fire. Then, just as he thought his limbs would pop from the exertion, Trenchard saw his chance. As he floated past a deeply creviced rock, he pulled a fragmentation grenade from his belt and shoved it deep inside the crack, pressing the activation button as he went. Slamming his back into an opposing rock wall took the wind out of his chest, but Trenchard hit the steering jets hard, counting in his head, nine, eight, seven...

This was what he had been saving his fuel for. He raced away from the primed grenade at breakneck speed. Just as the pirates rounded the corner and raised their rifles, the grenade exploded. Trenchard didn't look back. For a second, the dark interior of the asteroid was silently lit up like a summer day. The reflection from the sparkling minerals in the walls was almost blinding. Then the impact of the shrapnel and expanding gas of the explosion hit him, throwing him forwards with extreme velocity and shredding his suit. The fabric of his space-suit immediately began to self-heal, but there was no way to avoid the large boulder in front of him. He slammed into it and his right arm was instantly crushed. He could hear the bone break inside his suit with a loud snap and he dropped his rifle which spun away into the darkness.

The whole asteroid heaved outwards like the chest of a giant taking a deep breath. Then slowly the rocks began to collapse back inwards, dragged back by gravity. Boulders and lumps of iron began to smash randomly into each other. The interior of the asteroid became a whirling barrage of spinning splintered rock. *Must get out*, thought Trenchard through the pain of his broken arm, *must get free*.

Trenchard saw an opening and hit the jets again, shooting out from the asteroid like a cork from a bottle of champagne. He checked the mirror on his left hand. Two of the pirates were still following him. One of them had a rifle. The pirate slowly raised his weapon. There was nothing that Trenchard could do. He was a sitting duck. He was dead.

WHUMP!

With a blinding flash, the empty space near to the Might of Fortitude was suddenly filled by a massive, decelerating spacecraft. The gravity wave of the decelerating ship sent out a ripple that made the Might, the Onibaba and every nearby asteroid, bob like ducks on a pond. Trenchard looked up, his heart singing. It was the Breath of Vengeance, the ship that had dropped them off in the asteroid belt. Sivia's message must have got through. A large ship like the Breath of Vengeance shouldn't jump into the asteroid belt like that, certainly not so close to a smaller ship, but if they had come in further away, then they would have lost the element of surprise. It was a dangerous manoeuvre. Even now, the Breath was taking heavy damage from asteroid collisions as it veered towards the Might of Fortitude and the pirate ship Onibaba.

Inside the Might of Fortitude's control room, Captain Smiler's Executive Officer saw the Breath of Vengeance arrive on a monitor screen and swore quietly to herself.

'We're leaving. NOW!' she shouted, donning her helmet and racing up the exit ladder, closely followed by her quietly panicking comrades.

The top of the ladder opened out into a broad passageway that led to other areas of the vessel. The Exec and her fellow pirates stopped short, just outside the hatch, causing those behind to pile into their backs in their hurry to escape. The Exec stared in disbelief and raised her hands in resignation of surrender. The entire corridor was filled with the troopers of the Might of Fortitude, each one with a Vicar rifle levelled at a pirate's chest or face. At their head, a stern looking Stofan and a grinning McGagh met the Exec's gaze levelly.

'Drop your weapons. Don't move!' Stofan shouted threateningly.

'I would listen to the lady if I were you,' McGagh sneered. 'We've all had a particular pisser of a bad day!'

Every pirate threw their weapons to the floor and surrendered. Then suddenly the corridor lurched unsteadily, making the troopers stagger and grab for any nearby hand hold.

'What the hell is that?' said Stofan glancing up.

'Gravity wave from another ship arriving,' said McGagh. 'A big one too!'

The Might and the Onibaba were rocking dangerously, docked together as they were in a deadly embrace, pneumatic clamps straining with the effort. A couple of attack gun-ships that had been launched from the nearest hangar bay of the Breath of Vengeance were already speeding towards the scene, dodging and weaving between the random lumps of hurtling rock. The docking clamps of the Onibaba groaned like an angry bear and quickly disengaged from the airlock of the Might. The Onibaba hit full thrust, scraped along the Might's hull in a shower of sparks and then powered away from the area as fast as it could manage. The gun-ships were too small to take her on and the Breath of Vengeance was too slow and massive, but they both did a good job of chasing her off with a few rounds of plasma fire.

One of the gun-ships rounded towards Trenchard. He quickly hit the distress alarm on his suit's chest unit and began to wave frantically, warning lights attached to his wrists blinking furiously. The last thing that he wanted now was to be shot by his own navy. He could just see the pilot of the nearest gun-ship give him a grin and a thumbs-up through the cockpit window as they sped past. Then he heard the pilot contacting the command ship over the radio as his suit's communicator came within radio range and locked into the naval frequency.

'*Gun-ship kilo bravo zulu, niner fiver wun. Target acquired. Alpha mike foxtrot.*'

Alpha mike foxtrot was ancient radio jargon in the phonetic alphabet. It was a way of saying a fond farewell to an enemy target; adios mother-fucker.

A second later the gunner leased off a couple of rounds from the mini-guns that were mounted on the side of the gun-ship and turned the two remaining pirates that were chasing Trenchard into a thin red mist. Trenchard sagged inside his E.V.A. suit as the second gun-ship pulled carefully alongside him, finally feeling the searing pain from his broken arm as the adrenaline of the chase subsided.

CHAPTER 11

"DEBRIEFING"

The next day, Trenchard had showered, eaten and drunk well. He had also slept like a log in a temporary bunk that had been allocated to him aboard the Breath of Vengeance. His arm had been bone-welded and set in a carbon fibre splint. The drugs the medics had given him had assured him of a good night's sleep. Now he was sitting and waiting nervously outside Admiral Fife's office. Fife was the Admiral who oversaw the Wolverine prototype project. He was therefore Captain Bird's immediate boss for the mission. Trenchard could only wonder how Fife would react after having the prototype nearly stolen and Captain Bird murdered.

Trenchard was roused from his inner thoughts as another brightly clad Admiral swept abruptly along the corridor followed by a group of office flunkies. You could always spot Admirals very easily, dressed as they were in bright red uniforms. They always reminded him of a cooked lobster. Trenchard vaguely recognised the middle-aged woman as Admiral Turner, the officer who Bird had been ordered to report to after the Mars uprising. She had instructed Bird and Trenchard to forget about what they had seen in the insurgent's headquarters, but Trenchard would never forget the sight of the bodies, slain by the sword of the black-clad assassin.

Trenchard stood a little awkwardly with his arm in a sling and attempted a cursory salute. Turner completely ignored Trenchard as she passed and then she and her flunkies disappeared into a meeting room a little further along the corridor. What was she doing here, Trenchard thought with interest? There were rather a lot of Admirals aboard such a relatively unimportant ship like the Breath of Vengeance. Something big must be going on.

Further thought on the matter was curtailed by another figure with very shapely hips who marched quickly down the corridor towards him. It was a young woman in her mid-twenties. She was astonishingly beautiful; long dark hair tied back into a pony-tail, with black eye make-up and fingernail varnish. She was obviously a civilian, dressed in plain black combats, but she had the air of someone who'd had previous military training. As the woman drew nearer, Trenchard put on his best pulling smile and looked straight at her, making a conscious effort to look her in the face and not stare at her breasts.

'Good afternoon Miss. What's a lovely thing like you doing on a great big military star-ship like this?'

You twat, he thought instantly. That had to be the cheesiest opening line imaginable. Come on Joe, you're completely out of practice. You can do better than that.

The woman stopped and stared at Trenchard as if he'd just crawled out from under a log. She placed her hands petulantly onto her hips and said, 'What?'

Trenchard paused; the usual stuff wasn't working. Actually, come to think of it, it never really worked. Perhaps the direct approach would be better?

'Fancy joining me for a drink later love?' he asked with a cheeky wink.

The woman broke into a genuinely warm smile, seemingly amused. 'Is that the best you can do? That's a pretty lame chat up line for a Commander of the Space Navy, isn't it?'

Trenchard grinned. At least he was getting somewhere. She had smiled and she had a lovely accent, just a hint of something foreign, Chinese or Korean maybe? Trenchard was no good at identifying accents.

'It's the best I've got,' Trenchard replied. 'So, how about that drink?'

The woman pouted. 'Sorry Commander, no can do. I've got a very important meeting with old iron knickers.'

Trenchard stared at her blankly.

'Admiral Turner?' explained the young woman. 'You didn't happen to see which way she went did you?'

Trenchard chuckled and jerked his left thumb down the corridor. 'Down there, second on the left love.'

'Thanks... *love!*' said the young woman, mimicking his patronising tone. She made as if to move off, then she stopped and turned back to face Trenchard. 'Well done for not looking at my chest the entire time mate! Catch you next time Commander.'

With that the woman marched off down the corridor towards the room that Admiral Turner had just entered. Trenchard watched her go, paying particular attention to her backside as she walked away. Something about the woman intrigued him but he couldn't pinpoint it. He was interrupted from his happy ponderings by a polite coughing. A smart young admin assistant had exited Fife's office and was holding the door open and smiling at Trenchard.

'You can go in Commander Trenchard. Admiral Fife will see you now.'

Trenchard smiled politely and made his way into the room. The assistant closed the door behind him and Trenchard was left alone with Fife. Trenchard tried to salute with his left arm and Fife impatiently waived him into a seat.

'Forget the formalities Commander Trenchard,' Fife growled in his deep Scottish accent. 'The fleet owes you a great debt of thanks. Please sit down.'

'Thank you, Sir,' said Trenchard, feeling more than a little uncomfortable. 'What can I do for you Sir?'

Fife leaned back in his high-backed leather chair and crossed his fingers across his stomach. His bright red uniform with the four diagonal black stripes of an Admiral was impeccable, ironed and starched. Fife mustn't have done any proper work for years. Trenchard studied Fife's nails. They were manicured. He was a desk jockey now. Still, a lot of the officers had a great deal of respect for him. He was more down to earth, more straight-talking than some of the other Admirals of the fleet. He was fair.

'Firstly, I wanted to thank you personally for saving the Might of Fortitude from the hands of the pirates. It was an extremely courageous thing that you did.'

'Thank you, Sir, but I was just doing my duty,' Trenchard said, a slight flush coming unexpectedly into his cheeks.

He suddenly felt out of his depth. He wasn't used to chit-chatting with high ranked officers. He'd only ever run into Commodore Ciaputa once or twice aboard the Hand of Valour, certainly no-one further up the chain of command than her. Trenchard was also finding it hard to concentrate his mind upon Fife's words. He was distracted, his mind still filled by the woman in the corridor. She had beguiled him; he couldn't stop thinking about her.

'I think that you did a little more than that Joe,' Fife grinned. 'I used to command a platoon myself. I know how hard the job is aboard those cramped, smelly little boats.'

That was true. Everyone knew that Fife had come up through the ranks. He had seen his share of fighting, unlike Trenchard's last boss, Commodore Ciaputa. But Fife had just called him Joe, was he on first name terms now with the Admiral? What the hell was going on here? Why was Admiral Fife even aboard this ship? The Breath of Vengeance wasn't a flagship. Something smelled funny.

Fife leaned forwards and his voice took on a confidential, hushed tone. 'Can I speak to you as one sailor to another?'

Trenchard nodded silently, his mind suddenly sharpening and fixing steadfastly on the Admiral's words.

'We've been watching Captain Bird for a long while now Joe. We knew we had a leak somewhere in the ranks; someone was selling information to the pirates. We suspected Bird. That's why we put him in charge of the prototype Wolverine. Think of it as the block of cheese in the mousetrap.'

'You were deliberately trying to entrap the pirates?' said Trenchard, suddenly starting to catch up. 'You were after Harlequin?'

Fife nodded. 'We knew that Harlequin wouldn't be able to resist the chance to get his hands on the Wolverine prototype. If we could bring him down, then his whole organisation would begin to crumble. Intel thinks that Harlequin is ex-navy. He just knows too damn much. He second-guesses our every move. We knew that you and Captain Bird were old friends. We also knew that you were particularly trustworthy. So, I… *suggested* to Captain Bird that he choose you to be his X.O. He jumped at the chance too.'

Trenchard sagged in his chair. 'It was a set up?'

'Yes,' confirmed Fife, settling back into his chair once again.

'That's how you got to us so quickly,' Trenchard thought out loud. 'You were waiting nearby for our signal.'

Admiral Fife nodded. 'It was a shame that Captain Bird was killed. I believe that he was salvageable. He was a good officer, just a little misguided. His official record won't mention anything negative, just that he was killed in action. It's a shame they ditched his body, I would have liked to have given him a proper burial. But the operation wasn't a complete loss. We're tracking the exhaust trail of that pirate ship and we've got some prisoners who were left on board the Might to interrogate, maybe find out some more details about their organisation. More than that, I think you've proved that you're ready for command of a star-ship.'

Trenchard sat bolt upright, alarmed. 'Me?' he stammered, amazed. 'But I… I haven't even done the Perisher!'

'That doesn't matter,' Fife said with a smile. 'The Might still needs a good Captain and experience counts just as much as training. You've earned those dolphins, Joe.'

Fife nodded towards the shiny badge that adorned Trenchard's breast pocket. It was the last thing that Bird had given to him. Fife's face took on a serious expression once more.

'We're up against it here Joe. There aren't enough qualified officers to go around. I'm prepared to bend the rules a little in your case. The Might needs a capable Captain. The job's yours if you want it?'

'You're *asking* me?' said Trenchard carefully.

Fife raised an eyebrow. 'I would rather it was your free choice than a direct order Commander. I know your command style is a little… forthright? A Wolverine will suit your style. Think about it. Your own ship to command, your own crew and the freedom of the stars!'

Trenchard thought about it. 'What about Pugh and Schmidt?' he asked cautiously.

Fife fixed Trenchard with a steely gaze. 'What happened on that ship stays on that ship Commander. We can't allow the rest of the fleet to know that there was almost a mutiny on board our newest prototype on her maiden voyage. Morale is already low as it is. Confidentially, there are already some problems aboard other ships in the fleet. Vice President Chang's policies are not widely supported within the ranks.' Fife tailed off into a sombre scowl, then took a deep breath before carrying on. 'I'm sure that being under scrutiny from the rest of the crew will be punishment enough for Pugh and Schmidt. They're going to find life aboard very tough, until they prove themselves to be trustworthy once more.'

Fife looked down at a computer touch screen and tapped at the controls.

'Plus, I'm sure that you can come up with some ingenious punishments for Pugh and Schmidt. I have a report here… a complaint of unfair treatment from a young trooper, a "Mrs Fluffy Kitten"?' Fife raised a surprised eyebrow.

Trenchard shuffled uncomfortably in his chair for a moment before replying, skipping over the issue as quickly as he could. 'I would like to recommend one of the crew for promotion Sir. Lieutenant Devinder Sivia, the S.E.O. He acted above and beyond the call of duty.'

Fife nodded. 'Surely.'

'…and I'm going to need a new X.O.?'

'I already have someone in mind. Anything you want Commander Trenchard. Just name it and it's yours.' Fife leaned forwards and stared intently into Trenchard's eyes. 'Surely you want another crack at Harlequin and that smiling son of a bitch who murdered Bird?'

Fife's eyes sparkled as he studied Trenchard. He was sure that Trenchard would bite. The offer was too tempting. Trenchard was silent for a long time. Then he stood up and walked deliberately towards the door, as if to leave. Fife screwed his brow up and called after him. 'Commander Trenchard?'

Trenchard turned and looked back at Admiral Fife, smiled a tight smile and pulled a cigarette out from a packet in his inside pocket. Very slowly he reached into the pocket again, took out a matt black Zippo lighter and lit the cigarette, taking a long drag. It was very bad form to smoke in a superior officer's office without being invited but Trenchard was showboating and he knew it. For once in his life he had an Admiral in the palm of his hand.

Then Trenchard fixed one of the navy's highest ranking officers straight in the eye and said, 'If I'm going to put my arse on the line again by going after those sadistic bloody pirates for you, then I'm going to need a very big drink first!'

With that, Captain Trenchard of the Might of Fortitude walked out of the Admiral's office with a smile on his face, intent solely upon finding the nearest bottle of rum.

Trenchard walked out of Fife's office on a high. He was a Captain. How good was that? He strolled down the corridor, practically dancing on air. He entered the elevator at the end of the corridor and pressed the button for the hangar bay where a shuttle was waiting to take him back over to the Might of Fortitude. No doubt there would be all kinds of questions from the crew. He'd stop by the stores when he got there and pull a bottle of rum to share with the officers. After all, it wasn't every day you were promoted to Captain, was it?

When the elevator slowed, Trenchard was still smiling. Captain of a ship and chatting up a fit young woman in the same day, he was on a roll. He thought about the woman in the corridor outside Fife's office. Something about her was bothering him. He couldn't place it but he was sure that he knew her from somewhere. He had a sneaky feeling like déjà vu that was creeping up on him like the big, fat hairy spider in his dreams. The elevator doors slid apart and Trenchard stepped out onto the hangar bay deck.

As he walked towards the waiting shuttle he passed a group of technicians. They were working on an open panel in the deck, re-wiring some circuitry. The junior snipe of the group was bored and was standing holding a length of plastic insulation pipe, swinging it around him like a sword and making swishing noises. Trenchard stopped and stared open mouthed at the young tech as his mind finally dropped the pieces of the puzzle together and then it suddenly hit him like a ton of bricks. Something from his sub-conscious welled up and burst forth like a dam breaking.

"Catch you next time…"

The woman's accent wasn't Korean or Chinese… it was Japanese. The voice, *her* voice, was the one that had haunted him in his dreams since the Belatu-Cadros uprising. The woman meeting Admiral Turner was the one who had slit his throat with a sword and left him for dead four years ago.

The woman in the corridor was the assassin from Mars!

He looked around quickly for the deck officer and grabbed the man roughly by the sleeve. 'Hey, that woman who came to visit Admiral Turner, which shuttle did she arrive on?'

The man looked confused. 'What?'

'The fit Japanese bird! Ponytail, nice tits! Where's her shuttle?'

Suddenly the man's face cleared. 'Oh, her… She didn't arrive in a shuttle. That's her ship over there.'

Trenchard followed the man's pointing finger across the hangar bay towards a parked spacecraft. It was like no other that Trenchard had ever seen, sleek and black like a smooth pebble. The Japanese woman was just disappearing up the ramp into the ship. Trenchard let go of the deck officer and began to run at full speed across the hangar bay towards the black vessel.

'Stop! Stop that ship!' he shouted, much to the bemusement of the techs around him.

At that instant, the ramp was raised, the black ship fired up its engines and blasted out of the hangar bay at full speed. Trenchard was caught in the wash of heat from the powerful thrusters and had to hide his face behind his arms. When he looked back up, just for a moment Trenchard was sure he could see the young woman staring smugly at him out of the cockpit window and winking at him. Then the ship passed through the magnetic field at the end of the runway and disappeared into open space.

Trenchard was left standing, panting hard and staring after the rapidly diminishing ship. If that woman knew Admiral Turner, then there had to be some way of finding her. One day he would track her down. One day he would have his revenge and wipe that pretty smile off her self-satisfied young face.

'Don't worry love,' he said under his breath. 'I will catch you… *next time!*'

The circular chamber was gloomy, foreboding, constructed from stone and starkly lit from above. Huge stone pillars encompassed the central lighted area, where a glossy, black stone table was encircled by fifty, high backed, leather chairs. The table had a bold logo directly in the centre, a red and black Yin Yang with a single orbiting red planet instead of the usual eight that surrounded the yellow sun on the United Worlds emblem. The figures who were seated around the table were only partially lit by the distant overhead beams, their faces deeply contoured by dark shadows. An old man with skin like weathered leather, leaned into the light and spoke in a heavy Russian accent that was deep and commanding.

'Was the mission a success?'

Admiral Turner twisted towards him and nodded at the old man as she too leaned forwards into the light.

'Yes, completely,' she replied. 'I recently received confirmation from our agent while I was aboard the Breath of Vengeance. Captain Bird was killed in front of Trenchard and the Might of Fortitude is now in his hands. Fife promoted him, just as we had hoped. It went exactly as we planned.'

The old man nodded in satisfaction. 'Good. Trenchard is exactly what we were looking for. He has opened new pathways in the Mesh. The future is looking bright for him. He is destined to become a great hero.'

A new voice spoke. This man remained pushed back in his seat, his face in darkness. Only his hands and the cuffs of his shirt were clearly visible on the table. His gold cufflinks were encrusted with diamonds; his shirt was the finest silk and his fingernails were immaculately manicured. He spoke with a French accent and he sounded worried.

'But do you think he is ready for the next test? The Sentinel prototype is extremely dangerous and unpredictable. He may be killed.'

The Russian smiled.

'Do not worry so my old friend,' he assured the Frenchman. 'Trenchard's future has been mapped out carefully by the Mesh.' Then the Russian smiled like an undertaker before a battle. 'He won't be allowed to die until we require him to.'

CHAPTER 12

"HOW TO MAKE A MONSTER"

Mars.

Four years ago...

The woman's eyes flickered open. For a long moment, all was confusion. There was pain somewhere, dull and throbbing, but she couldn't place it. It was like a fog or haze all around her. The light was searing and bright. Then a face came into view, a pretty woman with dark brown hair. Her face was kind, the sort of face you could confide in. She was wearing a bright red lab coat with a picture of a poppy on the breast pocket. Could she be a doctor?

Where am I?

The words formed in the woman's mind but she couldn't vocalise them.

Must try to sit up...

No movement.

Am I paralysed? Have I been in an accident? What's going on?

The pretty young nurse smiled, not in a comforting way but more a smile of jubilation.

'Her eyes are open. There's brain activity, we've done it!' she said excitedly.

So, I can still hear, thought the woman. *Why can't I move or speak? I'm locked into my own body. Help me! For Christ's sake, help me!*

Panic overtook her like a wave. She was sucked under into a seething mass of fear.

Another figure came into view, a taller figure… a man. He too was wearing bright red coveralls but had a surgeon's mask across his face and blue nitrile gloves on his hands. His hands were held up, raised into the air to keep them clean and they were covered with bright orange iodine.

'Excellent,' he said leaning forwards excitedly. His voice had a thick French accent. His eyes smiled over the top of the mask, deep creases at the corners. '…the first time that a human brain has been re-activated successfully! This moment will live in history.'

His words sat in the woman's mind like a nesting spider and wriggled uncomfortably.

Are they talking about me? What do they mean by re-activated?

A memory flared in the woman's mind. It was a violent memory of heat and pain. It faded almost as quickly as it came. Another figure came into view from the side, a slender woman with long, dark hair. She was dressed all in black and had her hands placed on her hips. She scowled down at the immobile woman.

'It'd better be worth it Papaver.' said the slender woman in an accent that had a hint of a Japanese undertone. 'Stealing her body from the naval morgue was a real pain in the arse! The base was on high alert after the R.D. attack.'

Body? I'm not dead! Help me!

The man leaned closer. 'Don't worry my girl,' said the French man, 'with all the confusion during the uprising at

Belatu-Cadros, nobody will miss one body. If we can transplant the brain into the machine successfully, then it will definitely be worth the risk.'

'You really think this will work?' said the Japanese woman uncertainly. 'The Sentinel is powerful alright, but the A.I. is as dumb as shit. What good is a dead brain going to be?'

The Frenchman snorted. 'It's no longer a dead brain and it will provide the spark of ingenuity that was missing from the earlier prototypes, just what you said was lacking. This was your idea after all Miss Saito. She has you to thank for her second chance at life.'

'Hey, don't pin this one on me,' snapped the woman called Saito. 'This is your sick little project Papaver! I'm just the hired help.'

The Frenchman laughed. '…and it's no longer called the Sentinel. Your comments after the last battle testing gave me a better idea. The machine is now to be referred to as the *Morgenstern*.'

'Morgenstern?' said the slender woman with a scowl. 'Sounds like a German rock band!'

'It seemed apt,' said the man with a smile.

The man picked up something from a metal tray to one side and held it up. It was some sort of medical instrument with a long, curved, sharp blade that glinted in the light as the man studied it. He leaned forwards and his hands disappeared out of view. There was a wet sound like a knife cutting through lettuce and then a loud crack.

'By the way,' he said as he worked, 'did you have any trouble at the insurgent's command headquarters?'

The Japanese woman leaned in, studying what the man was doing with gruesome fascination. 'No, not really. I ran into that couple of United Worlds troopers you warned me about but I took care of them.'

The man looked sharply across to her. 'You didn't kill them I hope. You were explicitly ordered not to.'

'Don't worry,' snapped the woman. 'I did just what you said. They'll both live. I gave one of them a scar to remember me by though, Joe something or other. He won't forget his mission to Belatu-Cadros for a long time.'

The name Belatu-Cadros sparked a memory in the woman's mind of dust and thin air mixed with shouting and explosions.

I was there! I was a trooper. I was fighting the insurgents and then a bomb went off. What happened to me?

The Frenchman seemed satisfied with Saito's answer and went back to his work. 'This body is perfect, the head is entirely intact despite the shrapnel wounds to the torso,' he said. After a moment, he stood up and handed the blood covered instrument to the young nurse who placed it back onto the metal tray.

'There, that's the spinal column severed. Now we can crack open the skull and remove the brain.'

The Japanese woman leaned in even closer, intently studying something. 'I'm sure she just blinked,' she said. 'Are you sure that she can't feel anything?'

Yes, I can! Help me for fuck's sake!

'Certain,' Papaver affirmed. 'The brain and the body died once already and now the spinal column is disconnected. There's no way that the mind could have survived. It's like a blank hard-drive that has just been formatted, waiting for us to fill it with new data. There's absolutely nothing of Lieutenant Hawkins left I'm afraid. She'll never know of her part in this ground-breaking procedure.'

Hawkins? That's me! The woman's mind screamed. *I'm in here. I'm not dead. Please help me!*

The man picked up another device. It had a rotary saw blade that spun and made a piercing whine as the man activated the trigger. He leaned forwards and looked straight into Lieutenant Hawkins' cold, dead eyes.

'Right, let's get cracking!' he said with a smile…

CHAPTER 13

"SHAME"

Acrid smoke hung like a cloudy veil around the ceiling as the squad of troopers ran along the darkened metal tunnel. They stopped at a junction, sweating and breathless. The sound of distant rifle-fire echoed off the grey metal walls, reverberating and sharp like bolts dropped into a metal bucket. There was the distant boom of artillery and then the floor and walls shook furiously for a moment. When the deck had steadied, Lieutenant Commander Pugh looked towards the rest of his squad with unease.

'Ok, McGagh, Stofan, I want two stun grenades round that corner, followed by the rest of the squad in a two by two formation. Ready. *Go!*'

There was a marked lack of movement. Some of the troopers scowled, some had shifty, uneasy expressions on their faces or were staring fixatedly at their boots. One immense man standing at the front, had defiance written on his face as clearly as chalk on a blackboard.

'What's wrong with you? Get to it, that's an order,' Pugh shouted, his voice faltering slightly.

Not *here*, he thought. Not *now!* There was too much at stake. Most of the squad stared at the floor, ashamed but resolute, unable to voice what they were thinking. Only McGagh, the large Irish man with the bad disposition, met Pugh's gaze directly.

'That's not going to work,' McGagh stated coldly, his staring eyes glinting resolutely in the darkness.

'What?' snapped Pugh, the colour beginning to drain from his already haggard face.

'If we use that tactic, we're all dead. We should head around to the next junction and double back, take 'em from behind.' McGagh glared at Pugh, his eyes unblinking. 'Unlike some of us, I've done this sort of thing before…'

Pugh's jaw dropped and he did goldfish impressions for a moment. It was true. Out of anyone in the squad, McGagh had the most experience in battle. His reputation preceded him like a bad smell. But Pugh was his commanding officer nonetheless. He had to take control of the situation.

'This is not up for discussion Leading Spaceman McGagh, that's an order!'

Pugh's voice was lower now, more desperate. He started to sweat. There was the low rumble of another distant explosion, grenades exploding inside the metal structure. The deck shook and a light that was hanging from a chain on the overhead began to sway slightly. The smell of burning flesh wafted down the corridor, an unmistakable aroma to anyone who had been in battle; roast pork mixed with burning hair. The air between Pugh and McGagh practically sizzled with nervous energy. Then McGagh's eyes narrowed.

'We don't take orders from filthy *mutineers!*' McGagh stated flatly.

His voice was not taunting, it was cold and calculated, a simple statement of fact. The sentence hung in the air like the thick smoke, heavy and bitter. The words stung Pugh as surely as if they had been a physical attack. McGagh turned his back on Pugh. This was even more insulting than the words. One by one, the whole squad turned their backs on Lieutenant Commander Pugh and began to walk off down the corridor in the opposite direction, following McGagh.

'McGagh!' Pugh shouted after him, sweat dripping down from underneath his helmet, his hands holding his rifle so tightly that his knuckles had gone white.

At a nod from McGagh, the squad broke into a jog. He was one of the few among them who had seen any real combat, seen death. His comrades knew that he was a veteran of Belatu-Cadros, the first and bloodiest battle in the war against the insurgent terrorists. They were more ready to trust him than a man who had betrayed them all in mutiny just a few days earlier. The departing McGagh cast a venomous glance backwards as if to say "I've won". After a moment of deep introspection, Pugh reluctantly began to follow them. What else could he do? The enemy were close. They still had a job to do. His feet felt like lead as he made his way along the corridor a few yards behind his squad.

Ahead of Pugh, the squad rounded a blind corner when suddenly at least twenty heavily armoured pirates appeared from behind several make-shift barricades and opened fire. The troopers didn't stand a chance. Each trooper that was hit by the crossfire squirmed in pain as a massive jolt of electricity ran from their metal soled mag-boots straight up through their legs. Blue light arced over their bodies as they convulsed, teeth clenching and eyes staring in pain. In a second it was all over and the whole squad lay immobile on the greasy deck, twitching slightly and groaning in agony. Pugh rounded the corner a moment later to find his whole squad disabled. He stared at the pirates and his shoulders slumped in defeat. He dropped his rifle which clattered to the floor and dejectedly raised his hands. One of the pirates smiled at him and then his face fizzed slightly with a static burst, rippling like a reflection in a pond.

'*Enough!*' shouted a loud voice from seemingly everywhere in the corridor. '*Open it up!*'

'SIMULATION CANCELLED,' said the flat voice of the Guardian computer. 'OPENING TRAINING AREA.'

The holographic image of the pirates blinked off. With a rumble and grinding of gears, the wall slid slowly apart allowing searing white light to pierce the darkness and fill the smoking corridor. Pugh squinted into the light to see a figure standing, hands on his hips and tapping his foot impatiently. When the doors had fully opened and Pugh's eyes had adjusted to the light, he could finally see the form of his commanding officer scowling straight at him from the adjacent classroom.

The rest of the squad were picking themselves up off the floor and dusting their uniforms down, still wincing in agony. The electric shocks had been painful, but not damaging. They would all have bruises where the stun charges had contacted the skin, but they would fade in time. What was more damaged was their pride. Pugh was marginally pleased to see that McGagh had cracked his chin on something as he fell to the floor and a large purple welt was beginning to spread across his disgruntled face. Captain Josiah Trenchard scowled at the squad.

'What a pathetic bunch of useless arseholes!' he shouted angrily. 'I should have you all disciplined for disobeying a direct order from your ranking officer.'

'But Sir!' McGagh protested.

Trenchard's eyes fixed on McGagh like a steel vice. 'Two watches on painting duty McGagh,' Trenchard snapped, eyeballing McGagh and daring him to say another word. 'We'll see if twelve hours in an E.V.A. suit with a brush in your hand and sweat running down your arse crack will wipe that smug grin off your face. Anyone else for *nines?*'

McGagh fumed but remained silent, as did the rest of the squad. Pugh may not warrant their respect but they were at least intelligent enough not to annoy the Captain any further. Many hung their heads and avoided meeting Trenchard's steely glare straight on.

'Well, I see that you're all cowards as well as trouble makers. You're a disgrace, the lot of you! Dismissed,' Trenchard bawled in disgust. 'I want you back here by oh six hundred tomorrow for extra training.'

The squad began to file unhappily out of the training area.

'Not you Pugh!' snapped Trenchard as Pugh made a move to leave.

The two men waited in uncomfortable silence as the rest of the squad disappeared. When they were quite alone, Trenchard rounded angrily on Pugh.

'You have to get a bloody handle on this Pugh!' he snapped.

'Yes Sir,' replied Pugh, unable to meet Trenchard's eyes directly.

'This has gone on long enough,' continued Trenchard. 'So, you fucked up when you followed Captain Bird on his fool's mutiny, but he's dead now and it's time to move on. I understand that you've been having a hard time from the crew and frankly, you deserve every bit of it!'

Pugh shuffled uncomfortably as he thought about the living hell that the crew had made his life in the three days since they had returned from the asteroid belt.

'But the time has come to fight back,' continued Trenchard. 'If you're ever going to command the troops effectively, you must first command their respect! If you can't even do that, then I can't trust you in combat.' He paused and caught his breath before snapping, 'We can't afford to lose another good officer. Sort it out!'

With that, Trenchard turned on his heel and swept out of the classroom leaving Pugh alone, miserable, and praying for a miracle.

Just outside the classroom, Trenchard ran into Lieutenant Chertok who was waiting patiently for him with a placid smile upon his face.

'I changed the simulation mid-way through as you requested Captain,' Chertok said calmly. Then he raised an inquisitive eyebrow. 'Altering the location of the enemy during battle was a little unfair wasn't it Sir?'

Trenchard scowled. 'That bastard McGagh needed to be taught a lesson damn it!' he growled. 'He's a trouble maker and he's far too cocky already. Pugh's had it rough recently but he's no use to me if he can't command a squad. If Pugh won't step up, then I've got to step down hard on the biggest cockroach in the platoon and that's McGagh. Otherwise, he could get good troopers killed one day. I'll not have a repeat of what he did on Mars aboard my boat!'

Trenchard paused and took a deep breath, trying to calm down. He scratched at the long scar on his neck and wished that he could smoke in the training area.

'Come on,' he said to Chertok. 'Let's get back up to the Might.'

CHAPTER 14

"BAD NEWS TRAVELS FAST"

Far out on the edge of the solar system, beyond Pluto and just inside the Oort cloud, sat the moon-sized lump of rock named "Cairn". The surface of this barren and airless dwarf planet was crammed with shining pressure domes containing the military installations of the United Worlds Space Navy. In a high orbit of the naval base sailed a multitude of mighty leviathans, dark shapes that slid through space like colossal monsters in the deep sea. These mighty star-ships were simply vast tubes of engine. They were designed to suck in matter from space and blast it out from spherical engine cores to propel the craft faster than light between the furthest stars. Huge rugby ball shaped gravity pods rotated slowly like Ferris wheels around these mighty engine cores to provide gravity to the fragile human crews within.

Holding orbit dotted between these vast monsters were much smaller craft; Hunter search-and-destroy class. These missile-shaped vessels resembled submarines, with fins arranged around the centre of the ship like the fletching of an arrow. They were still referred to by the sailors of the navy as "boats" rather than ships, and their proud lineage could be traced back hundreds of years to the submarines that they so closely resembled.

One of the smaller craft was slightly different than its sisters. It looked newer and the weapons mounted on the hull of the vessel were more powerful as befitted the latest prototype in the fleet. This Wolverine class vessel, itself larger than a sea-going battle ship, sat in orbit revolving gently around its axis. It bore a long gash along its side, the scar of a recent run in with the pirate ship Onibaba. Painted on the hull, which was receiving a fresh coat from a grumbling, space-suited McGagh, was the proud name of the boat; the *Might of Fortitude*.

Captain Josiah Trenchard was sitting in the wardroom aboard the Might of Fortitude waiting for a mat-stat briefing and sipping on bad tasting, ship issue coffee. His recent promotion, after the death of the previous Captain, still hadn't quite sunk in. He stared with mixed feelings at the static holograph of the preceding Captain that still hung on the bulkhead opposite. Captain Bird had been a good friend to Trenchard, ever since the academy when Trenchard had first joined the navy. Sure, he was misguided and had tried to hand the Might over to the pirates, but Bird had received his just reward for that; a bullet through the head and his body flushed into space with the rest of the jetsam. It had been Trenchard that had put his life on the line to keep the vessel out of the clutches of Captain Smiler and the pirate leader Harlequin.

This then his reward for saving the navy's prototype hunter-killer; he was now Captain of the Might of Fortitude. He should feel greatly honoured but he had begun to wish that he hadn't been given the responsibility by Admiral Fife. He was finding out that being a Captain carried its own unique set of problems.

He stared down at the agenda for the "material state of the boat", or mat-stat briefing, on the green hologram that floated above the table in front of him. At the top was a long list of officers. He didn't know any of them well enough and yet somehow, he had to command their respect. Certainly, they all knew that he had saved the boat, but they also knew that his promotion had been a field promotion. He hadn't completed the Perisher officer's training course. He hadn't even earned his dolphins badge like every other sailor on board. Trenchard absent-mindedly rubbed the twin dolphin badge that was pinned above his left breast pocket as he thought about this. He would always be a skimmer to the crew; he could see the mistrust in their eyes. No, mistrust was too strong a word. It was more like they were waiting for him to slip up so they could point and laugh and say "I told you so!" He sighed heavily as his eyes ran down the list and took another sip of the foul-tasting coffee.

Warrant Officer Van Allen - Tactical
Petty Officer Hall - Communications
Chief Petty Officer Kittinger - Scanner Control

He had met all three. They were good solid officers but he knew very little about them. That was something he must put right soon. It was one of the reasons that he had called this meeting.

Warrant Officer Cochran - Weapons Fire Control

Cochran at least he knew a little about. She was very young and very keen. Her bright red hair had earned her the nickname "Scarlet" among the male members of the crew, with whom she had quite a fan club. There was nothing wrong with her but she was a little green and lacked experience. Like most of the crew, she was fairly fresh out of officers training at the academy. He still had to see how she would react under any real pressure.

Lieutenant Commander Sivia - Chief Engineer

Here was someone that Trenchard did know reasonably well. Sivia, the Might's only serving Sikh, had aided Trenchard when the pirates attempted to steal the Might of Fortitude. He had managed to send a distress message which had saved them all. Trenchard owed his life to this man. His actions had earned him a promotion at the recommendation of Trenchard.

Chief Petty Officer Schmidt - Navigation
Lieutenant Commander Pugh - Warfare Officer

Trenchard's eyes hovered over the last two names and he scowled. What to do with these two, he thought? They had both sided with Captain Bird in the mutiny that had nearly lost the boat to the pirates. They were obviously deeply misguided but Admiral Fife had insisted that neither were to be officially reprimanded. He had left their punishment and rehabilitation down to Trenchard. The crew had been particularly hard on these two and he knew that Pugh was at breaking point. If the haranguing from the crew wasn't enough, then today's refusal of Pugh's squad to obey orders had been the final straw. Trenchard sipped at the coffee, wishing that it was rum. He still had no real idea how to proceed. He took a cigarette from a crumpled packet in his inside pocket and chewed on the end reflectively. He wouldn't be able to light it aboard the boat, smoking was only allowed in designated areas on larger vessels, but it helped him to think. He sat for a while, pondering as he flicked the lid on his matt black Zippo lighter open and closed rhythmically.

(Position Vacant)- Executive Officer

Trenchard took another gulp of the particularly bad, plastic cup full of coffee that was burning his finger tips and he grimaced. Even three sugars had done nothing to sweeten the bad aftertaste. The cup almost tasted better than the coffee it held. Trenchard had himself been Captain Bird's X.O. and Admiral Fife had promised a replacement officer over three days ago. So far, he had heard nothing. They were bound to be sent out on a mission soon. The navy couldn't afford to leave ships lying idle, especially not in the present political climate. Who would Fife choose? Would they be any good? Could Trenchard rely upon them? Too many questions; it was out of his control for the time being. He snapped the Zippo shut and set it down on the table top, then he stared at it for a while hoping for inspiration. Trenchard's deep introspection was disturbed a moment later by a tentative knock on the wardroom hatch.

'Come,' he called, without making any effort to rise.

The space in the wardroom was limited at best and Trenchard was wedged in at the top of the long oak table that served for meals and officer's meetings. The hatch opened and Chief Petty Officer Kittinger stepped in, saluted and then stood to attention. He was the boat's primary radar and scanner watch-stander. He stood for a moment just outside the hatch looking slightly awkward.

Trenchard smiled, 'Sit down man, there's no need for ceremony.'

Kittinger broke a quick smile and shuffled along the bench seat towards Trenchard.

'You're the first,' Trenchard observed. 'Good. I value punctuality.'

Kittinger nodded curtly. 'Thank-you Sir. The others are on their way.'

Trenchard nodded and studied Kittinger. He was an American by birth, if such things mattered any more. Medium build, medium height, brown hair. Nothing about him seemed to be extraordinary.

'Kittinger… any relation to Colonel Joe Kittinger?' asked Trenchard as he chewed on his unlit cigarette.

Kittinger's eyes suddenly brightened. 'Yes Sir, he's an ancestor of mine on my father's side.'

Trenchard smiled warmly. He'd found something to connect with the man.

'Damn brave man that…' he said with a grin. '…the first man to leave the atmosphere of the Earth and enter outer space. And he did it in a *balloon* of all things. Then to top it off he returned to Earth by jumping off with a parachute!'

'Yes Sir. Fell to Earth at nearly supersonic speed and he did all that with a ripped glove in his pressure suit; nearly lost his hand,' grinned Kittinger. 'All of our family knows the story Sir. I'm surprised that you do. It was such a long time ago.'

'I studied everything about the space race when I was a child. I had posters all over my bedroom walls of the Apollo missions, the first lunar base and the crash of the Westerhope.' Trenchard paused for a moment as he remembered his childhood. Then his face cleared. 'Balls of steel that man,' Trenchard praised eagerly. 'I trust you've inherited the family jewels?'

Kittinger chuckled. 'I do my best Sir.'

'That's all I can ask of anyone,' Trenchard replied.

There was a moment of genuine warmth between the two officers. Trenchard had only known the crew for a little under a week. He was still finding his feet with them all. This was a good start.

Just then, the hatch swung open again and the rest of the officers filed slowly in. Pugh and Schmidt were noticeably last into the room and sat as far away from Trenchard as they could manage. Trenchard stared hard at them both. Neither one could meet his gaze, which was hardly surprising. When they were all seated, Trenchard cleared his throat and began.

'Okay. Let's get on with the mat-stat briefing then. As you are no doubt aware, we haven't received any orders yet as to the next mission. Nor have we received a replacement X.O. In the meantime, I expect all of you to keep the crew on their toes. We may be called in to action at any moment. I've scheduled another round of training in the simulator down on Cairn for this afternoon.'

Trenchard looked at the officer's faces. They were downcast and introspective, as they had been since the death of their revered Captain. He paused and took a deep breath. He was not looking forward to broaching the next subject but it had to be done.

'Look… I know that you're all grieving for Captain Bird,' he said. The sentence hung in the air like an unwanted bad smell. No-one could meet his gaze as it travelled around the table. 'I understand that he was killed by one of Harlequin's men and that you're all thirsting after revenge.'

Harlequin was the infamous and elusive leader of the pirates. It was a subordinate of Harlequin, only known as "Smiler", who had killed Captain Bird in cold blood. The pirates had jettisoned Bird's body and so the crew had been denied the chance for a descent funeral. The crew had not had the proper chance to say goodbye to their Captain and it had left a haze of disquiet hanging over everyone's heads.

'I promise you that when the time comes you will have your revenge!' said Trenchard as forcefully as he could muster. 'I'd like to rip off Harlequin's head and spit in the hole myself, believe me!'

There were a few eyes raised to meet his gaze. A few corners of mouths began to lift hopefully.

'But for now, I need you to shelve your grief and pain and save it for later. We have a job to do. We're about to be sent out on another mission, god knows where. I need you all to be sharp, professional. When the time comes, and it will, Harlequin will wish that he'd never pissed off the crew of the Might of Fortitude and he'll wish that he'd never been born!'

Trenchard let his words soak in. Then after a suitable pause, he looked towards the S.E.O., Lieutenant Commander Devinder Sivia. As the vessel's Space Engineering Officer, Sivia was responsible for everything from the nuclear engine to the laundry.

'How are we coming with the repairs?' he asked.

Sivia nodded his black turban-covered head towards his Captain. 'Everything's done bar the damage to the outer hull from the Onibaba scraping along as she made her getaway and that would require a stint in dry dock to repair properly. It's not structural, so there's no real problem. I've had the junior snipes replacing the stealth tiles and painting the hull in E.V.A. suits for the last three days. It's nearly done.'

Trenchard grinned. "Snipes" was naval slang for the engineers that worked in the dingy and cramped crawl spaces of the vessel. The juniors wouldn't have appreciated the painting duty but at least it kept them busy.

'How's McGagh liking his spell with a paint brush?'

Sivia laughed, idly stroking his beard. 'He grumbles a lot, but he's actually doing a good job. I think his bark is worse than his bite.'

Trenchard nodded. 'Just make sure that if he shits on the floor, you rub his nose in it. He needs to be taken down a peg or two,' he said, continuing the canine analogy. Then he turned to Van Allen. 'What about the tactical simulations that I requested?'

A chime from the control panel on the table in front of Trenchard interrupted him. He reached forwards irritably and pressed a control.

'Yes?'

A young woman's voice answered him. '*Communications here Sir, petty officer Hartmann on watch. We're picking up a breaking news report transmitted from Earth, Sir.*'

Trenchard rolled his eyes. 'I don't think a news report is worth interrupting a mat-stat briefing for, Hartmann,' he snapped. 'Save it to the data store and we'll catch up when…'

'*Pardon me Sir, but I think this is important!*' Hartmann interrupted urgently.

Hartmann's voice sounded stressed, almost panicked. Trenchard stiffened up. Something was wrong. 'On screen,' he commanded.

With a burst of static, the whole of the wall at the far end of the table became a holographic screen showing an Intergalactic News Network report. The camera was shaking, hand held and pointing at a young female reporter who was hanging, half out of the open hatch of a shuttle that was flying over wide, rolling blue ocean.

'*…can't believe what we're seeing,*' the woman screamed over the noise of the shuttle's whining engines and the rushing wind. There was another noise in the background, a deep ominous rumble, unseen for the moment but deeply unsettling. '*The cables are falling thousands of miles from space, coiling up as they drop and smashing the terminal building on Konstantin Island into dust!*'

The camera panned to the side. In the middle of the churning ocean stood the artificial island that had been built as the anchor for the Earth's one and only space elevator. From there, immense cables went straight up through the atmosphere into space and were tethered to a space station in orbit. This allowed huge payloads to be hauled into space for a fraction of the expense of rocket fuel. But something was wrong, seriously wrong. The cables were falling. Smashing down upon the island and turning the concrete buildings into dust.

'*Oh god!*' Cochran whispered, deeply shocked, voicing the thoughts that were going through everyone's mind.

All eyes were fixed steadfastly on the screen. A deathly hush had descended on the room.

'*There's no possible way that everyone managed to evacuate the island,*' cried the reporter. '*There are thousands of people… Oh no… I can see shuttles being smashed down as they try to escape, boats in the water being dragged down beneath the seething waves…*'

Huge plumes of dust spread out across the ocean, partially obscuring the view like a sinister, choking fog. The scene resembled a great Kraken waking from the oceans depths, flailing its tentacles at anything that moved. For a second the camera zoomed in to a landing platform on the island where a dozen people were desperately trying to cram themselves into an already packed shuttle. A coil of cable fell straight on top of the shuttle and all was obscured by a thick dust. Burning debris began to fall from the sky, trailing plumes of fire and smoke like meteors.

With a noise like an atomic bomb going off, the last of the massive cables smacked into the turbulent waves. The sea level dipped alarmingly as the suction from the mighty cables pulled it down. Then slowly, like a titan rising from the deep, the ocean welled up into a massive tsunami, hundreds of meters high. The waves spread out in a concentric ring and gained speed as they travelled towards the distant shores of several continents.

The camera panned back to the reporter's ashen face for a moment. '*I'm getting word… there has been a statement. The outer-system insurgents, known as the Rubente Dextera, are claiming responsibility. They're calling it a strike for liberty…*' The reporter's face fell and she dropped the microphone to her lap in shock, tears rolling down her ashen face. She could just be heard whispering a single word, '*bastards!*'

'Turn it off!' snapped Trenchard, his voice breaking.

The hologram blinked off. For a moment, no-one moved or even spoke. Each person was in a very dark place of their own, imagining the horrors that were unfolding even now on their home planet of Earth. The news footage would have been sent by a standard signal, hours ago. It had taken that long to reach the Might in orbit of the naval base on planet Cairn. What was happening on the Earth right now, nobody could bear to imagine. Trenchard looked up at his officers and cleared his throat, trying not to give away any emotion.

'Get to your stations. The crew will need you. They will all see that report sooner or later. They all have family and friends back home. From this moment, we are on red alert; crew to general quarters.'

The officers silently shuffled out. Cochran was the last and she paused by the door.

'Cochran?' Trenchard said softly.

Warrant Officer Cochran turned and stared at her Captain. Her face was pale and white and she was trembling. She looked Trenchard deeply in the eyes for a moment and then said in a quiet voice, 'My brother works as a baggage handler on Konstantin Island…'

Without another word, Cochran turned and left the room. Trenchard sat for a long while, stunned into inaction. He didn't know what the hell was going on but he knew one thing for certain. In the instant that the space elevator had crashed into the ocean, everything had changed forever.

CHAPTER 15

"GENEVIEVE NOIR"

A few busy hours later, Trenchard was once again sat in the wardroom staring at the hologram screen, only this time it was a one-to-one conversation with Admiral Fife. Unlike the news broadcast, the naval communication and intelligence network or N.A.C.I.N., was carried by a series of way stations that transmitted the data via similar technology that allowed the larger space-craft to travel faster than light. Communication was almost instantaneous within a single solar system, with slight delays when transmitting between different systems that were light years apart.

Fife was a dour Scot if ever there was one, but he was fair and dependable. He had helped Trenchard ease into his role as Captain of the Might of Fortitude after the untimely death of Captain Bird. Trenchard believed that he could trust Fife. He had been given no reason to doubt that trust so far. It was almost as though Fife had taken a special interest in Trenchard but he could only guess as to why. Fife had been filling Trenchard in on the recent events surrounding the destruction of the space elevator with a grim expression on his stony face.

'We still don't know the full extent of the devastation, but it is worldwide,' said Fife seriously. 'The tsunami caused by the cables falling into the ocean has killed thousands all around the Atlantic rim. It's a global catastrophe, coming so close to the assassination of President Smith.'

'Smith's *dead?*' Trenchard spluttered in shock.

'You haven't heard?' Fife's face was a picture of amazement.

'I've been too busy with the ship and the crew for the last few days to watch the news reports and keep up with gossip.'

Fife looked slightly affronted. 'Maybe you should start to take a greater interest in current affairs Captain,' said Fife with a clear undertone of displeasure. 'You're a Captain in the Space Navy now. You represent the United Worlds when out on mission. You'll find that politics plays as much of a part in naval matters as does oiling weapons and swabbing decks!'

Trenchard remained tight lipped. He was just beginning to realise that he was now playing a completely different game. Fife had just given Trenchard a verbal slapping down and it smarted.

'President Smith was killed by a roadside I.E.D. It was a mining charge that has been traced back to thefts made by Martian pirates working within the asteroid belt.'

'Harlequin?' ventured Trenchard.

Fife nodded grimly. 'It appears that they sold the explosives on to the insurgents who have already claimed responsibility for both terror attacks. They're demanding independent rule for the outer systems and proportional representation in the United Worlds government. Otherwise they've threatened to continue to target public heads of state and vital installations.'

'*Jesus…*' Trenchard swore under his breath.

The announcement from the insurgents amounted to an all-out declaration of war.

'Who's standing in for the President?' he asked. Although he already suspected the answer, he was still dreading hearing it out loud from Fife.

'Vice President Chang has temporarily assumed power,' Fife confirmed grimly.

The sentence echoed in Trenchard's mind like the heavy lid of a coffin slamming shut. Chang was, in Trenchard's own opinion, a vicious little prick. Chang had been responsible for Mars during the uprising. It was his policies that had brought back the death sentence for terrorists after centuries of clemency. It was his influence on Smith that had ramped up the pressure on the insurgents and had, in Trenchard's opinion, antagonised them into such desperate measures. Chang was dangerous and unpredictable. He had all the hallmarks of a military dictator in the making.

'Chang's pissed off,' Fife announced with absolutely no humour in his voice. 'He made a public announcement that there are going to be two new space elevators built to replace the first. He's already made a deal with the Papaver Corporation to build more military star-ships, bigger and meaner than before. He's cracking down hard on the outer systems. Several colonies have already been placed under martial law and he's increased security at all government buildings. The Hunter and Wolverine patrols have been put on constant revolving shifts with all leave cancelled.'

Trenchard's face belied his feelings. He looked shocked and worried.

'But the navy can't possibly cover all of that at the same time. The United Worlds encompass too many systems and we don't have enough personnel. We're underfunded and under equipped already. We can barely cope as it is!'

Fife nodded. 'High Command has already come to the same conclusion. Admiral Adisa has advised Chang to start a recruitment drive and apply to the United Worlds government for extra funding. Fortunately, the public outcry over the terror attacks is providing no shortage of candidates. Xenophobia towards the outer colonies is growing fast. The naval academy on Cairn is going to become very busy.'

Trenchard was silent for a long moment as he took all this in. Pushing recruits through training quickly meant more troopers but those troopers would be young and inexperienced. That could only make matters worse. Then he looked up and said, 'So what's our mission?'

Fife smiled at Trenchard's direct question. Trenchard was no fool and had already realised that Fife must have something special planned for the Might of Fortitude.

'A space elevator hasn't been built on *any* planet for many years,' Fife began. 'The Papaver Corporation facility that constructs the carbon nano-tube cables was put into mothballs years ago. It's located deep within the Kuiper belt.'

Trenchard raised a surprised eye brow. The Kuiper belt was an area of the solar system beyond Neptune. It was a region believed to be left over from the planet forming process, populated by thousands of chunks of ice. Pluto, once designated a planet, was now known to be just one of many planet sized objects that roamed the outer reaches of the solar system. It was a cold, dark and hostile place.

'The area of the Kuiper belt where the factory is located is too densely populated by fractured ice for a jump capable ship to get very close. The Might will have to be piggy-backed near to the area and dropped off. You are to proceed to the factory and maintain security until Papaver's permanent staff arrives to take over.'

'Why is the factory in the arse end of no-where?' Trenchard asked suspiciously.

'The carbon nano-tubes are made by a process called super growth Chemical Vapour Deposition.'

Trenchard gave Fife a blank look. He was not "well-up" on science.

'The process requires great quantities of water added to the C.V.D. reactor. There's plenty of water available out there,' explained Fife. 'Plus, room to build the extremely long lengths of cable needed.'

'And you suspect that the factory will be a target for the insurgents?'

Fife nodded. 'We don't think that the insurgent organisation has access to armed space-craft capable of attacking the factory as yet. But this recent attack on President Smith shows that they have developed an affiliation with the pirates. It's just possible that the pirates may attack on their behalf. With the space elevator destroyed, export from Earth has been crippled. Rockets are just too cumbersome. That makes the factory a top priority target for both us and the insurgents.'

'Right.'

'Your new X.O. will be arriving shortly with a data cube containing the mission details.'

Trenchard raised a surprised eyebrow. 'You've finally decided on a replacement?'

Fife sighed and rubbed his forehead. He was clearly exhausted. 'With everything that's been happening, it was more a matter of who was available. She's a damn good officer though. I'm sure that you will get on together. Good luck Captain. Fife out.'

The screen blinked off. Trenchard sat in silence and thought hard. The last remark from Fife was more of an order than a question. Trenchard was meant to accept the new X.O. and just get the hell on with the job whether he liked her or not. Fife obviously didn't have the time or the resources to argue. Things were clearly bad on Earth and Fife had other fish to fry.

Trenchard was old fashioned; some would say "sexist". Privately he didn't agree with women in the navy, he certainly didn't like working with them aboard a star-ship. But in his position of authority he had to set a good example. Great, he thought. A mission to the arse end of no-where to guard an empty factory and now a woman as his X.O. On top of that he had an inexperienced crew who were still mourning the death of their Captain and two mutinous officers that no-body trusted. Could things possibly get any worse?

The light above the main airlock changed from red to green and the hatch slid apart with a sharp hiss of escaping air. Trenchard and the gathered officers stared keenly towards the hatchway, eager to get the first look at their new executive officer. The woman who stepped briskly forwards from the airlock was in her mid-thirties, tall, and had a cold but not unattractive face. She stopped in front of Trenchard and saluted abruptly.

'Captain Trenchard?' she asked in a thick French accent.

'Good morning,' Trenchard replied, as brightly as he could muster, as he returned the salute. 'You must be Commander Genevieve Noir?'

The woman nodded.

'Let me introduce you to the crew,' said Trenchard, turning towards Lieutenant Commander Pugh who was desperately trying to look welcoming.

'I'm sorry Captain,' Commander Noir interrupted, 'but I have orders here for you from Admiral Fife. I will have to meet the crew later; the matter is too urgent. May we use your wardroom?'

Trenchard looked stunned for a moment but recovered quickly. Damn, she was keen. He could see why Fife had chosen her. He would have preferred it if she wasn't quite so pushy in front of the other officers, but there was time for her to learn that later. He waived his hand towards the end of the corridor.

'This way,' he said in a friendly voice with a tight smile.

Trenchard led Commander Noir towards the wardroom, leaving the other officers exchanging confused glances.

Trenchard settled himself into the wardroom bench seat for the third time that morning. He watched as Commander Noir drew a data cube from her pocket and inserted the small black cube into a slot on the control console in front of him.

'Right,' he sighed. 'Perhaps now you can tell me what's so damned important that this couldn't wait?'

Commander Noir sat down and smiled warmly at him. 'I'm sorry to step on your toes Captain Trenchard. I know how it must look to the crew. I promise it won't happen again.'

Trenchard felt himself unexpectedly flush red in the face. Noir's whole demeanour had changed. She was now being warm and friendly. She was not unattractive, quite the opposite and now that she smiled the coldness left her face like the melting snow in springtime.

'Apology accepted,' said Trenchard, a little less coldly himself.

Was he being manipulated? Would he have let a man get away so easily with acting that way in front of the other officers? Stop second guessing yourself Joe, he told himself. She's an officer of the navy and she has a job to do, just like you.

Noir operated a palm control that was set into the desk top and a glowing green three-dimensional hologram appeared above the centre of the table. Green text flared over the image which read, "Personal: for Commanding Officer." Then the tactical image of the space station appeared, resembling a container shipyard stacked on its side. The structure was made from huge rectangular pods that had been connected together to form laboratories and living quarters. They surrounded a central void, which

Trenchard assumed was where the carbon nano-tubes were constructed. The whole thing resembled a hollowed-out Rubik's Cube. Deep in the heart of the structure there was an area that was highlighted with flashing red.

'Apart from the ability to construct and cut the carbon nano-tubes, it has recently emerged that there is another reason that the pirates might be interested in this facility.'

Trenchard felt his stomach clench. Here it comes, he thought. His day was just about to get a whole lot worse.

'When it was mothballed, Papaver used the space station to store several prototype weapons systems that his company had been developing.'

'What?' Trenchard exclaimed in alarm.

'Papaver thought, an abandoned factory thats only use was to build cables for a space elevator that no-one thought would ever need replacing, was the perfect place to hide top-secret weapon prototypes.'

'Marvellous!' exclaimed Trenchard. 'What's he got there?'

Noir shrugged. 'Most of it isn't too impressive,' she said, scrolling a list through the air with her thumb. 'A lot of the technology has been superseded by now. But there is one item that Papaver is extremely worried about and he won't give us the details of the weapon. It's still classified. All we know is that it's code-named "*Morgenstern*".'

Trenchard racked his brain. His knowledge of German was not extensive. 'Morning... stone?'

Noir shook her head and corrected him. 'Morning Star. Sometimes used as a reference to Lucifer or Satan but also a medieval spiked mace. The truth is that we don't know why it was called that. The designers probably just liked the name. All we know is that Papaver is worried sick in case the pirates capture it.'

Trenchard leaned back in his seat and put his hands behind his head, then stared at the metal overhead. 'So, this isn't just a babysitting mission for an abandoned factory. This is a guard detail for high security, top-secret weaponry? Wonderful!'

'One more thing,' Noir said, lowering her voice. 'Because of the top-secret nature of the weapon, we can't let the rest of the crew know anything about it unless it becomes absolutely necessary. We are to protect the station until Papaver's technical team arrives to take charge but we are to stay out of the weapon storage facility. Admiral Fife was very clear on this point.'

Trenchard pulled a sour face. 'Why do we always have to pussy-foot around Papaver? You'd think he owns the navy the way that High Command simpers after him.'

Noir shrugged. 'He practically *does* own the navy Sir. His company builds and supplies all our weapons and ships. He built this prototype vessel Captain. He could make things very difficult for the navy if he wished to.'

Trenchard simply grunted and nodded. 'When do we leave?'

'The guided missile destroyer Art of Devastation is already preparing to take us there. We are to dock onto her immediately and leave A.S.A.F.P.'

The troopers of the Might of Fortitude were tucking into their evening meal. The quality of the food was much better tonight as fresh fruit and vegetables were plentiful, owing to the boat being docked at home port. Vast bio-domes had been built on Cairn; huge greenhouses inside which fruit and vegetables were intensively grown. Cox, Stofan and a group of others were already half way through their meals when McGagh pushed over to their table and elbowed his way down onto the bench. He looked tired and irritable and was covered with paint smears.

Stofan grinned at him. 'Hello Paddy,' she said. 'How come you've got paint on your uniform when you've been inside a protective E.V.A. suit for the last four hours?'

McGagh was hitting the bottom of a ketchup bottle, vainly trying to get the last dregs out and onto his beans. The choice tonight was between spaghetti Bolognese or egg, chips and baked beans. The big Irish man had gone for a portion of both. He was now covering the whole plate with red sauce.

'I was bloody clean until I got out of the damned suit and had to clean the spray valves,' he growled, pushing a forkful of chips and beans into his mouth. 'The flaming pressure hose broke free and covered me with paint. I've spent the last half hour cleaning the bloody mess up!'

Stofan and Cox chuckled.

McGagh stopped chewing and glared at Cox. 'I don't know what you're laughing at kitten boy!'

Cox stopped laughing and begun to absent-mindedly rub the kitten pin badge on his uniform.

Stofan glared at McGagh. 'Hey! There's no need to take it out on Cox. It's your own fault for being a smart ass to Pugh. I warned you not to.'

Paddy grunted and continued to eat. 'I didn't see you obeying his orders during the training mission. I could have sworn you were right behind me when we got zapped in the nads.'

Stofan stuck her tongue out at McGagh and continued to eat her own meal. Cox paused with his fork mid-way from his plate to his mouth and stared off into the distance.

'I keep thinking about all those poor people,' he said.

McGagh stared at him as he shovelled another large forkful into his mouth and made a grunting noise.

'What do you mean?' Stofan asked.

'Trying to escape that island when the space elevator fell and being crushed to death; thousands of them. Then the waves hitting the coast and drowning people.'

Stofan placed a comforting hand onto Cox's arm. 'Will your girlfriend be alright?'

Cox smiled. 'Nancy? Oh, sure. She lives well inland. I'm sure she'll be okay.'

'That's good then,' said Stofan. 'Try not to think about it. Try to think about our job. It's up to us to hunt down people like the ones that destroyed the space elevator.'

'I hope wherever we're being sent, we get the chance to give them fuckers back what for!' growled McGagh as he glugged down some coffee and wiped his mouth with his sleeve. 'Any idea where we're headed?'

Stofan shook her head. 'No idea, but I'm guessing it's somewhere inside the solar system.'

'How do you know that?' asked Cox, ever in awe of Stofan's seemingly limitless knowledge of naval matters.

'Because I saw them loading the supplies for the galley this morning. We haven't taken on nearly enough stores for a long voyage. They were loading in a bitch of a hurry too, so it must be an urgent mission. The logistics officer was in a right foul mood.'

'Maybe they found out who did it and we're being sent to hunt them down,' said McGagh with a gleeful grin.

'You have a bit too much blood lust for me Paddy,' snapped Stofan as she stared hard into his eyes.

'What am I supposed to have?' he said, still grinning. 'I'm a trooper in the Space Navy. It's my job to kick the insurgents' heads in. They're filthy rotten dirty fighters the lot of them. The sooner we've put a bullet into every single one of their thick skulls, the better!'

Stofan sighed. 'They're still *people* Paddy. They have families themselves you know. They believe in what they're fighting for, just like us.'

McGagh's eyebrows shot up. 'Sounds like you're trying to justify what they did! You're not a fuckin' sympathiser, are you?'

'No of course not!' Stofan exclaimed. 'It's just that you always deal with black or white, right or wrong Paddy. I'm just saying that it's usually more complicated than that.

There are grey areas where right or wrong gets blurred sometimes.'

McGagh cleared his plate and stood up, ready to go back for seconds. 'Just you wait till some insurgent has a rifle pointed in your face and your mate's body is lying in pieces on the ground next to you,' he snarled. 'Then we'll see if you still believe in grey!'

As McGagh stomped grumpily off towards the back of the queue for food, Stofan watched him go and sighed. Then she swigged down her coffee and turned to Cox.

'Come on then. We have a weapons prep to do before we get underway and I want to be ready, whatever this mission turns out to be.'

CHAPTER 16

"NERVES"

The huge docking clamps released with a hiss that reverberated through the vessel. The Might of Fortitude powered away from the Art of Devastation towards the Kuiper belt like a pilot fish leaving a shark. The area resembled a vast expanse of Arctic Ocean, chock full of massive icebergs and trailing frozen dust and debris. The largest object in this area was the dwarf planet Makemake, an ice giant that was two thirds the size of Pluto and composed from frozen methane, ethane and nitrogen gas. There was nothing on or near Makemake, but the dwarf planet dominated the horizon like an oversized dirty snowball.

The Papaver Corporation factory was much further into the arctic depths of the ice field. The Art of Devastation had dropped the Might off as close as she could but it was still almost a day's voyage into the ice field to the factory. It was far too dangerous for any Watters' Drive capable ship to jump into an area as densely populated as the Kuiper belt. The ship would have risked damage to her hull when she dropped out from the faster-than-light propulsion. The Might of Fortitude was relatively small and could dodge between the icebergs. She powered up her engines, as bright as a sun and then blasted at full thrust into the foreboding cold heart of the densest part of the Kuiper belt.

Twenty hours later, the watch crew in the control room gazed on as the space station finally drew near. Trenchard turned to the navigator.

'Schmidt. Bring us within five hundred meters of the station and then full stop. I want the troops sent across in the drop-ships. We can't afford to dock the boat in case trouble shows up. I want the Might on a constant watch, just out of sight from the station, hidden behind one of the ice formations. If a pirate cruiser shows up I want to take them by surprise.'

'Aye, aye Sir!' came the reply from several officers.

Trenchard turned towards his executive officer. Commander Noir was standing close behind him to his left. She stood expectantly, waiting for her orders to leave for the station.

'Commander Noir, you have the Conn. I'm going down there myself,' Trenchard ordered.

Noir was appalled. 'Sir!' she spluttered. 'Your place is on the ship, it's my job to command the troopers on mission. It's completely against regulations to…'

Trenchard raised his finger in front of his face, immediately silencing Noir. 'I don't need the regulations quoted at me Commander. I'm well aware of what the book says. I'm also well aware of your service record.'

Noir's mouth, which was hanging agape, snapped shut and her eyes burned with anger and resentment.

'Did you think that I wouldn't check you out?'

Noir remained steadfastly silent.

'You've had absolutely no practical experience of close combat, ground based tactics, zone clearance or anything that wasn't a simulation,' Trenchard began. 'You have however, excelled as a bridge officer in several battles and your understanding of tactics in ship-to-ship combat is second to none. Admiral Fife's recommendation was very clear on that! I've had years of experience entering hulks like that.'

Trenchard's finger shot out sideways, pointing at the looming space station that sat in front of the ship like a broken Rubik's Cube.

'It is my command decision that in this instance, you are better positioned as watch commander of the ship whilst I secure the factory; especially given the particularly delicate nature of the situation over there… and on my boat, my word is fucking law! Understood?'

Noir fumed for a moment and then simply replied, 'Understood.' Then when Trenchard refused to break eye contact, she added a terse, '*Sir!*'

'As I said, the Conn is yours Commander Noir. Pugh, you're with me,' Trenchard snapped.

Trenchard began to climb the exit ladder from the control room. Pugh gave Noir a reassuring smile and then followed Trenchard up the ladder. Noir stood for a moment, her face burning. Then she shook her head as if to clear her thoughts and turned back towards the officers who were all staring at her, open mouthed. At her stern gaze, everyone busied themselves about their watch stations once more. Noir walked over to the V.R. Conn, stepped up and began strapping her legs into the braces.

'Schmidt. Plot a course that puts us behind one of those blocks of ice. Helm, once the drop-ships are launched manoeuvre us into position, carefully. Then I want all non-critical systems powered down so that we're undetectable. *And some-one get me some damned coffee!*' she snapped.

Trenchard and Pugh reached the core of the Might where the ladder split into two, ascending and descending towards the fins that held the two drop-ships and the waiting squads of troopers. They paused for a moment, floating in the zero gee at the entrance to the shafts.

'Get your squad into the drop-ship and head for the starboard airlock on the station; I'll take the port side. Work your way in and post guards at any critical areas. Whoever gets to the station's control centre first, powers up the systems and brings the life support systems and defences on-line. Understood?'

'Yes Sir,' Pugh replied.

Trenchard stopped and looked Pugh straight in the eyes. 'Lieutenant Commander… Look, I know things have been difficult for you since the mutiny.'

Pugh dropped his eyes to the floor and muttered, 'Sir.'

'I understand why you did it, but I think that you were misled. Captain Bird could be… *persuasive.*'

Pugh looked back up into Trenchard's face, a tiny ray of hope lighting in his eyes.

'He was a hard man to say no to. He was commanding and authoritative. The crew will learn to trust you again, but you'll have to work at it. You must give them something to trust. This mission is your chance to shine. Show them a brave face son. Show them a leader. Actions speak louder than words. Make them understand that you're not afraid to put your balls on the line and they'll begin to trust you again.'

Pugh smiled and said, 'Thank you Sir.'

'But if you disobey even one of my orders, I'll cut your nuts off with a blunt old rusty knife and feed them to you! Understood?'

Pugh nodded. Trenchard made a move towards the ladder.

'Sir?' said Pugh.

Trenchard turned towards him again.

'Yes?'

'What did you mean by the "delicate nature of the situation over there"? What's in that station?'

Trenchard took a deep intake of breath. 'It's classified; direct orders from Admiral Fife.'

Pugh looked like he wanted to know more but didn't push it. He simply nodded.

'Let's just say,' Trenchard continued, 'that I wouldn't go opening any secured storage boxes in a hurry if I were you.'

The two, stubby drop-ships powered towards the space station, their thrusters glowing brightly in the darkness. Inside the leading ship, Trenchard was strapped into his seat as were the other troopers. The two pilots were concentrating on their heads-up-displays and tactical holograms. Trenchard looked about him at the white-faced troopers. They were mostly kids, fresh out of training. None of them had any real experience in actual combat, apart from McGagh. For the last few days he'd had Pugh drilling them in the simulator on Cairn but that was nothing compared to actual combat experience. At least they looked the part, dressed head to toe in black body armour with domed shoulder pads and a tough helmet with protective visor.

One young man caught his eye. He was only ranked as Able Spaceman. Trenchard had previously reprimanded him for wearing a pin badge of a kitten that had been given to him by his girlfriend. At Trenchard's behest, his unforgiving comrades now knew him solely as "Mrs Fluffy Kitten" or as these things were prone to evolve, "Pussy" or "Kitten Boy". The nickname would be hard to shake off.

'What's your name son?' Trenchard asked, being sure to make eye contact with the young man.

'Mrs Fluffy Kitten, Sir!' said the trooper, remembering the reprimand that Trenchard had given him.

'I mean your real name son,'

The nervous young trooper lifted his head and stared at Trenchard in utter terror. 'A.S. Gerry Cox, Sir!'

'This is your first time on a combat drop, isn't it?'

'Yes Sir,' Cox gulped, his lower lip trembling slightly.

The conversation was drawing attention from others nearby. Good, thought Trenchard. It was just what he wanted.

'Has your rifle been inspected and cleaned?'

'Yes Sir, twice. Checked by Lieutenant Stofan Sir!'

'Good. Remember your training. It's the discipline and procedure that will save your life. Just remember your combat drills and you'll be fine.'

'Yes Sir.'

The atmosphere inside the drop-ship was beginning to thaw a little but it needed a final push. They were no use to him if they were so worried that they panicked under fire.

'Know any good jokes?' Trenchard asked.

Cox shook his head, unsure where this was going. 'I can never remember them Sir, at least, not the funny ones.'

Trenchard smiled broadly and settled back into his seat. 'There was this young fella, just about your age, a real streak of piss…'

A few of the nearby troopers giggled. Cox started to smile but he was still unsure of himself.

'Anyway,' Trenchard continued, 'he sits down on a park bench next to a rough looking old bloke. After a while he notices the old bloke staring at his hair. See, the young fella has this brightly coloured Mohican hair do; nine inches high and all spiky and shit.'

By now everyone in the cabin was chuckling. Even the pilots had wry smiles on their faces, ear-wigging what was going on behind them.

'After a few minutes the young fella gets pissed off at the old man for staring at him, looks him straight in the eye and says, "What's wrong with you, you old fuckwit? Have you never done anything crazy in your life?" The old man chews this over for a moment and then finally replies, "Yes son. When I was in the Space Navy, I got really drunk one night and had sex with a parrot. I just thought that you might be my long-lost son!"'

The whole cabin exploded with laughter. Even Cox was laughing out loud by now.

While the cabin was still full of raucous laughter, Trenchard leaned across towards Cox and whispered, '*Follow your training son, and you'll live to be that old fella on the park bench. You'll be okay, don't worry.*'

Then Trenchard gave Cox a friendly wink. The atmosphere inside the drop-ship had eased considerably by now. The troopers were still on edge but they weren't dwelling on dark thoughts. Much better, thought Trenchard. Telling a joke was an old trick that he had learned from his days in old Skelat's platoon aboard the Hand of Valour. It had served him well over the years. He let his mind wander back to the old days and as usual, it wasn't long before the barren and dusty wastelands of Mars filled his mind.

He was shaken out of his meandering thoughts as the engine noise of the drop-ship suddenly rose and Trenchard could hear the steering thrusters on the nose and tail firing, turning the ship ready for docking.

'Okay everyone. Get ready,' he shouted.

All the troopers grabbed their rifles and placed their hands onto the buckle of their harnesses, ready to move. There were a series of sharp clicks as visors were dropped into place. There was a jolt and a clunk as the drop-ship docked with the space-station and a steady hiss of air as the air-lock was pressurised. After a few seconds the red light above the hatch changed to green. Trenchard looked towards the pilots. One of them craned his head around and gave Trenchard the thumbs up.

'You're good to go Sir!'

'First team, Lieutenant Chertok you're up front,' yelled Trenchard.

Twelve of the troopers released their harnesses and stood up. They headed towards the hatch, clanking on the metal deck in their mag-boots. They were followed by an officer with two red stripes, Lieutenant Boris Chertok, the Russian who Trenchard had met briefly during simulator training. He was tough as old boots and was one of the few who had seen a little combat. At a nod from Trenchard, Chertok operated the hatch control and the hatch slid open with the sound of grating metal, revealing only darkness beyond.

'Good god, it's cold,' Chertok announced, grinning back at the rest of the squad. 'I hope you all put your thermal undies on, because you're going to need them!'

CHAPTER 17

"COLD IRON"

Inside the airlock, it was indeed very cold. The space station had been shut down for years and the life support systems were waking up as slowly as a teenager on a school day. The airlock area was only just warm enough to support human life. The trooper's breaths came out in clouds of steam and a thick frost sparkled on every surface. There was no gravity inside the station, because the main systems hadn't been activated and the station was dead still.

The first team of troopers fanned out in the entry area with their weapons covering the exits. Their magnetic boots clanged on the freezing metal floor sending echoes down the foreboding connecting corridors and spraying clouds of sparkling ice crystals into the air. Lieutenant Chertok followed the squad through and waved them forwards. With a click, the motion detecting lights blinked into life, making the troopers squint for a few seconds with the brilliance of the light reflected off the iridescent frost. For some strange reason the lights were set into the floor.

Once the exits were covered, Trenchard strode through with the second squad of twelve troopers. He looked around himself, taking in his surroundings. The cold air smelled stale and musty like the damp basement of an old terraced house. It was low in oxygen and he was breathing heavily. He looked up and saw something that shouldn't be there; a dirty footprint on the ceiling above him.

'Shit!' he swore out loud. 'We've come in the wrong bloody way up. That's going to cause hell when we get the gravity started up again. I'll be having a word with the pilot when this is over.'

Looking about him he now saw other clues that they were upside-down. A warning sign next to a door, ceiling vents next to their feet and a fire sprinkler that he had almost trodden on.

Chertok looked expectantly at Trenchard. 'Orders Sir?' he asked.

'Split your squad into two and take the corridors to the left and right. Leave guards at every major junction and work your way around towards the main control room. I'll take my squad straight through and meet you there.' Then Trenchard looked over to a trooper who was carrying a small bag attached to his front harness. 'Release the omni,' he ordered.

The trooper opened the bag carefully and pulled out a small triangular device about five inches on either side. At the press of a switch, three fans, one at each corner, activated and the device floated up into the air above the trooper's heads like a child's toy helicopter. In the centre of the triangular device a clear plastic hemisphere glowed dimly.

Trenchard waved at the device, squinting into the dome. 'You got us?' he asked out loud.

In the control room of the Might of Fortitude, Commander Noir studied a glowing hologram that was being projected into the air at the front of the bridge. It showed the troopers from the point of view of the hovering triangular robot.

'The omni-bot is functioning within normal parameters,' she said rather coldly. She was still smarting from Trenchard's earlier reprimand.

'*A simple yes would have done Noir.*' Trenchard grumbled, never one to take any nonsense from a junior officer.

The Ocular Mobile Naval Intelligence robot, or "omni-bot" for short, was essentially a floating probe. It allowed the ship to keep track of the mission visually, whilst scanning for a range of other data simultaneously.

'*Keep your eye out for bogey men,*' the image of Trenchard said with a grin.

'I'll be the first to shout if I see any monsters Sir,' Noir replied through tight lips.

On the other side of the station, Pugh's squad had entered via another airlock the correct way up. They had walked through several frozen corridors to find themselves in an unusually shaped room. Pugh gazed around the room they were now standing in. It was a giant tube, like standing inside a massive baked-bean tin. Each end of the tin had an over-sized circular airlock. Right in the centre there was a circular ring or track that ran around the entire circumference, encompassing the room.

'Those are the biggest air-lock hatches that I've ever seen. What is this place?' Pugh asked out loud.

'No idea,' replied Lieutenant Stofan, Pugh's number two. 'Something to do with the carbon nano-tube construction maybe?'

'It's the cutting room,' came a gruff Irish voice from directly behind them.

Pugh and Stofan turned around to where the voice had come from. Standing behind them was the mighty frame of Patrick McGagh. He was looking rather smug.

'*What?*' Pugh asked, feeling more than a little confused.

'They pass the carbon nano-tube cables through one hatch and out the other. The ring in the centre is a sonic cutting device, specially designed to cut the nano-tubes. That's the control station,' said McGagh, pointing to a panel of switches on the wall.

Pugh and Stofan exchanged astonished glances.

'How do you know that?' asked Pugh.

McGagh shrugged. 'I watched a documentary on the telly about building the space elevator. They did a whole section just on this room. I had a lot of time on my hands when I was locked up…'

Pugh thought about this. McGagh had indeed been locked up in naval prison for fighting, just before he was transferred to the Might of Fortitude. His explanation had the ring of truth.

'You're a man of hidden depths,' remarked Stofan.

'I'd say more hidden shallows!' grinned McGagh.

'Come on,' said Pugh. 'We need to push on. There's a lot more of the station to cover.' With that, he headed for a hatch that was set into the side of the curved room, followed closely by the rest of the squad.

Back inside the main airlock, Trenchard looked around at the troopers.

'Move out,' he ordered. 'Keep in touch if you spot anything… *unusual.*'

'Define unusual?' Chertok asked with a grimace.

'Anything that looks like you shouldn't mess with it,' replied Trenchard testily.

Chertok diligently split his squad in half and each group clanked off down corridors to the left and right. Trenchard waved his squad forwards down the central tunnel. The omni-bot followed after them, humming very gently and bobbing slightly in the air as it went, having difficulty compensating in the zero gravity.

After making their way through several frosty corridors, Trenchard's squad eventually reached a door which said, upside-down at the bottom, "Main Control". The door opened after the second attempt with a shower of ice crystals that hung suspended in the air like freezing fog. The troopers stepped gingerly into the room. The control room, although upside down, was largely unimpressive and utilitarian. It held several consoles and bolted down chairs. At one end, there was a huge plexi-glass window that looked out across the cubic void enclosed by the station; the factory shop floor where the carbon nano-tubes were constructed before they were passed to the cutting room.

Trenchard made his way over to the wall and with effort, he clumped up the wall and then righted himself on the floor, the opposite way up to the other troopers. He scanned the main console and found the panel that he was looking for. He brought his left wrist up towards his mouth, pressed a button on a black wrist band and spoke into a small microphone.

'Trenchard to all troopers; I'm about to fire the retros and bring the gravity back on-line. Hold onto something. Out.'

All the troopers in the control room grabbed onto anything that they could get their hands on and braced. Most of them chose to stand beside a wall that they could conveniently slide down. Trenchard spoke again into the bracelet cuff-link communicator, '…and in three, two, one!'

He activated the control. There was a short pause and then a judder as the rocket jets fired and the station began to slowly spin around its central axis. Slowly and steadily gravity began to take hold. The troopers found themselves gradually sliding down the walls and ending up crumpled but unhurt in a heap on the floor. Trenchard checked that all the troopers were unharmed before examining the frozen control panel in front of him.

'Right, where's the on switch?' he asked out loud, as he brushed frost away with his gloved hand.

In a large storage room, next to another airlock, Pugh's squad had just recovered from the gravity coming back on.

Stofan suddenly shouted out, 'Lieutenant Commander!'

Pugh looked over in alarm. 'What is it Stofan?'

Stofan pointed excitedly to a pile of metal crates that were stacked against one wall.

'These are marked property of the Papaver Corporation but they're not parts or materials for nano-tube manufacture. They're not even supplies for the crew of the station. I think that they're weapons of some kind. Should they be here?'

Pugh rushed over. The crates did indeed look very out of place. They were cordoned off from the rest of the boxes and cargo. All these crates looked much more secure and well-built than the rest. Pugh even recognised some of them as the same storage boxes that held ammunition and missiles aboard the Might of Fortitude. Two crates in particular, caught his eye. They were metal containers about seven feet tall, shaped disconcertingly like coffins. They had clear plexi-glass covers that were frosted inside with ice. On the front of the containers were hand shaped palm-control devices, cutting edge technology for the time that the space station had been mothballed. The shapes inside the containers were instantly recognisable. There were humanoid figures inside the crates and just about where the heart should be, there was a steady glowing red throb inside one of the crates.

'Big fuckers aren't they,' McGagh observed as he peered through the plexi-glass cover of one of the crates and instinctively moved his hand up towards the palm control device.

'*DON'T,*' Pugh shouted.

McGagh's hand froze in mid-air and he met Pugh's steely gaze. Pugh looked deadly serious and McGagh brought his hand back down again, grinning mischievously all the way.

'Sir,' Stofan said quietly. 'This one has leaked something…. nasty.'

They all looked down. On the floor in front of one of the cases was a pool of liquid that was even now, thawing from its long freeze in the cold depths of space. The liquid was viscous, dark green and had one other identifying feature.

McGagh wrinkled his nose. '*It stinks!*' he said, backing away and holding his hand over his face. 'Awwww! It's all over my boots! It's worse than nappies and fish guts!'

Stofan pointed. 'The seal has been broken, must've been faulty. Look!' she said.

Pugh gingerly reached forwards with his gloved hand. He placed his fingers gently onto the rim of the cover next to where the green slime was leaking. With a sudden rush of movement, the cover unexpectedly swung forward under its own weight and crashed onto the floor, ringing like a bell. All three jumped back as something heavy, wet and smelly, fell forwards and slopped onto the floor. McGagh, Stofan and Pugh stared in horror at what lay on the floor. Whatever it was had now become a mass of mixed up components, covered in a thick dark green slime that stank to high heaven. Rigid structures stood out, gleaming under the slime; reminiscent of human bones but made from highly polished metal. Right in the centre of the stinking heap was one item that looked out of place, even though it was partially hidden by the sludge.

'What is that?' said Pugh with horrid fascination across his face.

McGagh pulled his combat knife from its sheath on his belt and leaned forwards. Carefully he pushed the blade into a recessed hole on the object and gently lifted it from the sloppy mess. As it was raised into the air in front of them, trailing thick strands of rubbery green slime, all three gasped in astonishment.

'Is that?' tailed off Pugh.

'Yep!' replied McGagh in a matter of fact tone. 'Some poor fucker's skull, or what's left of it. The jaw's missing…'

In addition to the jaw being missing, the top of the skull had been cut off in a clean circle, leaving the deep bowl that would have held the exposed brain. The brain had long since rotted away. As the three stared at the grimacing skull held by McGagh's knife which was plunged through the eye socket, the skull began to fizz and pop. Before their eyes the bone simply melted away to leave a thick, black goo dripping from the end of McGagh's shining blade.

'Damn I could have used that!' grinned McGagh mischievously. 'Halloween's coming up. I needed something to scare away the trick-or-treaters.'

Stofan rolled her eyes and sighed. Pugh brought his wrist up to his mouth and pressed the communicator button on his cuff-link.

'Pugh to Trenchard,' he said, a slight quaver in his voice. 'I think we found what you're looking for. Over.'

Behind Pugh, his squad's omni-bot zoomed in onto the second metal coffin.

'What the heck is that?' said Chief Petty Officer Kittinger, staring at the scanner control station aboard the Might of Fortitude. He was receiving information directly from the two omni-bots, straight to his station.

Commander Noir walked towards him and leaned over. 'What are you getting?' she asked quietly.

Kittinger screwed up his face. 'Hard to tell,' he said. 'There's the usual tell-tale chemical signature from the stored explosives and solid fuel but the tall box in the middle has some kind of cryogenic system in operation. Whatever is in there has been put into deep freeze.'

'Right,' said Noir.

Bingo, she thought. This must be the stash that Papaver was so worried about the pirates getting a hold of.

'There's one odd reading,' added Kittinger. 'I'm picking up a life sign inside the box. It's very faint and it's centred at the top of the box, but there's definitely something alive in there.'

Commander Noir straightened up with a worried expression on her face. *'Morgenstern…'* she whispered softly to herself.

'What sort of weapon has Pap-Corp built that has a life reading?' Kittinger enquired with a crumpled forehead.

Trenchard had just received the message from Pugh. He straightened up and spoke urgently into his communicator.

'Trenchard to Pugh. Do NOT touch anything! Place a cordon around those boxes and touch *NOTHING!* Understand? Over.'

Pugh's voice came back over the cuff-link communicator. *'Roger that Sir. WilCo and out.'*

'Sir!' Cox shouted abruptly across the control room. 'Look!'

Trenchard turned his head towards the direction that Cox's outstretched arm was pointing. Outside, through the plexi-glass window, in the huge space where the carbon nano-tubes were constructed, something was moving. It was black, almost invisible against the darkness of space in the unlit area in the central void of the space station. It shifted almost imperceptibly like a leviathan waking in the darkest depths of the sea.

Trenchard hurriedly looked down and scanned the control panel in front of him. 'Lights, lights, lights… come on!' he muttered desperately to himself.

Then he found the control that he was looking for and slapped the button down hard. Instantly, the central void was filled with searing bright white light from powerful spotlights. Illuminated at the centre was the ugly, black, leech-like shape of a pirate battle cruiser. The instant the lights came on, the cruiser began to build speed, heading out into open space.

'Bastards!' shouted Trenchard. 'They must have been here all the time, powered down.' He slammed the control on his wrist communicator. 'Commander Noir!' he shouted.

Noir was already strapping herself into the leg braces of the V.R. Conn.

'I'm already on it Captain!' she shouted as she lowered the black visor down across her eyes and metal electrodes extended and contacted her temples. Suddenly, the ship around her disappeared and she was plunged into a virtual world. It was as though she became part of the Might of Fortitude. Looking around her she saw the space station, now spinning slowly to produce gravity. From out of the central void the pirate cruiser blasted at full speed. Several gun turrets on the pirate ship swivelled towards the iceberg where the Might was hiding and fired. They already knew where the Might was concealed. Glowing balls of green plasma were thrown towards the Might of Fortitude's hull by powerful magnetic coils. The searing plasma simply melted holes through the ice without diminishing speed.

'Helm, evasive!' she screamed.

The Might of Fortitude lurched to port, just before the plasma could hit the hull. Noir moved her hands in front of her in the virtual world, feverishly operating controls.

'Steer thirty-five degrees port, down twelve degrees, full thrust.'

'Aye, aye Sir!' shouted the Planesman and Throttleman together.

Noir grabbed icons that represented the targeting for the Might's own plasma cannons and dragged them across towards the virtual image of the fleeing pirate ship. The target indicators changed from green to red as they locked on.

'Rig for red. Sound General Quarters. Weapons fire control; fire for effect!'

The lights in the control room dimmed and were replaced by a dim red glow.

'Aye, aye Sir,' shouted Warrant Officer Cochran. 'Firing now.'

The Might leased off a series of plasma burst from her forward cannons. The green plasma spun through space in a spiral due to the spinning motion of the Might of Fortitude. Most of the rounds missed the pirate ship which dodged and weaved between the floating chunks of ice.

'Tactical, compensate for spin and plot a course to bring us alongside the bandit.'

'Aye, aye Sir,' confirmed Van Allen, feverishly operating his station.

The Might of Fortitude began to move parallel to the slower pirate ship, ramping her engines up to full speed. Her forward and rear canons swivelled towards the starboard side preparing for a broadside. The ship's computers calculated the spin of the vessel and prepared to fire the canons in sequence.

'Fire at will,' Noir commanded, grim determination in her voice.

'Aye, aye, Commander. Target locked,' confirmed Cochran. 'Firing now!'

Each of the cannons of the Might of Fortitude now fired in rapid sequence as she spun through space like an arrow in flight. As each cannon revolved around with the hull and was brought to bear on the pirate ship, it released a deadly barrage of plasma. It then ceased firing as it spun out from line of sight, only to be replace a second later by the next cannon. Wave after wave of deadly green death flew across the void, smashing through ice chunks and ripping into the hull of the fleeing pirate ship.

The space station floated alone in the darkness, her lone guardian now far away, chasing the pirate cruiser. From deep within an immense ice cavern, in a nearby mountain of frozen methane, several lights blinked on. A massive dark shape crept forwards from the cavern towards the now unprotected station. It was at least four times larger than the Might of Fortitude and the entire hull was packed with weapons. The grim helmeted skull and crossed rifles of the Martian space pirates was painted boldly across the front of the ship. Within minutes, the large ship had crossed the void to the station and had begun docking, its clamps grasping onto the station like the clawed legs of a mighty black spider.

Trenchard was hectically working his way through the control panel, gradually switching all the systems back on line. He threw the last switch and all the station's lights came on, chasing the remaining shadows away. He relaxed for just a moment. He was convinced that Noir could handle the relatively small pirate cruiser. The Might would be back soon and the station would be fully secured. Time to find some coffee he thought to himself. That was assuming they hadn't cleared out the supplies completely when they had abandoned the station.

He was disturbed from his thoughts by his wrist communicator beeping urgently. He brought it up to his mouth and pressed the button. 'Trenchard here. What's up? Over.'

The voice that came back over the radio was Chertok's Russian accent and it sounded worried.

'*Sir. Have you looked out of a window recently? There's another pirate ship. It just appeared out of nowhere. It's massive, like a destroyer! It's docking! Over.*'

Trenchard paused for a moment before replying, his mind racing.

'Trenchard to all troopers. Prepare to be boarded. Set up defensive positions at all airlocks. Out.'

Trenchard turned towards Cox, who looked completely terrified.

'What do we do now Sir?' Cox asked, his voice trembling.

Trenchard took a deep breath. 'We fight!' he said simply.

CHAPTER 18

"QUOTH THE RAVEN"

Trenchard had returned to the airlock where he had originally entered the space station, but the right way up this time. The station was now comfortable; warm, well-lit and had gravity. That was the end of the good news. The drop-ships had been ordered to run. They were no match for the massive pirate cruiser. Trenchard had instructed them to wait at a safe distance, out of range of the weapons of the pirate vessel. The troopers had dragged several crates and tables into the airlock area to provide some cover but it wouldn't be much use if the pirates had high power rifles. It was more of a psychological prop than anything else. Trenchard knew that the same thing was happening at all the other airlocks in the station. The pirate ship could only dock at one of them but the pirates were quite capable of space-walking in E.V.A. suits to any of the airlocks to attempt to gain entry.

The troopers waited tensely. They were extremely nervous. For many of them this would be their first time in real combat rather than simulated. These pirates would be flesh and blood, not tricks of the light in the combat zone on Cairn. Trenchard studied the young lad Cox who was kneeling next to him. He was sweating. Looking down, Trenchard could see the boy's hands were trembling as he gripped his rifle. Trenchard caught Cox's eye with a wave of his hand.

'Toughen up there Cox,' he said with a wink, 'this'll be a piece of piss!'

Cox smiled back and relaxed ever so slightly. His smile faded quickly as a loud clang echoed down the corridor. It was the pirate ship docking. It sounded like the single, mournful, toll of a graveyard bell. The noise sent a shiver down Trenchard's spine. The station shook and vibrated slightly until the computers compensated for the extra mass attached to the outside hull. Then they adjusted the rotation of the station and the tremors ceased. Trenchard tensed as he heard the hiss as the airlock cycled and pressurised.

'This is it,' he shouted. 'Short, controlled bursts. I don't want any loose cannons! Wait for my order to fire.'

The airlock hatch hissed open. There was only darkness beyond. Trenchard gripped his rifle hard and his finger tensed upon the trigger. There was movement. Several space-suited pirates walked through the hatch into the light. As usual their helmets were spray painted with grisly skull designs and images of snarling animals and demons. Trenchard studied them closely through narrowed eyes. They were unarmed and one of them was waving a piece of white cloth.

'Hold!' Trenchard instructed as he raised his hand.

The pirates stopped just inside the hatch area and stood stock still. The man at the front, whose helmet was painted to resemble a bull, rounded on Trenchard and stared at him. Trenchard cautiously stood up and carefully lowered his rifle. He walked a couple of paces forwards and stared at the leading pirate who was holding the white flag of truce.

'Well?' he asked impatiently.

'*We have you outnumbered,*' said the bull pirate simply, his voice distorted by the speakers of his E.V.A. suit's communication system. It wasn't a threat, just a statement of fact. '*Our Captain doesn't want unnecessary bloodshed. He requests that your commanding officer comes aboard to negotiate terms.*'

'Negotiate?' Trenchard spat the word. 'Pirates don't negotiate. You're a load of bloodthirsty murderers! Why should I trust you?'

The pirate made no movement, although Trenchard got the distinct impression that the man was studying him.

'*You have no choice. Resist and there will be a battle, which we shall inevitably win. Most of your lot will die and we'll get what we came for anyway.*'

There was a long, cold silence. Trenchard had to admit to himself that the pirate had a point. He turned to Lieutenant Chertok.

'Chertok, I'm going aboard with bully boy here and leaving you in command of the squad. S.T.F.B. Hold your fire unless they try to board. If they do… give 'em hell!'

Chertok smiled. 'In Russia, we have a saying. If you are going to die, die with music!' he said with a wink. 'We'll give 'em hell alright Sir, you can count on that!'

The Might of Fortitude raced through the Kuiper belt at full speed. The smaller pirate cruiser was crippled and the Wolverine was moving in for the kill. Commander Noir shouted to Cochran at the weapons station.

'Cochran, target their engines and prepare to fire heat-seekers.'

'Aye, aye Sir,' Cochran replied.

'Sir!' Kittinger announced from the Scanner Control. 'Their E.C.M. system has just failed and the blocking signal has dropped. I'm now scanning the ship interior. I can't find any life signs. They must be controlling the ship remotely from a source near to the space station.'

Noir grimaced underneath her black visor.

'*Merde!* It's a decoy.' She turned her head instinctively towards where she knew Schmidt and Van Allen were seated. 'Schmidt, plot the quickest course back to the station. Van Allen, I want a tactical simulation of the whole area by the time we get back there. Kittinger, begin scanning for other enemy ships near the station. Cochran…' Noir paused and gritted her teeth. 'Fire fox two!'

A single heat-seeking torpedo burst from the forward tubes of the Might of Fortitude. It circled around in a wide, graceful arc, before locking in on the engines and explosions that were breaking out along the broken hull of the unmanned pirate cruiser. The missile ploughed headlong into the cruiser and it disappeared in a flash of blue and white light.

Trenchard allowed himself to be led into the bowels of the massive pirate cruiser by the pirate with the bull design on his helmet. It was surprisingly tidy and organised for a privateer ship; however, the whole ship looked like it had been put together from salvaged junk. No two bulkheads looked the same and every hatch was slightly different. Spot repairs and patches covered every piece of equipment and the whole ship had the feel of a mechanic's pit; dirty, greasy and dark.

Finally, he was shown into a conference room located in a central gravity wheel. Trenchard tried to relax and loose the zero-gee nausea he had been feeling as he looked around him. The room had a long oval table in the middle and several holographic projectors mounted onto the walls. One whole wall was taken up by a crudely spray-painted version of the pirate's emblem; the skull helmet and crossed rifles. Trenchard's escorts left the room and the hatch was then shut firmly behind them. Trenchard waited, the muffled sounds of talking and maintenance work coming through the bulkhead next to him from somewhere distant. He was wondering what the pirate Captain would demand. Would Trenchard even get off this ship alive? He had allowed himself to be taken, unarmed, deep into an enemy vessel. He knew that he was just buying time. Papaver's people were supposed to be on their way and the Papaver Corporation built the best weapons in existence. Everybody knew that. They would hardly arrive unarmed, would they? But would they arrive in time to help?

Trenchard was disturbed from his pondering as the hatch swung slowly open and in walked a tall figure, fully space-suited and helmeted. The guards posted outside the hatch were holding rifles. Clearly, he was now a prisoner rather than a guest. The hatch swung shut with a resounding clang and the two Captains were left alone to stare each other out. Trenchard studied the pirate Captain. He, if it were a he, was tall and extremely broad shouldered; a titan of a man. His space-suit was sprayed matt black and his helmet had been painted to resemble the gaping maw of a sinister black Raven. Trenchard stared at the figure defiantly.

'Nice helmet,' he sneered. 'Very… ornithological.' The pirate remained silent and made no movement. After a moment Trenchard jeered, 'Are we just going to stand here and stare at each other like a couple of twats?'

The pirate Captain remained steadfastly silent. He reached up and undid the clasps that held his helmet in place. With a twist, he pulled the helmet slowly off. The face underneath beamed a broad smile. It was a face that Trenchard knew well; one that he was absolutely certain he had seen killed by a bullet through his forehead in the control room of the Might of Fortitude.

'*Bird!*' spluttered Trenchard in shock.

'Hello Trench,' replied Bird. 'Long time no see old fella.'

Trenchard couldn't believe his eyes. He had quite definitely seen Bird killed by the pirates, shot through the head at point blank range by Captain Smiler.

'How?' he stammered, anger welling within him, his fists clenching tightly.

Bird smiled. Obviously, he was taking great pleasure in his old friend's discomfort.

'It was staged. Micro blood packs that were triggered by the blank firing pistol that Captain Smiler used. You had to believe that I was dead Trench old mate. Looks like it worked.'

Trenchard exploded. 'You son of a bitch!' he spat, taking a step forwards, enraged beyond the point of self-control.

Captain Bird brought a small pistol up from his side and waved it threateningly at Trenchard.

'Ah, ah!' he warned. 'This one isn't loaded with blanks.'

Trenchard backed down and as he fumed he growled, 'Why?'

Bird shrugged and sat down wearily on one of the conference room chairs, swinging his heavy boots up onto the oval table with a clunk.

'It was always my intention to defect. If High Command knew that I was still alive, then they'd throw everything they had at trying to track me down. I'm too much of a security risk. Shame we couldn't steal the Might. We could use a ship like that.'

Trenchard leaned forwards over the table, his fists clenched in fury, his knuckles white.

'You fucking traitor!' he shouted. 'I trusted you. You betrayed the whole crew.' Then in a softer voice he said, '*You betrayed me…*'

Bird's face became deadly serious. 'You sound like my bloody ex-wife! I told you my reasons. Vice President

Chang is bad for the United Worlds. He's rotten to the core.'

'How can you be so sure?' Trenchard asked with genuine interest. 'He's just another power-hungry politician, isn't he?'

Bird looked uncomfortable. 'I did a little digging,' he said. 'After Mars, after Lorna…'

Trenchard blushed bright red and averted his eyes. There was an uncomfortable moment between the two old comrades.

'…after we went our separate ways I tried to investigate what really went on. There wasn't much to go on. It always bugged me where the R.D. insurgents got all their weapons and explosives from. I know the inquiry found that Papaver Corp exec guilty but I think he was just a scapegoat. I found a guy on Mars about a year ago who was ex R.D. He swore blind that Chang was supplying the weapons to the R.D. via an intermediary.' Bird fixed Trenchard with a hard stare. 'Care to guess who he said sold them the weapons on behalf of Chang?'

Trenchard shrugged. 'Astound me.'

'It was a young woman. Japanese. Long dark hair. She always carried specialist weapons including a sword. Sound familiar?'

Trenchard stared at Bird, dumbfounded. Bird nodded back.

'Chang is devious. I think that he deliberately caused the uprising on Mars in order to gain power. He's a fucking dictator and now he's in charge of the whole game! Sure, he's only "acting president" for now, but it's only a matter of time before he takes absolute control. I would lay odds that he was behind the assassination of President Smith. There must be someone to stand up to his rule but we're badly under resourced. If we're to stand any chance then we need weapons, we need what Papaver is hiding on that space station.'

Trenchard's face suddenly cleared, realisation dawning.

'You already know what Papaver has stored over there, don't you? But you didn't know the location of the factory, did you? The Kuiper belt is vast. It would take you years to search it manually. So, you let us lead the way, straight to the station.'

Bird nodded. 'It was fairly straight forward to arrange. We have sympathisers within the navy. They informed us of the destination of the Art of Devastation and that it was carrying the Might to a top-secret mission. Plus, I know that you're Admiral Fife's errand boy.'

Trenchard's eyebrows shot up, affronted. He could feel stinging bile rising in his throat.

'I knew Fife would send you after the Morgenstern, Trench old chum. You led us right to it. We were just about to board the station ourselves when you arrived.'

Trenchard was silent for a long time, then he straightened up and folded his arms across his chest. 'No matter how bad you think Chang is Bird, this isn't the way to do things. You're a traitor to the United Worlds and your pirate friends tried to kill me in the asteroid belt. I should kill you right now with my bare hands but I expect that my life expectancy would be fairly fucking short thereafter?'

Bird nodded gravely.

'…and I don't suppose that you want to surrender and come back with me to face a court martial?'

Bird shook his head solemnly.

'So, what's the next move?' Trenchard asked.

Bird's face became even more serious.

'Two choices mate. One, you surrender. We collect what we want and leave. I promise that your crew will come to no harm so long as the Might stays well out of missile range of my ship. We'll leave quietly and everybody's happy, except perhaps for Papaver and Chang.'

'…and choice number two?' snarled Trenchard.

190

'We take the station by force. There's a battle. Lots of people die needlessly. It's your choice Trench.'

Trenchard's answer was simple. It comprised of two short words, and the second one was "off!"

CHAPTER 19

"IT'S ALIVE"

A few minutes later, Trenchard was deposited, rather roughly, back in the airlock. He picked himself up off the floor, dusted his uniform down and turned around to face the departing pirates.

'Thanks lads!' he shouted angrily after them. 'I hope you die a slow death from venereal disease!'

The bull helmeted pirate stopped and turned to face Trenchard. *'You've got three minutes.'* he said coldly, before closing the hatch behind him.

'What happened Sir?' Lieutenant Chertok asked with worry written across his face.

Trenchard held his finger up to silence him and looked up at the hovering omni-bot. He brought his cuff-link communicator up and pressed the call button.

'Trenchard to Noir. Are you reading me? Over.'

In the control room of the Might of Fortitude, Commander Noir had removed the V.R. Conn visor and was watching Trenchard on the hologram suspended in the air in front of her.

'Here Sir,' she replied.

The holographic Trenchard narrowed his eyes. *'I want you to keep the Might out of range of the pirate vessel for the time being. She's too big; you wouldn't stand a chance against her. Remain at a safe distance until reinforcements arrive. We'll hold off the pirate force in here.'*

Noir's cheeks burned with fury. 'But Sir!'

'No buts,' snapped Trenchard. *'Follow my orders. Trenchard out!'*

Trenchard released his communicator button and the signal went quiet. Noir could still see Trenchard on the hologram from the perspective of the omni-bot, ordering the troops into defensive positions. She fumed for a moment before turning towards the front of the bridge. 'Helm. Thrusters at station keeping.'

'Aye, aye Sir!'

Then Noir disengaged herself from the Conn's leg brace and walked casually over to the scanner control station where Kittinger was sitting. She leaned over his shoulder, trying to remain nonchalant and whispered into Kittinger's ear so that the rest of the crew couldn't hear her.

'Can you scan anything from here?'

'Not much Sir,' Kittinger whispered, playing along with Noir. *'They have their electronic counter measure screens up. The E.C.M. is blocking everything; I can only perform visual scanning of the outside of their hull.'*

Noir nodded. *'I want you to scour the surface of that ship for any weaknesses. Concentrate on the welds and seams. These pirate hulks are badly maintained and they're usually stitched together from old salvaged vessels that were scrapped for dangerous structural defects. There are bound to be some physical weaknesses.'*

'Aye Sir.'

Then Noir turned to Cochran.

'Cochran, I want you to keep target lock on that vessel. Pay particular attention to anything that Kittinger finds. If that ship so much as twitches, I want to be able to cripple her, or at the very least even the odds.'

'Aye, aye Sir!' Cochran replied with a broad smile on her face.

Three minutes passed; then five, then ten.

'What the hell are they playing at?' Trenchard said to himself.

'Perhaps they're having lunch?' Chertok joked. He was kneeling behind an upturned table next to Trenchard, idly polishing his rifle.

'They're up to something,' Trenchard scowled, bringing his communicator up towards his mouth. 'Trenchard to Pugh. See anything?'

Pugh's voice came back, echoing and distant. *'Not yet Sir… wait.'*

There was an agonisingly long pause.

'Pugh here. There's noise on the outside of the hull. I think they're walking across the hull in pressure suits. Over.'

Damn, thought Trenchard. He had expected them to attack in force through the hatch in front of him. It would be easier for the pirates to attack directly from their own ship. Some would die, but they had the advantage of numbers. Bird must have known that; he knew how Trenchard thought. He'd sent the pirates in the hard way, marching across the outer hull of the station in space suits with magnetic boots. What other tricks did Bird have up his sleeve? He was teaching these pirates military tactics. Or did he simply already know the location of the Morgenstern in the storage bay where Pugh was located?

'Chertok, I'm taking half of the squad with me to Pugh's location. You stay here and keep an eye on that hatch.'

'Yes Sir. We won't let any of those buggers through!'

In the storage area, Pugh and his squad of twenty-five troopers were hidden behind packing crates and boxes. Across the room, they could hear the air in the entrance airlock cycling through. The light above the hatch turned from red to green.

'This is it!' Pugh shouted. 'Get ready.'

Pugh stared pointedly at McGagh. McGagh nodded in recognition, his expression deadly serious. He'd been in combat many times before; he knew what to expect. Unfortunately, McGagh was probably Pugh's best trooper, his best chance of surviving this battle. He might be undisciplined and unpredictable, but right now Pugh wouldn't trade him for the world.

The hatch swung open. Nothing moved in the darkness beyond. Then a small metal cylinder arced through the air. It landed with a "dink, dink, dink" sound and then rolled across the floor, spraying a thick yellow smoke as it went.

'Suck rubber!' shouted Pugh.

Each trooper reached behind their neck and pulled a thin breathing mask up over their face beneath their chin guard. The masks were attached to the neck of each uniform and then tightened quickly by Velcro straps. Several space-suited pirates began to file through the hatch, rifles raised and ready, partially obscured by the acrid smoke.

'Fire at will,' Pugh yelled, his voice slightly muffled by the mask.

Red hot metal seared through the smoky air from each trooper's rifle. Dark shadows danced over the walls from the bright muzzle flashes. Several pirates fell screaming to the floor but many more flooded the airlock area and managed to find cover behind storage crates and heavy machinery. Several more grenades were thrown, this time stun charges. They exploded with enormous force and the troopers nearby were thrown off their feet by the pressure blast. The air became thick with bullets, smoke and screams.

Pugh aimed a volley at a pirate that tried to charge his barricade. The case-less rounds hit the pirate at waist level and cut the man in half. He grasped at his guts as they spilled out onto the ground before crumpling into a twitching heap on the floor.

Next to Pugh, McGagh was rushed by another pirate and the two rolled onto the floor. McGagh rose up through the smoke and clubbed the pirate in the face with the butt of his rifle until it broke through his visor. After a few more blows, the pirate ceased moving.

Silently in the corner, the coffin shaped case of the Morgenstern lay forgotten and alone in the maelstrom next to the puddle of slime that had once been its comrade. The soft red glow from the heart of the creature within, penetrated gently through the frosted plexi-glass cover and cast sickly red shadows through the swirling smoke of battle. From out of the smoke, the black gloved hand of a trooper reached up carefully. The hand inserted itself snugly into the palm control device on the front of the case and deftly operated the controls, unnoticed by anyone else in the chaotic room. Then the hand withdrew and disappeared into the smoke from which it came.

The mind awoke, screaming…

The screaming was unceasing and became thought. It had no concept of time elapsed or of flesh. It knew only pain, searing and unrelenting. The brain of the thing had no flesh to touch or feel. It could neither hold nor comfort. It had neither eyes to see nor a mouth to speak and yet it screamed. The scream became thought and the thought was "kill!" Neurons connected, circuits surged with power and the thing became aware; not in a conscious way, but somehow it could sense the soft flesh that was nearby. It longed for the warmth of flesh, it became jealous of the flesh and the jealousy became rage. Hate upon hate, wrath upon wrath. The creature awoke with but one thought… KILL!

A huge black fist punched through the plexi-glass front of the coffin-shaped container and it shattered into a thousand spinning shards. Steam poured forth from the metal casket as the frozen interior bit at the warm air outside like a shark. The fist clenched. The forearm, as thick as a tree trunk, flexed and became a mass of lethal silver spikes. The Morgenstern stepped sluggishly out from its sarcophagus like Boris Karloff's creature rising from his creator's slab. It was roughly humanoid in shape but grotesquely muscular. The face bore no features other than dark semi-circular receptors where eyes should be. It seemed to be made from flexible black rubber that creaked and groaned as the creature moved. A soft red glow emanated from the chest, illuminating the area in front of the creature like a crimson searchlight. The top of the skull was transparent and pulsing within was the unmistakable shape of a human brain, severed and kept alive in a tank of nutrients. Truly the Morgenstern resembled the dark creation of a cackling mad scientist.

The creature relaxed as its covering warmed up and then it flexed its body. The muscles swelled and the whole surface of its upper torso and arms became covered by hundreds of vicious metal spikes that pushed up through the rubber skin like grotesque body piercings. The thing walked heavily forwards, its feet thudding on the metal floor like gold bars dropped from a height. One of the pirates saw the thing moving through the smoke and aimed a volley of fire straight at the creature's chest. The bullets sank into the rubber-like flesh and then slowly popped harmlessly back out again, the flesh re-sealing like putty and leaving no trace. The pirate stared at the thing in front of him, too terrified to move, like a rabbit caught in head-lights. The Morgenstern turned slowly to face the petrified pirate and then in a lightening movement, it swung its club-like forearm straight at the man's chest. The pirate was at the same time both crushed by the blow and skewered by several of the vicious spikes. His shredded and battered corpse dropped to the floor in a pool of blood, twitched for a moment and then became still. Trenchard skidded into the room just in time to see the Morgenstern rise through the steam like a mighty titan and slay the unwitting pirate.

'Back! Back! FALL BACK!' he shouted over the rattling noise of the rifle fire.

The United Worlds troopers began to retreat backwards, giving covering fire to their comrades as they went. This left the Morgenstern surrounded by an ever-growing horde of space-suited pirates, filing determinedly through the airlock.

The creature went wild...

It began to swing at anything that moved. The pirates nearest to the beast were literally diced by the furiously whirling spike covered clubs. In a short time, the floor became a mass of shredded corpses, twitching and gibbering, with the Morgenstern standing victorious over the heap of minced flesh and bone looking like Satan himself. Those pirates fortunate enough had retreated, back towards the airlock, out of reach of its terrible arms. Trenchard and Pugh were the last out of the storage room on the opposite side. Pugh stared at Trenchard, his face ashen, terrified out of his wits.

'What is that thing?' he shouted.

'One of Papaver's experiments,' Trenchard shouted back.

'What do we do?' Pugh asked urgently.

Trenchard looked around him. 'The pirates seem to have its attention for now. How strong do you think this hatch is?'

Pugh nodded in understanding and the two men slipped through the hatch, closing and locking it behind them.

CHAPTER 20

"TRAPPED"

On the other side of the thick hatch, the sound of battle was reduced to the distant and muffled screams of the dying. Trenchard turned to address the troopers as he scratched irritably at the long scar that ran from his neck down towards his chest.

'Someone find some welding gear or a plasma torch. I want that hatch welded shut and a whole pile of heavy stuff pushed up against it,' he shouted. 'Double time. Move!'

Several sweating troopers rushed off in different directions to find what they could.

Pugh turned worriedly towards Trenchard. 'Papaver made that?' he asked in astonishment.

Trenchard shrugged. 'It must've been one of his prototype weapons that didn't work properly. You can see why he mothballed it here, frozen in the middle of nowhere. Imagine if the insurgents got hold of that and dropped it off in the middle of a major city on Earth? How many people do you think it would kill before they could stop it? Imagine if they could duplicate it, make an army of them? It would make the space elevator disaster look like a picnic in the park.'

There was a long, uncomfortable silence.

'Bullets don't seem to have any effect on it. What do we do?' Pugh asked. Worried at the best of times, he was now as white as a sheet.

Trenchard snarled. 'We kill it.'

'How?' Pugh gasped in amazement. '…and if we do, won't Papaver be upset? Won't he want it back?'

Trenchard railed. 'I don't give a flying fuck what Papaver wants! I'll give him back the pieces in a bag if necessary. This mission is under *my* command and out here my word is fucking law! If that abomination gets out of that room, it could wipe out every living thing on this space station. These troopers are my responsibility. We kill it and then we piss on the remains and set fire to them, got it?'

'Aye Sir!' said Pugh, grinning a little, 'but shouldn't that be set fire to it and then piss on the remains, Sir?' He asked with a wry smile on his face.

For a moment, Trenchard smiled. He was finally getting through to Pugh. Their relationship so far had been troubled at best. Trenchard knew that there was genuine warmth in Pugh's grin. Pugh was finally starting to trust him, if only a little. By now a trooper had found some welding gear and was diligently melting a seam around the hatch. Several other troopers were hauling heavy gear down the corridor to barricade it.

'If only we could get a good look at it,' Trenchard said, thinking out loud.

Pugh's face suddenly brightened. 'The omni, it's still in there!'

'Right,' said Trenchard, bringing his wrist communicator up towards his mouth. 'Trenchard to Noir. Are you still reading me? Over.'

Commander Noir was pacing back and forth across the control room of the Might of Fortitude. Her brow was furrowed and her expression dark. She looked up as Petty Officer Hall at the communications console called out.

'Commander! Captain Trenchard is calling, audio only.'

'On speaker!' commanded Noir.

'*...to Might of Fortitude. Repeat. Trenchard to Might of Fortitude. Are you reading me? Over.*'

'I'm reading you loud and clear Captain. What is your situation? We lost track of you with the omni. Over.'

'*Our sleeping guest woke up,*' Trenchard explained.

Noir looked shocked. '*Baise-moi!*' she swore under her breath.

'*It's running amok in the storage area. We've managed to barricade it in for the moment, but I don't think it will last long. Is the omni still operational? Over.*'

Noir looked over to Kittinger for confirmation.

He nodded. 'We're still receiving the signal but there's a lot of smoke in there. It's hard to make anything out.'

'*Right,*' came back Trenchard's voice. '*Get the omni as close to the thing as possible. I want a broad-spectrum scan. I want to know everything there is to know about that thing. We have to find a way to stop it. Call me when you have something. Trenchard out.*'

Noir walked back over to Kittinger. 'Can you single out the creature from the pirates?'

Kittinger shook his head. 'Not visually, there's too much smoke and movement. The motion scan is off the scale.'

Noir thought for a moment. 'There was a small life sign from the creature's head when we performed the initial scan, probably human tissue of some kind, maybe brain tissue.'

Kittinger looked up at her, appalled. 'It's cybernetic? Is there someone's brain inside that thing?'

Noir gave nothing away. 'Switch to thermal. The creature should be the only one with a tiny heat source at around head height.'

Kittinger nodded and obediently operated the controls.

Inside the storage area the Morgenstern stood still, surveying the scene. The pirates had hurriedly retreated through the airlock and locked it behind them. Their comrades inside the room were all slain and splashed across the floor. Entrails and blood covered every surface like a gory Jackson Pollock painting. Their deaths hadn't been clean. The tactical programming in the Morgenstern's software was trying to decide what to do next. The Airlock was strong, reinforced and locked. It scanned the room and located the inner door. Before it could budge, it spotted movement. The small, triangular omni-bot hovered out of the smoke towards it and hung in the air, just in front of the creature's face. The Morgenstern studied it quizzically with its crescent shaped eyes. It could detect no life signs. There were no obvious weapons on the floating device.

Pain…

There was no threat.

So much pain…

The two robots stared back at each other like a child staring at a chimp through a glass wall at the zoo.

Random images flashed through the creature's mind. Memories and experiences from a woman's life flickered across the thoughts of the creature like moths against gaslight. The memories sparked new pathways across redundant circuit boards. A little girl played on a red bicycle. She fell off and grazed her knee. Her mother comforted her. A boy kissed her lips for the first time at the school graduation dance. Now a grown woman she felt the surge of rocket power as she left the Earth for the first time and headed into space. The feeling of the powerful engines exploding beneath her was exhilarating.

Then the images changed, became darker and more intense. The woman was on a dusty planet with orange soil and a purple sky. A

*city in the desert stretched out before her. There was a name…
"Belatu-Cadros". A crowd charged the gates of the military base.
Barrels rolled towards her. Her riot shield was simply useless. There
was a searing explosion and then blackness…*

'Come on. Just a few more minutes,' Kittinger whispered
under his breath. He was feverishly operating the controls
in front of him, taking every scan possible.

Noir leaned in. 'Are we there yet?' she asked in a
hushed voice.

'Nearly… nearly!'

*The memories sparked again in the swirling black smog of
nothingness. A man's face peered down at her. He was holding a
surgical device. He spoke as if she was dead already. He cut into her
flesh. She felt every slice, every tear. She felt the numbing,
uncontrollable intensity of pain…*

The Morgenstern zoomed its optical receptors in on the
omni-bot for a closer study.

Revenge…

It saw the scanner sphere in the centre of the triangle.
Someone was watching it. That gave them a tactical
advantage.

Kill!

The crescent shape receptors flared bright red. The
Morgenstern suddenly swung its mighty battle club
through the air and obliterated the tiny omni-bot in one
foul swoop. As the broken pieces hit the nearby wall and
crashed to the floor, the Morgenstern turned its mighty
body and started to stomp towards the inner door.

Flesh!

'Damn!' Kittinger swore, as the signal from the omni-bot went blank.

'Did you get enough?' Commander Noir asked urgently.

'One moment,' said Kittinger, desperately scanning over the results. After a moment, he turned to Noir and said, 'I'd like the Chief Engineer to look at this.'

'Right,' said Noir, looking up. 'Guardian. S.E.O. Sivia to the Control room immediately,' she ordered.

Trenchard and Pugh were waiting in the corridor outside the store room for the results of the scan. The hatch was now welded shut and a reasonably large pile of equipment was stacked against it. Suddenly, there was a mighty thump from the other side of the doorway and several thick spikes pierced right through the solid metal hatch.

'Jesus Christ!' shouted Pugh. 'What's that thing made from?'

Trenchard shook his head. 'No idea, but it's one tough son of a bitch! It must have finished with our pirate friends and now it wants more.' Trenchard turned to address his troops. 'Prepare grenades and get ready to fall back to the next intersection. I want the hatches welded shut after us as we move. Maybe we can buy some time.

'But why is it just killing indiscriminately?' Pugh enquired. 'What's the use of a weapon that you can't control?'

Trenchard thought for a moment. 'Most probably it would have been designed to be dropped behind enemy lines and kill anything that moved until it received a signal from the attacking force to turn it off,' he postulated. 'Either that or the thing's simply knackered! It's probably malfunctioning. There's a good reason it was decommissioned and locked away in the arse end of nowhere.'

Pugh screwed his face up. 'But if it was decommissioned, how did it suddenly become activated again Sir?'

Trenchard glared back at Pugh. 'That's a bloody good question.'

Captain Bird, the mighty Raven, was standing on the bridge of the pirate battle ship watching what remained of his crew return across the hull of the space station. A fully space-suited pirate rushed onto the bridge, sweating and exhausted. He stood shamefacedly in front of Bird.

'Report,' said Bird curtly.

'It's no good Sir,' said the pirate between pants of breath. 'The robot has been activated and there's no way of stopping it. We've already lost thirty men and now it's gone after the United Worlds troopers.'

Bird nodded. 'Very well; we'll have to abandon the mission. Shame...' Then Bird turned and stared pensively at the image of the Might of Fortitude on a screen in front of him. 'Still,' he began thoughtfully, 'it would be nice to return not completely empty handed, wouldn't it?

In the control room of the Might of Fortitude, Noir, Kittinger and Lieutenant Commander Devinder Sivia were studying the data received before the omni-bot was crushed into oblivion.

'Can you make anything out?' Noir asked.

Sivia pursed his lips and scratched at his turban covered head. 'The basic frame and power source is similar to the shifters and loaders used in cargo stations,' he said thoughtfully. 'I can't make sense of the covering though, it's something new. It's probably a prototype formula from Papaver, it'll still be classified.'

'What about the head casing?' Kittinger queried. 'Maybe there's a weakness there?'

Sivia shook his head. 'The organic component is encased in a special plasti-steel formula. It's the same stuff they use for observation windows aboard luxury cruise liners. You can make a window twenty foot across out of the stuff and it'll withstand bullets, grenades, asteroid hits. You might as well try and break through a steel wall with a tooth pick.'

'There has to be something!' complained Commander Noir.

Sivia suddenly raised both eyebrows. 'Hang on, there's an interesting result from the thermal scanner. Look here!' he said, pointing to an area on the display in front of them.

The scan was a thermal image of the creature. The hot areas appeared in white through red and yellow to cold areas in green and blue. There was a small area on the creature's leg that was so dark blue as to be almost black.

'That part of the outer skin is still frozen from the cryo-tube that it was discovered in; it must be a manufacturing fault in the skin.'

'So what?' shrugged Noir.

'Soooo… the motion scanner shows that area to be completely static. Frozen stiff! The outer skin is obviously susceptible to temperature change. If you lower the temperature…'

'It'll become stiff and immobile,' finished Noir. She walked over to the communications console. 'Noir to Trenchard. Come in please.'

Trenchard was running again. The Morgenstern had almost made it through the first barricade. Shredded metal lay in ragged ribbons on the floor around a gaping hole in the welded hatch. Most of the troopers were already through the next hatch and standing by to weld that one shut too.

As Trenchard ran, he drew his hand up towards his face. 'I'm a little busy right now Commander! Leave a message at the beep…' he shouted into the microphone.

Trenchard looked towards Pugh, who was the other side of the hatch. Pugh nodded. Trenchard pulled a grenade from his harness and turned towards the beast. The thing glared at him as it struggled to pull itself through the jagged hole.

'Hey, you ugly twat!' he shouted.

The creature raised its head instinctively towards the noise.

'Catch this, you son metal of a bitch!' Trenchard shouted, throwing the grenade straight at the thing's head.

Trenchard leapt through the hatch and it was slammed shut a millisecond before the grenade exploded. The whole station shook and the lights flickered momentarily. Instantly, two troopers began to weld the next hatch shut.

Trenchard held up his communicator again as he caught his breath. 'Right then Commander Noir. What's up?'

'*You have to freeze it Sir. It's susceptible to extreme cold!*'

'Cold?' repeated Trenchard.

Trooper Cox jostled past Trenchard, manhandling a large piece of equipment over towards the door and throwing Trenchard's concentration momentarily.

'Careful there sonny!' he snapped, before turning his attention back towards Pugh.

'How the hell are we supposed to freeze the damned thing?' he snapped. 'Fire extinguishers? Chemicals?'

Pugh thought for a moment. 'We are in deep space Sir. If we could get it near an airlock…'

There was the abrupt sound of tearing metal and a piercing scream. Trenchard and Pugh spun around. The Morgenstern had already reached the hatch and instantly begun to tear straight through. Cox had been placing the heavy equipment next to it and had been caught across his right arm by the deadly spikes. He fell to the floor, clutching his arm in agony as blood poured through the tattered shreds of his uniform's sleeve. Trenchard instantly grabbed Cox and began to drag him away from the door. McGagh rushed to the door, picked up a heavy metal bar from the barricade and began to beat the creature fiercely about the arm until it pulled back through the hole. Red light from the creature's chest spilled through the opening, illuminating the trooper's frightened faces.

Pugh turned towards the troopers. 'Ten rounds incendiary through that hole, now!' he screamed.

A helmeted trooper stepped forward; removed his armour piercing magazine from his rifle and clicked into place one that contained incendiary rounds.

'McGagh, move it!' Pugh ordered.

McGagh dived out of the way just before the trooper raised his rifle, took careful aim and fired ten rounds, straight through the torn metal hole and into the creature's chest. The rounds could be heard impacting and exploding on the other side of the door. Fire burst forth from the jagged maw and the creature retreated momentarily from the searing hot flames.

Trenchard gently pulled Cox's helmet off and threw it aside. He looked into Cox's terrified eyes and spoke as seriously as he could. 'Brace yourself son, this is going to hurt like hell!'

Cox nodded, his eyes streaming, scared stiff. Trenchard undid the Velcro cuff of Cox's sleeve and peeled back the shredded cloth which was sticky and soaked with blood. Cox winced and moaned in agony. His arm looked like it had been mauled by a lion. The muscles hung limply in shreds from ivory white bone that shone through the tattered flesh. Trenchard fought to keep his lunch down. He had seen serious injuries before but he never got used to the sight of someone's insides.

'Field kit!' Trenchard called urgently.

Stofan rushed over with a plastic box of medical supplies. Trenchard hurriedly opened the box and took out a small vial, some antiseptic fluid and a bandage.

'Brace yourself,' he said gently to Cox, who nodded as bravely as he could manage.

Trenchard stabbed the vial onto Cox's arm, injecting an anaesthetic. Then he opened the bottle of liquid and poured the entire contents all over Cox's arm. Cox writhed and screamed in agony as the antiseptic stung every severed muscle and nerve.

'Hold him!' shouted Trenchard.

McGagh and Stofan dropped to their knees and steadied the struggling young man as the anaesthetic began to work.

'Steady there Jez mate!' said McGagh in a surprisingly comforting tone for the usually hard-faced Irish man.

Quickly, Trenchard placed a sterile dressing over the injuries and then wound a bandage tightly around Cox's arm. Cox was weeping and incoherent by now. Trenchard grabbed his face with both hands and forced Cox to look at him, staring straight into his eyes.

'Be brave son. Think of your girl back home. What's her name?'

'*N, nnnn, n Nancy,*' Cox managed through the tears.

'Be brave for Nancy son,' Trenchard coached with a warm smile. Cox smiled through the pain. Then Trenchard turned to the two troopers that were holding Cox down. 'Take him back, well out of range. Set up a temporary area for the injured. There's going to be more.'

'Aye, aye Sir,' said McGagh and Stofan together.

Trenchard stood and watched as the two troopers carried Cox's limp form away. He turned towards Pugh.

'What was that idea you had about an airlock?' he asked grimly as the Morgenstern began to batter furiously upon the hatchway once more.

CHAPTER 21

"REVENGE"

On the bridge of the pirate ship, Captain Bird turned to his communications officer and spoke softly. 'Open ship-to-ship hail,' he ordered and then dropped his raven painted helmet down over his face.

The officer nodded back. 'Hail open, aye, aye Sir!'

'Captain Raven of the pirate vessel Cour Valant to the Might of Fortitude. Come in please,' said Bird, his voice reverberating and sounding tinny through his suit's communication system.

A floating green hologram snapped into existence in front of Bird, showing Commander Noir standing in the middle of the Control room of the Might of Fortitude. Her hands were on her hips and a foul expression across her face.

'*Commander Noir here. That's a very polite hail for a filthy pirate, Captain Raven,*' she snapped. '*To what do I owe this... displeasure?*'

Bird chuckled. 'I wish to discuss terms,' Bird announced simply.

Noir raised an eyebrow. '*Terms? What terms?*'

'Why, the terms of your surrender of course,' Bird said gleefully.

Noir tried not to let her surprise show. '*What are you talking about?*'

Bird gathered himself before replying. 'You are out-gunned Commander Noir. You will surrender your vessel to me.'

'*Ridiculous,*' Noir spat back. '*You may have a larger ship with a greater quantity of weapons, but your ship is old and ready for scrap! I can out manoeuvre you in any battle!*'

Bird smiled smugly. 'But can the space station out manoeuvre our missiles Commander Noir?'

Noir was quiet for a long time before her eyes narrowed. '*What?*'

'It's very simple,' Bird replied with an even smugger tone of voice. 'If you don't surrender your ship to me, I will destroy that space station and all of your brave troopers, including your illustrious Captain Trenchard.'

There was a long cold silence from Noir. Her eyes raged with fire.

'*You know that I cannot do that,*' Noir replied after what seemed like an eternity.

'I'll give you three minutes to think about it before I open fire,' Bird stated, before nodding to the communications watch-stander.

The hologram blinked off, just as Noir was about to say something terse in reply.

Back aboard the space station, the troopers had retreated through another three hatches and the Morgenstern was still coming, fuelled by fury and hatred. They had deliberately taken a route that had led the Morgenstern towards the tubular cutting room where they were laying a trap. Pugh was pulling on an E.V.A. suit that had been hung on a rack near the massive airlock alongside three others.

'Are you sure about this?' Trenchard asked with deep concern in his voice.

Pugh pulled another leg of the suit over his uniform. 'Positive,' he replied. 'The Might can't afford to lose another Captain,' Pugh looked pointedly at Trenchard. 'Your safety is my responsibility and I'm not asking anyone else to volunteer. This is my duty. Plus…' Pugh fell silent and looked down for a moment, ashamed. 'I feel that I owe it to the crew.'

Trenchard nodded and grasped Pugh's shoulder to comfort him. 'Just watch your arse. Get that thing as near to the airlock as you can before popping the hatch and then stay out of reach. That suit won't stand up to those spikes; you can't afford to get any tears in the fabric.'

'I'll do my best,' Pugh insisted. 'These are the biggest airlocks on the station; if that thing can't be sucked out through one of those, then it's not going anywhere and we've lost.'

On board the Might of Fortitude, Commander Noir was sweating, deep in thought. The crew's lives were in her hands. Either she gave up the ship, or the whole platoon on the space station would die. The crew in the control room were staring at her, waiting expectantly. If she made a bold move and attacked the Cour Valant, then the Might of Fortitude would undoubtedly be damaged or even destroyed. She couldn't rely on help arriving; reinforcements might be hours or even days away. Her three minutes were nearly up.

'Schmidt,' she snapped, as she began to fasten herself back into the V.R. Conn, 'Plot a course that takes us directly away from the pirate ship.'

Schmidt's eyebrows shot up. 'We're running? We should give them the ship. Surrender is a reasonable…'

Noir gave him the sternest look that she could muster. 'Just do it mister!'

Schmidt nodded meekly and began to program his station as Noir pulled the black visor down over her eyes, submerging herself in the virtual world once more.

'Cochran, I want a firing solution for the Cour Valant's engines in thirty seconds, full salvo of heat-seekers.'

'Aye, aye Sir,' Cochran shouted back as she too began to feverishly operate her controls.

'Sir, we're receiving another hail from the pirate ship,' Hall announced from communications.

'Audio only,' Noir instructed.

There was a pause and then Captain Bird's disguised voice filled the control room. '*Commander Noir, your three minutes are up. Shall I prepare you afternoon tea in my cabin, or are we going to do this the hard way?*'

Noir grinned. 'Ever played hide and seek with a five-year-old Captain Raven,' she shouted. 'They can always find hiding places that you could never fit into. Come and get me, ready or not!'

The Might of Fortitude fired up her main engines and powered away from the space station at full thrust. On the bridge of the Cour Valant, Captain Bird watched the sleek vessel on his screen, smiled and turned to his command crew.

'Chase her, full thrust. Target the space station, full salvo.'

'Aye, aye Captain!' returned the crew in unison.

'Sorry Trench old chum,' he muttered under his breath, 'looks like you'll never get back to Mike's Bar again…'

Pugh waited nervously beside the huge circular airlock. The inner hatch had been braced open and the safety circuits disabled. It would simply be a case of operating the outer hatch mechanism when the Morgenstern was nearby and the thing should be sucked out into open space. Trenchard and a handful of troopers stood just inside the hatch on the far side of the room, waiting to lure the creature inside. A steady thump, thump, thump came from the opposite door as the metal was gradually shredded by the beast's mighty spiked club.

Pugh could feel the sweat trickling down the small of his back. His legs had become wobbly, like jelly. He knew that this was a risky manoeuvre; he knew that he would probably die. He'd strapped a few grenades to the front of his space suit which would shorten the agony if the Morgenstern caught him and maybe even damage the creature in the process. With a last mighty crash, the Morgenstern plunged through the shredded metal door and stood for a moment, just inside the room as it made a tactical evaluation of the situation.

Pain...

There was a single target standing by one exit, armed with three grenades. Across the room were four targets armed with high powered rifles and at least twenty grenades. They were a greater threat.

Revenge!

The Morgenstern turned towards Trenchard, the red glow from its chest piercing the gloom.

Trenchard put his fingers into his mouth and whistled. 'Hey ugly!' he shouted. 'Why don't you come over here and kiss my furry arse crack, you revolting cybernetic fuckwit!'

Trenchard leased off a few rounds from his rifle and the creature began to stomp angrily towards him.

'Fall back,' Trenchard ordered as he cast a last glance towards Pugh who gave a cautious thumbs-up.

The troopers closed the hatch and immediately began to weld it shut. The Morgenstern stomped closer to the door, ignoring Pugh, just as they had planned.

'Come on,' urged Pugh from inside his suit. 'Just a little further!'

The Might of Fortitude sped towards a cathedral sized ice formation, the Cour Valant hot on her tail. Gradually the larger pirate ship gained distance from the space station. The Might reached the side of the ice mountain and disappeared behind it.

On the Bridge of the Cour Valant, Captain Bird narrowed his eyes and commanded, 'Fire missiles!'

The weapons station watch-stander shouted 'Aye, aye Captain!' and operated a control.

Four missiles sped from the forward tubes of the pirate hulk. They bent around in a graceful arc and then headed at full speed towards the defenceless space station. Suddenly, the Might of Fortitude rounded the other side of the ice mountain, gunned her engines and sped straight towards the Cour Valant at ramming speed. Captain Bird's grin disappeared and his face rapidly became deadly serious. He motioned to his communications officer, who nodded back to him.

'Commander Noir?' began Bird. 'Playing Chicken now? What good will that do you and your gallant crew? If you ram us then both ships will be damaged, your ship will probably not survive. Power down and surrender. I promise that your crew will come to no harm.'

Bird waited patiently but there was no reply.

'Commander Noir?'

Then Noir's voice came through on the radio, grim and determined. '*Alpha Mike Foxtrot, you smug bastard!*'

The Might of Fortitude ploughed straight towards the ugly black pirate hulk. The Cour Valant began to steer to starboard in a desperate attempt to avert a collision. The plasma cannons that were dotted all over the hull of the pirate ship began to rain glowing green balls of plasma in the direction of the Might. Her hull scorched, spewing stealth tiles, but it held.

Noir gritted her teeth and spoke to the junior officers seated at the helm. 'Lose the bubble! Now!'

Both officers pushed their control yolks to the extreme position, as far as they would go. At the last second the Might of Fortitude veered off and swung around the rear of the pirate ship. The turn was so tight that the Might's tail fin scraped along the Cour Valant's hull with a shower of sparks.

Commander Noir's eyes narrowed under her visor. 'Cochran, full salvo now! Fire for effect!'

Cochran nodded and operated the weapons fire control. 'Firing Fox two!' she called. 'The fish are in the water!'

Four heat-seeking torpedoes screamed from the forward tubes of the Might of Fortitude. They swung around as the Might sped behind the larger pirate vessel and the missiles headed straight for the Cour Valant's engines. The Cour Valant let off counter measures of chaff and flares. Three of the missiles exploded harmlessly in space but one sped onwards. The lone missile impacted directly into one of the Cour Valant's engines, sending plumes of white heat exploding into the void.

The Cour Valant, crippled but still alive, began to list to starboard. It crawled away from the space station like an injured fox on a motorway hard shoulder, leaving a floating trail of burning debris in its wake that gradually extinguished in the airless vacuum.

Captain Bird smiled as he watched the image of the Might of Fortitude diminish on his screen. Around him was chaos. The bridge crew of the Cour Valant were attempting to regain control of the ship, extinguish fires and affect damage repairs. One of the crew rushed over to Captain Bird and stared anxiously at him.

'Should we go after her?'

Bird smiled. 'No. We're too badly damaged. She's a damned good officer, a worthy opponent. Trenchard will have his work cut out with her.' Bird settled back into his command chair. 'The Might will have to wait till another day. Let's get some distance while they still have their hands full with the Morgenstern.'

The Might of Fortitude steered towards the missiles that were still speeding towards the space station.

'Target those missiles Cochran,' ordered Noir. 'We can't afford to let any of them get through!'

Cochran began throwing all the Might of Fortitude had towards the missiles. Two of them exploded in a hail of green plasma but two more sped on.

'The Cour Valant is running!' Van Allen called excitedly from the Tactical station.

Noir allowed herself a brief satisfied smile. 'Let her go. We have to stop those missiles.'

The Morgenstern had reached the middle of the room and was now parallel to the huge circular airlock. Now's the time thought Pugh, as he moved towards the airlock controls. The Morgenstern instantly spun its head around to follow the sudden movement.

Flesh… Kill!

Pugh activated the opening mechanism and a spinning orange warning light began to flash accompanied by an alarm klaxon. The Morgenstern changed its course and began to make a bee-line straight for Pugh.

The Might of Fortitude picked off the third missile in a hail of green fury but the fourth closed relentlessly on the space station's hull.

'Cochran!' screamed Noir.

Cochran stared up from her station, her eyes wide. 'I'm sorry Commander. The missile is out of range. There's nothing that we can do!'

Commander Noir ripped off the black visor and threw it angrily across the control room. '*Salaud!*' she shouted angrily and stared helplessly at the sight of the missile closing on the space station on the hologram in front of her.

The circular airlock hatch began to inch open, agonisingly slowly. A fierce wind built up as the air began to be sucked out from the room. Pugh swayed unsteadily and grabbed the hatch frame next to him, hanging on for dear life. The Morgenstern swayed too, unsure of itself for the first time.

…and then the missile hit the station.

The whole station rocked as the missile found its target. Gravity failed for an instant as the station's spin was interrupted and the lights went out. Pugh was left in near total darkness with only the sickly orange flashing of the warning light to accompany him. The power had failed and the outer airlock door had stuck half open. Pugh could see the Morgenstern approaching slowly, a series of monstrous snap-shots as the beast was illuminated by incandescent flashes of orange light. It was almost upon him and the door was not open nearly wide enough to suck the damned thing into the vacuum of space. Terrified, Pugh looked towards his chest where the three grenades sat on their harness. There was only one option left.

Pugh ripped the grenades from his chest and quickly armed them for a short fuse. He pushed them hurriedly into the narrow crack around the outer hatch and dove headlong toward the looming Morgenstern, hitting the steering thrusters on his E.V.A. suit's backpack at he went. The Morgenstern lashed out towards him as he sped past, catching him with several of its vicious spikes across his left leg. Pugh howled in pain inside the helmet of his suit as his body barrelled over and he smacked straight into the opposite wall, smearing the floor and wall with fresh blood as he went.

Lights blinked on the top of the three grenades, on, off, on, off. Then they exploded in a searing blast of heat and light, ripping the outer hatch completely apart in a white-hot ball of spinning molten metal. The Morgenstern was thrown clear across the room by the multiple explosions. It landed in a crumpled heap in the centre of the deck. The howling wind of the escaping air grew to a hurricane. As the Morgenstern struggled to its feet it began to be dragged relentlessly towards the opening into space. Its body instantly became sluggish as the cold vacuum took hold, its rubberised flesh started to frost over, creaking and groaning like a rotten oak tree in a storm.

It's working, Pugh thought elatedly.

Clinging to a control panel to avoid being sucked into space himself and ignoring the searing pain from his leg, Pugh shouted in victory and relief as he saw the beast being dragged relentlessly away. Then there was a sudden noise like ripping flesh. Several curved spikes, like eagle claws, shot out from the creature's feet and dug deeply into the metal deck plate, rooting it to the spot.

Pugh's face fell. The creature slowly turned its head to stare at him as the howling wind gradually subsided. The chance to expel the creature into the void had passed. Several nozzles by the hole had popped open and a spray-foam had begun to fill the void left by the destroyed hatch. The breech sealant foam instantly hardened and blocked the hole with solid polyurethane creating a temporary airtight seal. Air began to be pumped back into the room by the automated systems and the temperature began to rise. The creature un-clasped the curved hooks from the floor and stomped around to stand square on and examine Pugh.

Victory!

It took a couple of paces forwards. Pugh felt his stomach turn to liquid. He was going to die. The Morgenstern was now standing squarely in the middle of the room, right in the very centre. It was studying Pugh with its evil, crescent shaped eyes. Pugh could almost swear that it had a smug expression on its solid metal face. He lay there bleeding, crying and expecting nothing but a grisly death.

Then Pugh looked up as something caught his eye and sparked a recent memory. The creature was right in the middle of the circular, sonic cutting device; a device that was used to cut straight through the hardest substance known to mankind. He took in the situation in an instant as he looked from the creature, to the sonic cutter ring, to the control panel that he was still grasping on to for dear life. With a last desperate burst of his remaining energy, his torn and shattered leg seeping blood and unconsciousness taking hold, Pugh slammed his hand down on the big red button that was labelled "Activate". With a searing whine, a sonic blast ripped around the circular frame and the creature's black rubber skin sizzled for a moment.

Pugh stared at the monster in disbelief. It seemed completely unaffected. He had failed. Then slowly the creature collapsed, falling into two distinct halves, sliced cleanly into two pieces from head to toe. As it buckled and the red light inside its chest became gradually fainter and fainter, the last thought that surged through its poor, tortured and tormented mind was;

Peace…

Exhausted, Pugh allowed himself one last satisfied smile before finally passing out from the pain.

On board the Might of Fortitude, Commander Noir looked over towards Kittinger at the Scanner Control. 'Where's the Cour Valant?'

Kittinger looked up from his screen. 'She's out of range of our weapons and heading away as fast as she can manage. We only damaged her conventional engines. I doubt whether we could catch her before she's out of the Kuiper belt and able to engage her Watters' jump-drive.'

'Damn!' swore Noir.

Raven would get away. No matter, she thought, the troopers on the station were her priority now. The station had been badly damaged and there was still the rampaging robot to deal with. She turned back to stare at the space station out of the front view slit.

'Sir!' Kittinger called, even more excited than before.

Noir swung around. 'What is it now?' she snapped.

Kittinger's eyes were wide as saucers. 'I'm picking up another ship approaching. She's *massive*, but somehow she's managing to drop out of Watters' drive, straight into the middle of the Kuiper belt!'

'That's impossible,' Noir sneered, 'no ship can...' Then she tailed off as she saw the massive space-craft appearing out of thin air, right next to the space station. 'Who the hell is that?' she asked, in a small awed voice.

Hall spoke up this time. 'I'm getting a handshake signal...' There was a pause. 'It's the Papaver Corporation flag ship Sir. It's the S.S. Bertrand!'

CHAPTER 22

"THE WARMONGER"

The mighty space-craft exploded out of Watters' Drive right next to the crippled space-station. Somehow it had emitted a massive pulse of heat that simply melted away the surrounding ice lumps into gas. No other ship could have done what this ship had achieved, but then again, no other ship was the flag ship of the mighty Papaver Corporation. The S.S. Bertrand was the best that money could buy, quite literally. It had been built with no budgetary limits, unlike the ships of the Space Navy fleet. The hull gleamed with white and gold and was covered with the most powerful and most up-to-date weapons in the whole of the United Worlds. Some of the weapons were prototypes, still classified and not due to be rolled out to the rest of the fleet for perhaps years to come. No expense had been spared to make her a beautiful, but deadly sight.

Aboard the Might of Fortitude, Commander Noir was receiving an incoming signal from the Bertrand. The face of her Captain appeared on screen, a gentlemanly figure in a Papaver Corporation uniform, white braided with gold. He had the look and air of sea-captains of old. The white-haired gentleman turned towards Noir on the hologram and smiled as if they were old friends meeting for coffee.

'*Commander Noir?*'

Noir nodded.

'*Good morning. I am Captain Grissel of the Papaver Corporation star-ship Bertrand. We stand ready to assist you.*'

Noir's eyebrow shot up. 'Assist?'

'*Yes Commander,*' smiled Grissel. '*We have excellent medical facilities on board to treat your wounded. They will be returned to you good as new; or perhaps even better.*'

Grissel grinned. Noir returned a false smile. She didn't like this man. There was something shifty about him. He was too well oiled; his eyes were hiding something.

'Our troops are still…' began Noir, but she was cut off mid-sentence.

'*I am fully aware of the situation Commander Noir. My crew are boarding the station even as we speak. Everything will be taken care of quickly and efficiently, I can assure you. We will attend to your injured and Captain Trenchard will be returned to you safe and sound.*' Grissel paused and his face became like steel. '*This facility is under Papaver Corporation protection as from this moment on. Do not approach closer than one thousand meters or we will be forced to take protective measures. Thank you for your co-operation Commander Noir. Grissel out!*'

The hologram blinked off leaving Noir fuming. 'Protective measures!' she shouted angrily. 'Just who the hell does he think he is?'

Petty Officer Hall at the communications station piped up. 'We've just received a message from High Command via N.A.C.I.N.,' she said. 'Orders from Admiral Adisa.'

'Adisa?' Noir exclaimed.

Adisa was the top-ranking officer in the Space Navy. He was the Admiral of the fleet and even out-ranked Admiral Fife. Why was he sending personal messages to a small boat like the Might, Noir pondered apprehensively?

'What's the message?' she asked carefully.

'To Captain Trenchard, Might of Fortitude,' Hall began, reading the message out loud. 'Papaver Corporation ship S.S. Bertrand arriving immediately to assume control of space station. Do not interfere. Stand down and accede to their requests. Military supervision is no longer required or necessary. Admiral Adisa, etcetera, etcetera.'

'Are the drop-ships back on board yet?' Noir asked with concern.

'Aye Sir.'

'Get me Captain Trenchard. Now!'

Trenchard had problems of his own. The Papaver Corporation crew had boarded from every single airlock simultaneously. They had then fanned out and begun rounding up his troops at gun-point. The security officers of the Bertrand were dressed in bright white shiny armour and helmets, picked out in gold. They carried a new rifle design that Trenchard had never seen before. One of them raised his rifle and pointed it straight at Trenchard. Trenchard in turn raised his rifle in defence. He was in no mood for this.

'Please lower your rifle Captain Trenchard,' said the white clad security officer from behind a gold tinted visor that masked his eyes and his identity. His words were polite but there was a definite underlying tone of menace.

'Lower yours!' Trenchard shouted, nodding to Chertok.

Chertok and the rest of the squad raised their rifles. The air resounded to the clicks of safety catches being turned off. The room was gradually filling up with even more white clad security officers. McGagh stared down at one of the white guards and growled at them, baring his teeth.

'I've got a man in that room who is most likely badly injured, or perhaps dead!' Trenchard barked irritably. 'Get out of my way or I'll put my boot up your arse!'

The man in front of Trenchard grimaced. 'By order of Admiral Adisa at High Command, we are assuming control of this facility. You are to vacate immediately and return to your ship. Military assistance is no longer required or necessary.'

'Required?' spat Trenchard, full of dismay and anger. 'You fucking son of a…'

Trenchard's communicator beeped suddenly. He lowered his rifle and raised his wrist to his mouth.

'Trenchard here,' he growled.

'*Captain,*' came Noir's voice over the radio. It had a certain air of concern and anger. '*We've received orders from High Command.*'

'Yeah, I know,' said Trenchard, still eye-balling the white guards. 'What about Pugh?'

'*Apparently, Papaver's people already have him in their medical facility on board the Bertrand. He's being worked on by their surgeons.*'

Trenchard's expression became thunderous. 'Get Pugh back as soon as he's fit enough and get the drop-ships over here pronto. I don't want to spend another fucking second in this shit hole! Trenchard out.' Trenchard lowered his rifle and Chertok motioned the rest of the troopers to do the same. 'Well?' Trenchard asked. 'What's next?'

The white guard motioned with his rifle. 'We will escort you to the main airlock and ensure that you exit safely.'

Trenchard smiled a sickly smile. 'You mean make sure that we get the fuck off this station?'

The guard remained impassively silent.

Trenchard waved at the troops. 'Move out,' he ordered.

The troopers began to shuffle unhurriedly away. The injured lad Cox was carried gently past by two other troopers.

'Do you want our medical staff to have a look at your injured man?' the white guard asked in a conciliatory tone.

Trenchard placed his fists onto his hips and scowled. 'I'd rather slide stark bollock naked down a banister covered with rusty razor blades into a bath of piss and vinegar than let one of you miserable twats…'

Lieutenant Stofan carefully laid a restraining hand onto Trenchard's arm and spoke in a soft voice. 'Sir, forgive me, but we don't have the greatest medical facility aboard the Might. It might be better to let them treat him?'

Trenchard scowled at her, uncomprehending for a moment and then he let out an exasperated sigh. 'Fine,' he said, turning to the white guard and prodding him in the chest with his finger, 'but make sure you take fucking good care of him! He's a damned, brave, young…'

Trenchard tailed off in astonishment as he saw a group of scientists from the S.S. Bertrand sweep through the room at that moment, on their way to some urgent destination. They were all dressed in bright red lab coats and escorted by even more white-clad security guards who carried even larger weapons. Trenchard stared coldly at them as they passed. The man at the front was dressed smartly in a grey suit. He was middle aged and had untidy dark hair which flopped across his eyes. He smiled at Trenchard as he passed and even gave him a friendly wave. Trenchard stood dumbfounded. He had seen the man many times before on the I.N.N. news reports. He was one of the richest and most powerful men in the entire United Worlds, the head of the Papaver Corporation, Claude Papaver himself.

Trenchard snapped his mouth shut when he realised that it had been hanging open in amazement. The fact that Papaver himself was here on the station explained the heavy-handed approach of the white guards. It also meant that whatever secrets were hidden here were more valuable to Papaver than they were letting on. Trenchard's shoulders slumped and he turned away, resigned to the fact that there was nothing more he could do here. If Admiral Adisa was involved, then any complaints that he might make would be like pissing into the wind with his mouth open. He was extremely tired and needed a good meal and a wash. His casualties were being treated, even if it was by Papaver's people. Trust them or not, Stofan was right. They would get better care aboard the S.S. Bertrand than on board the Might of Fortitude. Trenchard trudged slowly and disconsolately back towards the main airlock feeling like he'd won the battle, but lost the war.

Papaver's team entered the tube-shaped cutting room and stood, surveying the scene. A group of technical staff were already repairing the damaged hatch, welding a temporary sheet of metal plate over the foam-covered hole. Blood was smeared across the floor and pooled around the control panel where Pugh had clung on for dear life. In the middle of deck, the two halves of the Morgenstern lay where they had fallen. Even now a foul smelling green slime had begun to leak out from the innards of the machine and seep across the metal deck.

Papaver looked around. 'Everybody out! Now!' he shouted, clapping his hands and waving his staff away.

The technicians immediately downed tools and headed for the exit, as did all the guards. Papaver grabbed the arm of a young woman with dark brown hair as she passed.

'Not you Elaine,' he said quietly. 'I need to talk to you.'

The two waited for the room to empty and all the doors to close tight. Then Papaver turned to the pretty young woman and smiled.

'Do you remember when we built this unit Elaine, four years ago, on Mars?

The woman smiled and nodded. 'Yes of course Sir. I've been with you throughout the whole of the Sentinel project.'

Papaver chuckled. 'Sentinel. Morgenstern. Whatever it's eventually going to be called, I think we can safely say that this was a successful test of its capabilities. What we need now is a way to improve the bio-links and ensure complete control. The subject was clearly unstable. Mental control is the next step.'

He paused for a moment and studied Elaine. She had been with his company for many years, since before Mars and before the Sentinel project ever began. He felt that he could trust her, but just how far?

'Have you heard of the Providence project Elaine?'

Elaine smiled. 'Only the name Sir. I've heard some rumours in the staff canteen but nothing detailed. Why?'

'Because I think that you're ready for a little more responsibility. The Sentinel project is dead in the water for the time being. We can't go any further with this military automaton until we develop Providence further. You've been an invaluable member of my team while we developed the Sentinel. I'd like to bring you on board.'

Elaine flushed with pride. 'Thank you, Sir,' she said, beaming a broad smile.

'Plus,' continued Papaver, 'we have just been gifted with the opportunity to take the Providence project to the next level.' Then he fixed her with a serious stare. 'It's a top priority project Elaine. Once you accept, there's no going back. You may not like what you find.'

Elaine shrugged. 'I'm a scientist Sir. My quest is for the truth; however ugly it may be. I leave moral questions to the politicians and philosophers to argue over.'

'Good,' said Papaver. 'Then let's get the team back in and clean up this mess. I want to see you in my office aboard the Bertrand in an hour to get you up to speed on the project.'

With that, Papaver spun on his heel and headed away. Elaine watched him go with a sense of pride and more than a little trepidation in her heart.

A couple of days later, the Might of Fortitude was back in orbit around Cairn. Her damaged tail fin had already been repaired and the snipes had replaced the damaged stealth tiles and re-painted the hull. The crew were already down on the surface getting some well-earned leave. Pugh and Cox were safely in the naval hospital facility. The ship was almost empty, cold and virtually soundless, as still as the grave. Trenchard was sitting in the wardroom doing some overdue paperwork when there was a knock on the hatch and he looked up.

'Come,' he called.

The hatch swung open and Commander Noir gingerly stepped inside.

'Noir,' said Trenchard in what he hoped was a friendly voice. 'Thank you for coming. Please sit.'

Noir looked a little taken aback. The Captain wasn't usually this friendly. In fact, their relationship had been on the cold side of frosty ever since she had been posted to the Might. Noir settled down warily onto the bench.

'What can I do for you Sir?' she asked cautiously.

Trenchard leaned back and smiled. 'Nothing really... I just wanted to catch up. How's A.S. Cox?'

'He's been patched up and is resting in the infirmary at the base. The Morgenstern shredded his arm pretty well, but Papaver's surgeons have managed to re-connect all the tissue. He'll have some scarring, but he will get the use of his arm back fairly quickly.'

Trenchard nodded in what he hoped was an affirming way. '...and Pugh?'

Noir shuffled uncomfortably. 'He seems fine,' she said, 'but it must be hard to lose a limb. The replacement that Papaver gave him is top of the line though, a sort of thank-you for defending his factory. Physically he's fit for duty. Only time will tell if he is psychologically well adjusted.'

'He's a brave man,' Trenchard stated simply.

'Yes Sir, he is,' Noir agreed.

Trenchard nodded and stared off into the distance, deep in thought. 'I have something that I want to tell you Commander,' he said finally after a long pause.

Here it comes, thought Noir. What have I done wrong this time?

'I've just reviewed the ship's logs from the last mission,' said Trenchard. Then he fixed her with a steely glare. 'You did a damn fine job Commander Noir. I couldn't have asked for a better X.O. I just wanted you to know that.'

Noir stared blankly back at Trenchard for a moment before she realised that he was waiting for a reaction. She blinked. 'Thank you, Sir,' she managed. 'I just did my job.'

Trenchard nodded. 'But you did it well. Everyone did. I was seriously concerned about this crew when I was first given command of the Might. But I guess that first impressions can be misleading. There's still some work to be done here but I think that these people are shaping up to be one damn fine crew.'

There was a moment of silence as they both digested this. Then Trenchard sat up and became business like once more and Noir relaxed. She wasn't used to personal moments with a commanding officer. It made her feel more than a little uncomfortable.

'Do you have any idea what happened to that thing?' Trenchard asked.

'The Morgenstern?'

'Yes. I was pushed into the drop-ship soon after Papaver's lot arrived. What happened?'

'I'm not sure. Several shuttles visited the station after you left. I'm fairly certain that they cleaned up any trace of the stuff that they had stored there, including the Morgenstern.'

'So, Papaver still has it? Makes you wonder why they'd be so interested in a failed prototype doesn't it?'

'Yes…' said Noir, tailing off into a retrospective silence.

Trenchard stretched and clicked the bones in his neck. He pushed himself up from the table with his palms and looked down at Noir.

'I've given the whole crew some time off. I know it's against regulations but High Command can go jump! Every man and woman on this boat needs a bloody good drink and that includes me.' Trenchard started to move towards the door. 'Coming?'

Noir looked up at Trenchard. 'In a short while, I still have a few personal matters to finish up here first.'

'Suit your-self,' said Trenchard, grabbing his jacket from off a hook on the wall and heading out of the hatch, whistling a happy tune. 'I'm going to visit Pugh and Cox and then I have a debriefing with Admiral Fife. After that I'll be in Mike's.'

Noir stared after him as he left. It was as though the man she had just been talking to was a completely different person to that which she had first met. She had decided that Trenchard was grumpy and annoying. Now she had seen a different side to his character. Maybe she had misjudged him?

The naval medical facility on Cairn was immaculately clean and orderly. White covered beds were arranged in neat, military lines along a pristine white ward. The injuries of the troopers in here were mostly from insurgent's I.E.D.'s. Many of the troopers had lost limbs. The replacement limbs that the navy could afford were basic. Trenchard stared at Pugh's state-of-the-art leg in awe as a nurse cleaned the seam where the appendage met raw flesh.

'How's your leg?' Trenchard asked as delicately as he could muster.

Pugh grinned and rapped his knuckles on his left leg producing a hollow metallic sound. 'Good as new Sir,' he said, smiling.

Trenchard looked up at the nurse questioningly.

'He's still on the happy pills that Papaver prescribed him and also a pretty high dose of Morphine. I don't think that he even realises properly what's happened yet,' she explained. 'I'm all done here. Don't be too long, he needs his rest.'

Trenchard nodded and turned back to Pugh as the nurse walked away. 'That was a damned brave thing that you did Pugh,' he said. 'If it was up to me you'd get a medal.'

Pugh grinned inanely back, his eyes glazed and his pupils wide. 'I'm just happy to be alive Sir,' he said, 'back to fight another day!'

'You sure you're okay?'

'I will be Sir, soon as I get out of here. The food's terrible,' he said, winking conspiratorially. 'But don't tell the pretty young nurse that I said that.'

Trenchard looked over towards the bed next to Pugh where Cox was lying comatose. His arm was bandaged, but he looked strangely calm.

'Do you know how Cox is?' Trenchard asked.

Pugh shrugged. 'They've had to keep him sedated,' Pugh explained. 'Every time he wakes up, he just starts screaming and shouting. He's such a young lad and I think the shock of the battle really screwed him up. He'll need some psyche evaluation but I think he'll be alright.'

Trenchard nodded and then something caught his eye. As he leaned closer he saw a small patch on the back of Cox's head that had been shaved completely bare. There was a small scar about an inch long at the base of his skull.

'I don't remember Cox hitting his head, do you?' Trenchard asked.

Pugh looked over. 'It got confusing for a while back there. He could have had his head banged when he was carried away.'

Trenchard nodded his head, seemingly satisfied with the explanation. 'Well you rest up mate. Fife will want to send us out on another mission very soon. Until then, make the most of the company,' said Trenchard, nodding his head towards the young nurse.

Pugh smiled. 'Don't worry Sir. I'll be back on my feet soon, ready to rock!'

Trenchard smiled, stood and walked away. Pugh might be physically fine now, but he would need some psychological support himself when the drugs wore off. Losing a limb was no easy thing. Trenchard wouldn't be surprised if he would be looking for a new warfare officer soon. He hoped not. Pugh had begun to shape up to be a solid officer. Only time would tell.

CHAPTER 23

"A DRINK AND A THINK"

'...and then Papaver showed up and his fancy security team turfed us off the station,' said Trenchard as he finished his story. 'You know the rest.'

Fife sat back in his chair and arched his fingers together across his lap. Then he let out a long sigh through his nose and stared at Trenchard.

'You're pissed off with me,' he stated in a matter of fact tone.

Trenchard had done reasonably well to conceal his feelings up to now, but somehow Fife could see through his thick skin.

'Yes Sir,' he replied.

'You do know that the order came down from Adisa directly? I had nothing to do with it.'

Trenchard remained stubbornly silent for a moment. Then he let out a burst of anger.

'Then what was the fucking point of sending us on that mission? What were we, dispensable?'

Fife sighed.

'Half of my job is politics, Captain Trenchard. The other half is trying to do right by the ship Captains under my command. Papaver holds a great deal of sway over the navy. His company builds all our weapons and spacecraft. We have contracts with him that run into hundreds of trillions. He's reliant on us for business, but conversely, we are dependent on him for *everything*. He could withhold vital supplies at any moment.'

'So we're puppets of Pap-Corp now?' Trenchard snarled.

'No, but we have to occasionally accede to some of his wishes,' Fife snapped back. 'His ship was across the galaxy on other business when the space elevator was destroyed. That abandoned facility in the Kuiper belt suddenly became a vital war asset. He asked Adisa directly for help to secure the facility until such a time as he could arrive and take over.'

'We were caretakers then?'

'If you want to put it that way, yes,' Fife grudgingly agreed. 'The point is that you did your job and then his people took over. There's more in that facility than you realise. Papaver is developing new weapons all the time in order to keep one step ahead of troublemakers like the insurgents. The stuff stored there is above top secret and that's why you were "turfed off", to use your colloquialism.'

Trenchard fell grumpily silent as he digested this. Then he looked back up at Fife and asked the question that had been eating away at his insides.

'What about Bird?'

Fife sighed again and rubbed his aching brow.

'That's the most troublesome part of this. It's just like him to think up a scheme like that; to fake his own death and return under the guise of Captain Raven. He's clever and dangerous. That's why I'm ordering you never to speak of this outside of this room.'

'What?' Trenchard asked in extreme puzzlement.

'The thought of Bird's death at the hands of Captain Smiler was bad enough. But if word gets around that Bird has defected and joined the pirates because he doesn't agree with the decisions of the United Worlds government…'

Fife tailed off, clearly troubled.

'The situation is getting worse. None of the veteran troopers like Chang very much or agree with his politics. I can't say I blame them. Sympathy is growing for the insurgents. But we must remain united at all costs. If Bird's mutiny and defection becomes public knowledge, it could persuade others to do the same. We could be facing a deep split in the ranks and maybe even a military uprising against Chang's leadership. That can't happen, at least, not until the time is right.'

Trenchard studied Fife carefully.

'What do you mean by that?'

Fife fixed him with a stony glare.

'There are many ways to influence politics, Trenchard. Chang is bad for the United Worlds, but a bloody coup would be catastrophic at the present time. Suffice it to say that a lot of people don't like Chang or what he stands for, but the time is not right to depose him. News of Bird's defection could ruin everything. Forget Paul Bird and forget everything I've just told you. Go and have a drink. Then tomorrow, carry on as if you never saw Bird alive on that pirate ship. That's an order!'

Trenchard glared back at Fife and narrowed his eyes.

'Yes Sir!' he said with a low growl.

Mike's Bar was rowdy as usual. Trenchard entered the door of Cairn's favourite pub and paused for a moment, taking it all in. It had been a long time. The air smelled of stale beer, sweat and bodily gasses. It was like perfume to Trenchard. The lighting was dim and the floor sticky with spilled drinks. Along one wall was the bar, which was made to look old fashioned even though it was constructed from modern materials. The optics shined with different coloured spirits and the traditional hand pumps poured a frothy selection of real ales that the owner Mike brewed in a micro-brewery on the premises.

Trenchard pulled a packet of cigarettes out from his jacket pocket, lit one, looked about and found some of his crew sitting around a table in the far corner. He went over to the bar and bought a pint, before heading over towards the table. At the sight of Trenchard, Kittinger stood up and tried to perform a drunken salute. Trenchard waved him back to his seat, taking a deep drag of his cigarette and blowing a smoke ring.

'Sit down man. My rules…' he paused to make sure that everyone was listening, '…in here we're all equal. Rank doesn't apply when you have a drink in your hand.'

Kittinger gingerly smiled and sat back down again. It was most unusual for your commanding officer to sit and drink with the lower ranks so casually but Trenchard wasn't your usual Captain. Trenchard took a seat and looked around the table. Most of the control room crew and some of the troopers were here, with the notable exceptions of Commander Noir, Stofan and the red-head Cochran. By the looks of the empty glasses and bottles piled into the middle of the table, the rest of them were all half cut already.

'Where are the others?' Trenchard enquired gently.

'On their way,' replied Lieutenant Commander Sivia, sipping on a Coke. He didn't usually drink alcohol and was the only sober one here.

'Where's Commander Noir?' McGagh asked, swigging down a large glass of Irish whiskey.

'On the ship, finishing up,' said Trenchard. 'She'll be down here soon.'

Chertok leaned forwards across the table and spoke to Trenchard. 'How are Pugh and Cox?' he asked with a slur in his voice, his Russian accent thicker than usual.

'Pugh seems fine,' Trenchard explained. 'We'll know better when the drugs wear off. Cox was out cold when I saw him. The nurse said that it'll be a few days before I can speak to him.'

'A toast!' said McGagh, standing up and looming over the table. 'To Lieutenant Commander Pugh; never a braver man sailed the black void!'

Trenchard met McGagh's eyes with a steely glare. 'I'll drink to that,' Trenchard said and bashed his glass into McGagh's. There was a round of cheering and clinking of glasses. McGagh nodded to Trenchard confidentially as he sat back down as if to say "everything's alright now". Pugh's act of bravery had obviously settled his debt to the crew.

'Well, it's about fuckin' time you showed your sorry arse in here again!' a broad Geordie voice suddenly barked from directly behind Trenchard.

Trenchard turned abruptly to find his old buddy Dasilva standing right behind him with a smug grin across his face. Trenchard pulled a couple of notes from his jacket pocket and threw them onto the table, turning to his crew.

'The next round's on me. I have to catch up with my old ship-mate here.' Then he nodded and accompanied Dasilva over towards the bar where a couple of empty stools were waiting. It was pointless to sit at a table when he was drinking with Dasilva, they got through the rounds too quickly. It was simpler to just sit right at the bar itself.

It was dark in the hospital. All the patients were asleep, many troubled by dark nightmares; most were heavily sedated. A figure in a red lab coat walked silently down the rows of beds and stopped beside Pugh and Cox. She bent forwards into the soft night light that shone gently onto Cox's face, brushing her dark brown hair out of her face and tucking it behind her ear. She reached inside a pocket and took out a small device.

Looking around her to make sure she was unobserved, the woman placed the device next to the fresh scar on the back of Cox's head. She pressed a control and a light on the device started blinking. Cox's eyes flickered open and he stared, unseeing, straight at the ceiling. The woman deactivated the device and straightened up, smiling to herself. Then she pulled a long needle from her top pocket and gently took hold of Cox's unresisting hand. Carefully she pushed the needle into the soft muscle of Cox's palm at the base of his thumb and straight out the other side. Cox didn't even wince or struggle. He just lay there with a blank expression on his passive features. Satisfied, the woman pulled the needle out and placed it back into her pocket. Then she took a small communicator from another pocket, dialled a number and held the device up to her ear.

After a few seconds, a thick French voice said, '*Hello?*'

'Sir,' the dark-haired woman said quietly. 'It's Elaine. The Providence chip has been activated successfully!'

'So, how's things with you?' Trenchard asked as he settled onto the stool, holding up two fingers to the barkeeper Mike in order to buy another round.

'Not bad,' replied Dasilva. 'Same shit, different day. Admiral Turner has us training the new recruits. It's some grand idea of Vice President Chang's. Since President Smith was assassinated and the space elevator dropped in the ocean, he's started recruiting like fuckin' crazy. Chang says he's going to wipe out the insurgents. Can't see it ever hapenin' though, I mean, how do you fight a guerrilla force that's hidden in small numbers across every populated system?'

Trenchard nodded with understanding as the two beers were duly delivered. He took a long swig before replying.

'If Chang keeps it up, he's going to piss off every veteran in the navy. They were going to send us straight out again, after we've only just returned from the last mission. Our wounded haven't even been properly rested yet, for Christ's sake.'

Dasilva gulped his pint down in one and ordered two more. 'So, how does being a Captain of a star-ship suit you?' Dasilva asked with a grin before belching loudly. 'It must be champion being your own boss out there?'

Trenchard smiled at Dasilva's Geordie accent which was becoming broader and broader the more he drank.

'It's not all it's cracked up to be mate, believe me. My crew are eager, but they're mostly inexperienced youngsters. Then when you think you've got enough trouble with pirates shooting your bollocks off, the damn Papaver Corporation forgets to tell you they have a homicidal robot on ice in the middle of your combat zone.'

Dasilva's eyebrows shot up. 'Papaver?'

Trenchard looked around nervously to make sure that he wouldn't be overheard. 'This is classified mate, so don't go spreading this about…'

Dasilva made a motion as if zipping his lips shut.

'We were supposed to be protecting a facility that makes cables for the new space elevators that Chang wants built. It turned out to be an experimental weapons dump for Papaver.'

Dasilva pulled a sour face. 'That fuckin' French twat!'

Trenchard nodded. 'There was some kind of robot or cyborg on ice there. It was activated during the battle and went crazy, I have two troopers in hospital, and poor Pugh has lost a leg.'

Dasilva turned to look at the table where the crew of the Might were drinking. 'Jim's brother? Has anybody told Jim yet?'

Trenchard shook his head. 'I don't think so. Pugh's still recovering on drugs. Barely knows his arse from his elbow.'

'I'll tell Jim what happened,' said Dasilva, taking a long deep drink of his beer. 'That slimy bastard Papaver! I don't trust anything that he does. You know that he killed my brother?'

Trenchard gently put his hand onto Dasilva's shoulder. He remembered only too well when Dasilva had received the news of his brother's death, killed by a prototype rifle that had exploded in his face. The Papaver Corporation built all the navy's weapons. Dasilva held Papaver personally responsible.

'Well, there's definitely something shifty going on. That robot was designed to kill indiscriminately. There would be no other use for it. It just went berserk. What would Papaver want with a weapon like that? Certainly, the navy would never use it.'

Dasilva raised an eyebrow. 'You think not?' he said. 'I think those arseholes in High Command would do anything if it saved them some money. They're probably desperate to replace us with fucking robots. Mark my words, if Papaver is playing about with killing machines, then it's only a matter of time before us poor fuckin' munters pay the price!'

Trenchard stared fixedly into his pint. It was dark and swirling, just like his future. He didn't want to believe it, but he couldn't help but feel that Dasilva was right. Chang's regime was becoming more and more militaristic every day. The navy were no longer peacekeepers; they weren't policing the colonised systems; they were subduing them under martial law. The one thing that kept the balance was people like him and Dasilva. They had minds of their own and wouldn't follow orders blindly or without question. If they could be replaced by obedient machines then there would be no stopping President Chang from clamping down on the entire United Worlds, a military dictator in charge of cowering and terrified subjects.

Trenchard shook his head to clear the dark thoughts and held his hand up to get Mike's attention. 'Two double rums please Mike,' he asked.

Tonight, he was going to get steaming drunk.

In a darkened cabin aboard the Might of Fortitude, a slender female hand operated a small electronic device. The tiny hologram communicator was cutting edge technology, far beyond anything the navy or any of its recruits could afford. The small rectangular device was held flat on the woman's palm and a flickering full colour hologram blinked into existence above it. The face of the man in the hologram beamed broadly as he flicked the mop of untidy dark hair out of his eyes.

'*Bonjour mademoiselle. I was waiting to hear from you. I take it that you are alone?*' said Claude Papaver in his thick accent.

There was a pause.

'Quite alone,' a soft feminine voice replied.

'*I congratulate you on the success of your mission. The test was extremely successful. The Morgenstern operated better than could have been expected.*'

'I'm glad that you're pleased,' said the voice, without any real emotion.

'*You are ready for the next part of the operation?*' Papaver asked with his eyes wide.

'Yes.'

'*Good. Remember, the safety of Captain Trenchard is paramount. He is the one that we need. The rest of the crew are expendable. If it becomes necessary, then they must be sacrificed.*'

There was a longer pause.

'Don't worry. I'll do my part. You can count on it...'

Papaver beamed and then the hologram blinked off.

There was an exhale of breath. It was more of a release of pressure than of relaxation.

'… even if I have to kill every single member of this crew myself with my bare hands!'

EPILOGUE

"GENESIS OF THE MORGENSTERN"

Four years ago, on Mars...

Orange dust hung in the air, illuminated by shafts of sickly purple light. The woman moved cautiously along another silent corridor in the abandoned factory. It was close, she could feel it. For such a large thing, it could certainly move silently when it wanted to.

The pistol felt comforting in her grip, the cold steel a solid reminder of her skills. She had been trained for this. All those years at the naval academy and then the hours she had spent in the private simulator on board the S.S. Bertrand had paid off. She was a highly trained, agile killer. She had never met anyone, or anything, that could better her. Not yet. Perhaps today would be the day, but she doubted it.

She passed by a room that was filled with abandoned cattle pens. Dried-up straw and dung wafted across a floor that was caked with orange dirt. This was where the poor beasts had lived out their short lives before being sent to the abattoir. Food production was what Mars was all about these days. Nowadays the cattle could graze outdoors on the newly planted fields of grass. At least they were fattened in the open before their throats were slit. The Red Planet was finally becoming green and blue. Soon there would be a great flood and then life would spread out across new continents. For now, the planet was for the most part a barren dusty ball of rock with a feeble atmosphere. Soon it would be paradise.

The assassin coughed and spat up a ball of thick brown mucus. She should be wearing her respirator mask but in combat it was a nuisance, a distraction. It just got in her way. She could do without the extra oxygen for a short time. At least the lower gravity of Mars made it easier to move around. The effort of breathing in the fine particles of dust was balanced by easier movement.

Straining to hear the slightest noise, she moved on. Her feet left clear footprints down the corridor which made her easy to track. It probably made little difference to her adversary. It could see by infra-red, radar, sonar and all manner of other technological marvels that gave it a clear advantage. All she had were her eyes, her ears and her wits.

Something scurried across the floor in front of her and she instantly levelled the pistol. The dark shape froze momentarily. It was a huge spider from the Tarantula family. Had they been brought to Mars as pets or maybe in a banana consignment, who knew? However, they had travelled here, they had escaped and prospered. They fed off the rats that had also followed the colonists and their grain supplies. The lower gravity of Mars had allowed the exoskeleton endowed creatures to grow larger than they ever could on Earth. A few short seasons and evolution had done its job. The one staring at her now was over a foot long. It gave a brief shudder and scurried off into the darkness. She let it go. It would be a waste of ammo and the shot would give away her position.

She moved further along, past the abattoir which was still stained by the blood of cattle, congealed black stains on the concrete. The huge hooks that would have held the slaughtered beasts still hung from the ceiling and rattled slightly in the hot Martian breeze. In one corner was a huge steel bath for collecting the blood and turning it into black sausage. Nothing was wasted. Food was too precious these days. Her stomach rumbled at the thought. She hadn't eaten today. She didn't like to eat before battle. A bacon sandwich and a strong coffee were definitely in order if she survived this test.

Something made her stop and stare, transfixed. Amongst the blood spatter on one wall was some fresh graffiti. The local kids had obviously broken in to the abandoned meat plant and they had been busy with a can of red spray paint. There was the usual juvenile mixture of names, swear words, and pictures of skulls and phalluses. One phrase though, made her stop dead and stare.

"*Beware the fifty sisters!*"

She had no idea what the hell it meant but it stirred something deep within her. She felt a memory; no, a lost part of herself stirring inside.

Without warning, the glass-brick wall next to her shattered into a billion lethal shards as an arm the size of a tree trunk smashed its way through. The assassin reacted instantly and leapt out of the way, up onto a stainless-steel bench, scattering rusty butcher's knives left and right. She spun around and fired three shots straight at the creature's chest.

The thing that walked through the broken wall was huge. Matt black rubber armour that had the appearance of car tyres covered a robotic frame that stood over eight feet from head to toe. Huge metal fists were clenched and ready to strike. A menacing metal face stared at her through glowing red, crescent-shaped receptors.

'Thought you could sneak up on me, did you?' the assassin called from her lofty vantage point.

With a strange sucking noise, the rubber coating on the robot's chest spat the three rounds back out and they dropped to the floor with a metallic rattle. The chest then sealed over completely as if nothing had ever happened.

'Fuck!' swore the assassin. 'He really went to town on you this time, didn't he?' she cried.

The robot leapt with surprising agility for its great size. The assassin only just got out of the way before the steel bench that she was standing upon was crushed flat. She grabbed onto a ceiling hook and hung there for a second, aiming this time at the thing's head. Five more rounds bounced off the metal skull and dropped to the floor.

The robot shook with rage and let out an electronic roar of fury. Why its designers had decided to give it vocal circuits was beyond her. Perhaps they thought that it would appear more intimidating to its adversaries? Who cared? It was just another tin man with a bad temperament. It raised itself to full height, pistons popping, and then tensed its body. Hundreds of lethal spikes were slowly pushed up through the rubberised skin all over the chest, arms and legs of the robot.

'Right…' the assassin said to herself, as she stared at the vicious spikes with wide eyes. 'You're a fucking hedgehog! Time to leave.'

She turned and ran. This was not a tactical withdrawal or even a clever trick. She was simply running for her life. She dodged and wove through the room of metal benches while the robot simply tore straight through them, flinging the heavy slabs of metal across the room to smash into the concrete walls. The assassin raced through a set of double doors and slammed them shut behind her. She glanced around and found a fire point on the wall. Wrenching the fire axe from its brackets she thrust it through the door handles to hold the door shut and then turned and ran.

She needn't have bothered. The door simply exploded behind her. The fire axe handle splintered and the blade embedded itself in the far wall. The flimsy interior door was simply no match for the hydraulic pistons and motors of the creature. It powered after the assassin, clawed feet tearing into the concrete floor.

'More space…' the assassin thought out loud to herself. *'Must find more space!'*

She weaved her way through corridor after corridor, the robot always close on her tail. Then she found what she was looking floor. One corridor opened out into what must have been a refectory of some kind. Metal hatches at one end gave a view through to abandoned kitchens and the room was filled with cheap plastic tables and chairs. Discarded red plastic trays were strewn about. Here and there were styrene cups, stained with long dried out coffee. The assassin skidded to a halt in the middle of the room, relaxed, eased her breathing and turned calmly to wait for the robot.

With a crash, the door to the refectory flew off its hinges. The robot stomped heavily into the room and came to an abrupt halt. It could see the target directly ahead but the target was not moving. This was illogical. Targets ran, they always ran. Was this a trap? The creature scanned the room with every electronic device at its disposal. There was nothing unusual. It took a cautious step forwards.

'Come on then dick-less!' shouted the assassin, throwing her useless pistol away across the room with a clatter. 'What are you waiting for? Come and get me!'

The woman spread her arms out wide and motioned the robot to come closer with her fingertips. It took another tentative few steps, continually scanning the room for danger.

'Hey dick-less! What do you call a robot that picks on defenceless women?' she shouted provocatively and then she grinned mockingly.

The robot surged towards her suddenly and swung its spiked arm through the air like a mighty battle club. The assassin leapt through shafts of dusty air. She grabbed onto the robot's arm, narrowly missing the multitude of spikes with her slender fingers and vaulted onto its arching back. In a lightening move she pulled her trusty Wakizashi short sword from the sheath on her back and thrust it through a small chink in the robot's armour at the base of its skull. As the robot thrashed wildly about, the assassin ground the sword from side to side, slicing circuitry and wires, disembowelling the machine's guts and severing its artificial spinal cord.

'...*scrap!*' she shouted jubilantly, answering her own question.

With a groan, the machine collapsed into an immobile heap on the floor sending up clouds of orange dust. The assassin jumped off and landed nimbly next to it and carefully re-sheathed her sword. Then she noticed some blood on the side of her hand where one of the spikes had nicked her flesh and she began to suck gently at the wound.

'You're hurt?' echoed a man's voice from across the room.

The assassin stopped licking her wounds and gave the man a disparaging glance. 'Only my pride. It took me over ten minutes to finish this one off. You're getting better at building these bloody things.'

The man was followed into the room by a team of technicians in bright red lab coats, led by a pretty young woman with brown hair. They proceeded to fuss over the fallen robot as if it were an injured child.

The man walked up towards the assassin. 'I could have someone look at that for you Aska,' he said in his thick French accent.

'No thanks Papaver,' she replied. 'I've seen what your people do. I'd rather take care of it myself.'

The man sighed dejectedly. 'I'm only trying to be polite Mademoiselle.'

'Well don't!' said the woman. Then she threw him an angry glance and snapped, '…and it's Saito to you. *Miss* Saito. Let's keep this professional!'

The man raised an eyebrow and nodded towards the wreckage on the floor. 'Then what is your "professional" opinion of the Sentinel prototype?'

Saito shrugged. 'The weapons are fine. I like the spikes. Nice touch. Kind of reminds me of a medieval mace, simple and effective. The problem is with the brain. Robots are too logical; they don't have human instinct or creativity. No matter how well you programme the A.I. software, it will always lack that human spark. You could almost do with a real human brain in there!' she said and then Saito chuckled at the terrible thought.

Papaver opened his eyes wide as he thought about it. 'Perhaps you're right? A human brain you think?'

Saito gave Papaver a dirty look. 'Hey, I was only joking, for god's sake! You can't just go stealing someone's brain and sticking it in there.'

Papaver shrugged his shoulders. 'Why ever not?'

Saito shook her head in despair and began to walk away. 'You're a sick fuck Papaver, do you know that?'

Papaver stared after her. 'I have a present for you Miss Saito.' He paused for effect as he watched her stomp away. 'It's parked outside.'

Saito turned to stare at Papaver with her hands on her hips. 'What do you mean "parked"?' she asked.

'You'll see,' said Papaver. It's a prototype; a gift from an old friend of mine. You said you wanted a better ship?'

'It had better be a bloody good ship,' she retorted and spun on her heel again, making for the exit. '…and you should lose the robot's name! "Sentinel" sounds like something from a comic book. It's fucking stupid!'

She took a few more steps. Papaver made her skin crawl. She was desperate to be away from the man. She almost made it to the door.

'*They* have another mission for you Miss Saito,' Papaver called after her. 'The insurgent leaders have outlived their purpose. They must now be eliminated.'

Saito stopped and looked back exhaustedly. '*Today?*'

'No,' called Papaver. 'There will be a battle soon. The people of Belatu-Cadros are ready to rise up against the United Worlds. It must be done under the cover of the fighting, but you mustn't harm any United Worlds troopers. Mr. Kapol was very insistent on that point. What happens during the battle is crucial to the next stage of the Mesh.'

'Right,' said Saito simply. 'Call me when you want it done. Until then, I'm going to find a snack van. I feel a full cooked breakfast and about three really, really sugary coffees coming on. I might even have some fried black pudding.'

Saito stormed out, slamming the door behind her. Papaver watched her leave; his mind was a raging turmoil of emotions. He wanted to tell her how he felt, but she could never know the truth about his feelings for her. With a deep sigh, he reached into his jacket pocket and pulled out a small tablet device. After tapping a few keys, he brought up the search results for "medieval spiked mace". One result peaked his interest.

Medieval Spiked Mace — Morning Star or "Morgenstern" (German)…

He smiled to himself and put the device back into his pocket. There would be plenty of fresh brains available after the battle for Belatu-Cadros. Many troopers would die. Perhaps one of their brains would give some tactical experience to the battle robot? Turning abruptly, he addressed an olive-skinned scientist who was overseeing the retrieval of the defunct Sentinel unit.

'Farouk my friend. Do you happen to know where the nearest naval morgue is?'

THE END.

Josiah Trenchard will return in the "Space Navy Series - Books Three & Four" compilation...

Captain Josiah Trenchard has become known as the "Fixer" because of his growing notoriety for solving the Space Navy's most difficult, and dangerous problems. After insurgent terrorists attack the headquarters of the mighty Papaver Corporation, Trenchard's ship, the "Might of Fortitude", is sent on a mission to police the planet where the deadly gas used in the attack is produced. Meanwhile, one of his crewmembers who was injured in a previous encounter with the Morgenstern battle robot, is experiencing terrifying waking nightmares. To put a cap on Trenchard's day, he is forced to realise that there may very well be a traitor amongst his crew.

On their return, the crew of the Might of Fortitude are then sent on a desperate rescue mission. All communication has been lost with the scientific research vessel S.S. Seishi. Proteus Pharmaceuticals' boss, Akihito Nakamura, is desperately concerned for his son who is aboard, inspecting the science vessel. Nakamura makes a personal plea to Admiral Fife that Captain Trenchard should be sent on the rescue mission. What lies in wait for the troopers of the Might of Fortitude this time? What terrors shuffle in the darkness, snarling and clawing and lusting after human flesh? What is the terrible truth behind the miracle drug Ōnamuji?

If you have enjoyed this book, please leave a review on Amazon. Thank you. Honour, strength and unity!

OTHER WORKS BY THE SAME AUTHOR

The Space Navy series, in chronological order:

1) Josiah Trenchard and the Might of Fortitude

2) Josiah Trenchard and the Morgenstern

3) Josiah Trenchard and the Berserkergang

4) Josiah Trenchard and the Onamuji Zombies

5) Josiah Trenchard - Belatu-Cadros

6) Unity - Warrior of the Space Navy

7) Josiah Trenchard - Arkhangelsk

8) Josiah Trenchard and the Ghosts of Christmas Future

9) Josiah Trenchard - Prototype

10) Josiah Trenchard - Wargame (coming soon)

11) Josiah Trenchard - Roh-Tang (coming soon)

12) Unity - Protomorph (coming soon)

Twitter: @JonGardener

YouTube: Evilgenius1972

Goodreads: http://www.goodreads.com/JonGardener

Pinterest: http://pinterest.com/unitynovels

Web Site: https://sites.google.com/site/unitynovels/home

Facebook: jonathonfletcher.336

E-mail: unitynovels@gmail.com

GLOSSARY

Alpha Mike Foxtrot: A fond farewell to an enemy; Adios, mother-fucker!

Atmosphere Processor: A huge factory that pumps gas into the atmosphere of a planet to correct the balance and make the air breathable. They are manufactured by the Papaver Corporation.

Baby shit: Yellow, evil smelling engineering grease.

Black Void Rum: Trenchard's favourite tipple.

Boat / Ship: Ships carry boats. A submarine is always a boat not a ship. This tradition has clung on and so Hunter and Wolverine class vessels are referred to as boats.

Breech Sealant Foam: An instantly setting foam that is sprayed into hull breaches to seal them.

C.C.N: Central Computer Network. The future equivalent to the World Wide Web.

Cold iron: The whole ship shut down.

Cuff-link Bracelet Radio: A communications device worn on wrist with built in emergency beacon and G.P.S. Also capable of projecting tactical holograms.

Data Cube: A digital storage device, usually a black cube about one inch on each side.

Dolphins: Hunter-killer vessel basic training badge. On completion, there is a ceremony on deck where the Captain gives the sailor a glass with their badge in. The Captain puts his fingers into the glass and the rum is filled to the top of his fingers. The sailor then drinks the rum and catches the badge in their teeth.

Drop-ship: A vessel to surface shuttle for ferrying troopers into battle. It is capable of reaching escape velocity after a slow climb to high altitude. The vessel has four wing mounted jet engines placed on the tips of two wings. The configuration of the craft leads to the nickname "H-lifter" or "big H".

E.V.A. Suit: Extra-Vehicular Activity, space suit.

FUBAR: Fucked up beyond all recognition.

Guardian Computer: A software-based artificial intelligence that automates many systems aboard Space Navy vessels. It is installed onto every ship in the fleet and linked to the C.C.N.

Gun-ship: Capable of flying in space or an atmosphere. A variety of weapons and missiles can be mounted onto these versatile attack craft.

Goldilocks Zone: That area of a solar system where the conditions are just right for life. Not too hot, not too cold; liquid water and temperatures within acceptable limits.

Heavy Suit: An inner suit worn underneath regular clothes with heavy weights sewn in and elastic straps to keep the muscles under tension. It increases load on the body in micro gravity and helps to prevent muscle wastage on long trips.

High Command: The highest ranked officers of the Space Navy, headed by Admiral of the Fleet Adisa with Admirals Fife, Turner, Thomas, Mahmood and Lee.

Honour, strength and unity: The proud motto of the space navy.

I.E.D.: Improvised Explosive Device. Bomb.

I.N.N: / Intergalactic News Network. Daily news reports are sent to every colonised planet. The show is usually hosted by anchor-man Alexander Robertson.

Insurgents: Terrorists who want to break the colonies away from the rule of the United Worlds and become independent and self-governing. Also known as the R.D. or Rubente Dextera.

Mag-boots: Metal soled boots that can be magnetised electronically to stick to the deck of a ship or its outer hull. They automatically disable when gravity is restored.

Micro Pressure Body Suit: A thin jump-suit that is worn underneath regular clothes that can exert pressure upon different parts of the body. Used primarily in hologram simulations within the combat zone on Cairn to add realism.

Mike's Bar: Local hang-out for the troopers on Cairn.

Morgenstern: Prototype battle robot, built by Pap-Corp. Also known as the "Sentinel project".

N.A.C.I.N.: NAval Communication and Intelligence Network. Messages are carried by a series of way stations that transmit data via Watters' space.

Nines (two weeks): Punishment. Extra duties and leave cancelled, possibly including a fine.

O.M.N.I. / Omni-bot: Ocular Mobile Naval Intelligence, flying robot equipped with cameras and sensors. The robot can also project holograms and provide navigational assistance. In extreme circumstances, this flying drone can be turned into a small bomb.

Old Speckled Gobshite: Trenchard and Dasilva's favourite beer which is served in Mike's Bar on Cairn.

Papaver Corporation: The biggest manufacturer of weapons, ships and technology in the United Worlds. Owned and run by Frenchman, Claude Papaver.

Perisher: Hunter killer Commander training course. If you fail, you never serve on one again.

Rubente Dextera: The original terrorist organisation from which the galactic wide insurgent movement sprung. Referred to as the R.D. or the "red right hand of Mars" they were responsible for the uprising in Belatu-Cadros.

Section 42: An amendment of the criminal code allowing the arrest, rapid trial and public execution of criminals.

Sewage pipes: Term of endearment used by sailors to describe the hunter-killer vessels. It refers to the smell that develops when water is rationed on board and washing is limited to a quick rub over with a wet cloth.

Skimmer: Crew of any ship other than a hunter-killer. The term refers to an ancient rivalry between surface crew and submariners; "He's a fucking skimmer!"

Space Elevator: Cargo is carried up carbon nano-tube cables which are stretched between a base station on Konstantin Island in the Atlantic Ocean and the Buoy space-station in orbit of Earth. Transit into orbit is slower than by rocket, but much cheaper and more reliable. The first S.E. was destroyed by the insurgents. The disaster is referred to as "the drop".

Star-spires: Headquarters of the U.W.S.N., located on Unity Island, in the middle of the Pacific Ocean on Earth. Named after the motto "Aspirare Astra" - aspire to the stars.

Technologists: A trans-humanist religion. Followers do not believe in god but rather the improvement of one's self by technological augmentation.

United Worlds: The term used to describe the colonised planets, ruled from Earth.

United Worlds Space Navy (U.W.S.N.): A military police force that was raised to keep order throughout the United Worlds. The navy has the same rank structure as the British Royal Navy and is governed by High Command.

VICAR Assault Rifle: Void Capable Case-less Assault Rifle. A semi-automatic, case-less round firing rifle, fitted with an internal warming mechanism to allow the rifle to be fired without jamming in the freezing vacuum of space.

Virtual Reality Command Chair (V.R. Conn.): The Captain's command chair which sits at the centre of the control room or bridge. The Captain's legs are strapped in to braces allowing their torso and arms to move freely and operate virtual controls. A black visor with electrodes fitted to the temples allows the computer to interact directly with the brain.

Wardroom: Officers mess and meeting room, often decorated with photos of ancient underwater vessels. On a large ship there will be a "dirty shirt" wardroom where most of the aircraft crew eat and working uniforms are permitted.

Watters' Drive: A method of propulsion that enables starships to travel faster than light. It is a variation upon the Bussard Ramjet, combined with an Alcubierre drive. Particles of hydrogen are taken in via a huge collector at the front of the ship. They are then compressed by magnetic fields until thermonuclear fusion takes place and then the energy is shot out of the rear exhaust at incredibly high speeds to propel the ship forwards. Inside a star system, the Ramjet is sufficient for slower than light speed propulsion. During interstellar travel, the fusion power is used to create an Alcubierre metric field which contracts space in front of the ship and expands space behind it. This shifts space around the star-ship so that it can "surf" a wave in space-time and may therefore arrive at its destination quicker than the speed of light. At full speed, one light year distance takes approximately twenty-four hours to traverse. Large vessels frequently have to drop out of Watters' in order to traverse obstacles such as asteroid belts. They are particularly susceptible to attack by pirate vessels during this time. Steering is impossible during Watters' drive, where navigation is undertaken by a "point and go" method. Steering is only possible at slower speeds during Ramjet operation and usually requires augmentation by gravity slingshot around planets.

We hide with pride: The motto of the hunter-killer service.

17670217R00161

Printed in Poland
by Amazon Fulfillment
Poland Sp. z o.o., Wrocław